"I won't lose ~~~~
I'll do an~~~~

Wyatt flinched and look~~~~
best."

"I know." Charlotte bold~~~~ ~~~~ing his
gaze back to her. "Thank ~~~~ The time had come. "Will
you help me again?"

Confusion clouded his expression. "How?"

She opened her bag and pulled out the wallet. "Charles
left me some money. Whatever Mr. Baxter paid you, I'll
pay double."

He pulled back. "It's not that simple."

"Of course it is."

"No, it's not. The Orphan Salvation Society has an
agreement with Greenville. If the judge rules that the
children must go to Greenville, then I have no choice
but to take them."

Charlotte shook her head. He didn't understand. "I'm not
talking about all the children. I'm talking about Sasha."

Instead of walking away or shouting at her, he spoke
firmly. "There's nothing I can do to help you keep Sasha."

"Yes, there is."

He stared at her. "No, there's no~~~~

"You can marry me."

ORPHAN TRAIN:
Heading west to new families and forever love

Books by Christine Johnson

Love Inspired Historical

Soaring Home
The Matrimony Plan
All Roads Lead Home
Legacy of Love
The Marriage Barter

CHRISTINE JOHNSON

A small-town girl, Christine Johnson has lived in every corner of Michigan's Lower Peninsula. She loves to travel and learn about the places she visits. That puts museums high on her list of "must see" places and helps satisfy her lifetime fascination with history.

A double finalist for RWA's Golden Heart award, she enjoys creating stories that bring history to life while exploring the characters' spiritual journey—and putting them in peril! Though Michigan is still her home base, she and her ship captain husband also spend time exploring the Florida Keys and other fascinating locations.

Christine loves to hear from readers. Contact her through her website at www.christineelizabethjohnson.com.

The Marriage Barter

CHRISTINE JOHNSON

HARLEQUIN® LOVE INSPIRED® HISTORICAL

Special thanks and acknowledgment
to Christine Johnson for her contribution
to the Orphan Train miniseries.

Recycling programs
for this product may
not exist in your area.

™ LOVE INSPIRED BOOKS

ISBN-13: 978-0-373-82964-4

THE MARRIAGE BARTER

www.LoveInspiredBooks.com

Printed in U.S.A.

And we know that all things work together for good
to them that love God, to them who are the called
according to his purpose.
—*Romans* 8:28

For those who've lost earthly parents,
may Our Heavenly Father hold you close.

My deepest gratitude to fellow authors, Allie Pleiter
and Linda Ford, whose gracious guidance and
assistance helped me through many a rough patch.
You taught me so much!

Also, thanks go to Elizabeth Mazer,
whose insights opened my eyes to new possibilities.
It's been a pleasure working with you.

Above all, the glory goes to God,
without whom there would be no story.
For out of weakness, He brings strength.

Chapter One

∼✦∼

Evans Grove, Nebraska
Late April, 1875

*G*et in, do the job and get out.

It sounded simple, but Wyatt Reed knew that "simple" jobs seldom turned out that way.

All he had to do was escort a bunch of orphans to Greenville. That's what the town's wealthiest citizen, Felix Baxter, had told him. Apparently, the kids had gotten off in Evans Grove when robbers held up their train. They were supposed to continue on to Greenville the next day. Two weeks had passed, and still no sign of the children.

Baxter had sent telegrams and only got excuses. The town was fed up with waiting, and wanted the children now. That's where Wyatt came in.

The thing he couldn't understand was why. From what he could tell, the orphans had been rounded up out of Eastern cities and sent west by one of those do-gooder charities, the Orphan Salvation Society. Families were found for the children along the way, and Greenville was the final stop. They'd only get the worst of the lot, the children that hadn't been taken in anywhere else. Logic said this would be a rough bunch of kids, yet Baxter, claiming to speak for the town, had pounded his fist on his desk when demanding they come to Greenville as promised. The town wanted those children badly—too badly.

It made no sense, but Wyatt wasn't hired to ask questions. He was a tracker. He found what needed finding, and he wasn't about to turn down the kind of money Baxter had spread out in front of him.

Get in, do the job and get out.

With luck, he'd finish before the catch in this supposedly simple job reared its head. If not, he'd hightail it out of Evans Grove on his trusted mount, Dusty.

Wyatt dismounted in front of the hotel, his bum knee stiff after the twelve-mile ride from Greenville, and surveyed his surroundings. Baxter said he'd find the orphans here. The town was quiet, cozy, the kind of place where everyone knew everyone. No place for him.

He could spot a few signs of last month's dam break that he'd read about in the newspapers. Water stains marked the wood siding of the hotel at porch height. The lower floor must have escaped flooding. The front door stood open and a couple of gnarled old men sat on the bench outside spitting into a cracked chamber pot that served as a spittoon. Otherwise, the place looked deserted.

"Hotel open?" he asked. Locating eight missing orphans would take more than a couple hours. Any hitch, and he'd need a room.

The men on the porch eyed him warily before the one with a mangled ear managed to grunt in the affirmative.

"Thank you." Wyatt tipped a finger to his well-worn Stetson. "Got a town hall?"

The cabbage-eared man pointed north, across the street and toward a grove of hackberry trees. Beyond them stood a single-story building large enough to house a meeting room.

Must be the place, but would the mayor be there at four-thirty in the afternoon? In towns this small, the mayor usually worked his business by day and officiated in the evening.

He absently patted his ill-tempered Arabian. The horse nipped at his hand as if to tell Wyatt that he should settle them both for the night, but he wanted to see what he was up against. When a boy came bounding out of the hotel, eager to set Wyatt and Dusty up with quarters, Wyatt let him lead the horse to the livery but told the lad he'd register for a room later. For now, he had business to attend to.

First step in tracking is to get your bearings. Wyatt looked past the hotel to a saloon. Piano music tinkled out the open door. Some men fell prey to the lure of whiskey and gambling. In the end, they always lost. Wyatt should know. He'd done his share of stumbling in the war, but he hadn't touched a drop since the march through Georgia. He set his jaw against the swell of memory.

He had a job to do. The sooner he got it done, the better. Baxter had only given him a quarter of the fee up front. The rest would come upon completion.

He looked past the saloon to the creek. Piles of brick and lumber stood between the grain mill and the other creek-side buildings that had suffered the greatest damage. Rebuilding had already begun.

In the opposite direction, the street stretched east toward a pretty little church with a white steeple pointed high into the blue sky. It could have been plunked down here from any New England town. That old longing for the faith he used to know welled up out of nowhere. Wyatt pushed it aside. God wouldn't want someone like him.

Beyond the church loomed an unmarked building and then the general store. Wyatt strolled in that direction. A wagon rumbled past, and several women picked their way around muddy potholes. One glanced his way, and he nodded politely. She looked away and whispered to her companion, probably wondering who he was. This sure wasn't a town where a stranger could go unnoticed.

The cries of children rang out in the distance. The orphans? Or just the local boys and girls? He had no way of knowing. Orphans didn't wear signs. They didn't look any different than any other child. Except, like him, they didn't have a home. Like him, they belonged to no one. Like him, their future looked bleak, and they'd know it. They wouldn't be laughing and squealing. Those playing children couldn't be the orphans. No, orphans didn't belong in a hopeful town with scrubbed buildings and spring blossoms any more than he did.

He absently patted the front of his buckskin jacket and his too-thin wallet. After this job, he'd have enough to settle in San Francisco. He wouldn't have to track another fugitive or desperate soul. Maybe he'd open a shop, do something respectable. Yep, once he got paid in full, he'd never again have to take orders from men whose honor he couldn't trust. But he hadn't gotten paid yet.

Wyatt had lived in Greenville less than two months, but it was long enough to hear rumors about Baxter that made him doubt the man's sunny promise of a simple, quick and completely legal job.

"Mamaaaaaa!"

The plaintive cry halted Wyatt in his tracks. A child. Very young. Female. His tracker's instinct clicked into place. Her hiccups and wordless sobs came from very close, between the church and the unmarked building. These weren't the ordinary cries of childhood. This girl was terrified.

He slipped into the narrow alley between buildings, but a pile of empty crates blocked his view.

"Ma." Hiccup. "Ma."

Wyatt paused before the crates. What was he doing? He

didn't know the first thing about children, and he didn't know a soul in this town. Where would he take her once he found her?

He started to back away until a string of unintelligible words came out at a fevered pitch, followed by what sounded like choking. If someone didn't calm that child down, she'd stop breathing. Seeing as he was the only one nearby, that someone would have to be him.

He skirted the pile of empty crates, but she wasn't there. He followed the sobs to the back of the building and a muddy lane where a small, thin child with raven-black pigtails sat in the dirt. He wasn't much of a judge of children's ages, but she looked younger than school-age. Maybe three or four. Too young to be wandering around on her own.

Wyatt hesitated, unsure what to do as she lifted her tear-stained face to take in his considerable height. The sobs stopped. Her blue eyes widened so big they seemed to take over her whole face. One grubby hand went into her mouth, just like...

Wyatt stared.

By all the stars in the sky, she looked just like his kid sister, Ava, had at that age. Same pigtails. Same blue eyes. Same need to suck on her fingers.

The girl examined him with curiosity. She'd probably never seen such a tall man.

He knelt, his knee protesting. "Howdy, there. My name's Wyatt. What's yours?"

The hand didn't budge out of her mouth, but those sky-blue eyes continued to stare at him. What lashes! They practically brushed her eyebrows. One day this little girl would break men's hearts.

Today he needed to find out why she was crying and where she belonged. "Do you have any scrapes or cuts?"

She just stared.

He tried again. "Can you move your legs?" They looked fine, not obviously broken, but he wasn't a doctor.

She didn't budge. Clearly she wasn't going to answer him. Either she was too scared or too shy.

"Are you lost?"

Nothing again.

This was getting frustrating. "Can't you nod yes or no?"

Naturally, she didn't move her head one inch.

He rubbed his chin and attempted to ignore his aching knee. He'd try the obvious. "Did you lose your mama?"

"Mama," she echoed, somehow getting the word out despite the fingers in her mouth.

"Great." Finally, he was getting somewhere. He stood to take the pressure off his knee. "Where did you last see her?"

She went back to staring silently.

"Of course she doesn't know that, Reed," he chided himself. Some tracker he was if he couldn't remember that a lost child would be disoriented. Trouble was, he couldn't quite figure out what to do. Missing children weren't his specialty. He'd never worked with children until this job. Could this child be one of the orphans? He shook off the idea. She'd called for her mother. This girl had a family. In a town as small as Evans Grove, someone would know where to find her ma or pa.

He crouched again, ignoring his knee's protest. "If I pick you up and walk around town, do you think you can point to the last place you saw your mama?"

The girl answered by sticking out both arms.

She trusted him.

The knowledge kicked him in the gut. No one trusted Wyatt Reed. Not since before the war, anyway. If this girl only knew what he'd done. If she'd heard the screams of terror, she wouldn't trust him now or ever. But she didn't know who he was or what he'd done. She just trusted him.

"Get ahold of yourself, Reed." The girl didn't know anything about him. She trusted him to get her home, and he'd do it, the same as any paying job.

His big hands more than encircled her tiny waist. He lifted, and her thin arms wound around his neck. So trusting. This girl would crack his tough veneer if he wasn't careful.

He cleared his throat. "Let's find that mother of yours."

And soon. He couldn't take much more undeserved trust.

Charlotte Miller fingered the paltry selection of ribbons in Gavin's General Store. The emerald-green one shone against her pale fingers. The lovely ribbon would match her best dress, but she must buy the black. Custom dictated she hide beneath heavy black crepe for the next year or more while mourning the husband she'd never loved.

Charles Miller had treated her kindly, but all his love had been reserved for his deceased first wife. His marriage to Charlotte had been a business arrangement. She'd needed a husband when her parents died months after they arrived in Evans Grove. He'd needed a housekeeper and cook. Simple and sensible. Yet deep down, she'd hoped their marriage would one day develop the warmth and love that would usher in a large family.

She sighed. At least he'd agreed to take in one of the orphan girls. If not for Sasha, she would have no one.

Charlotte cast a glance toward the toys where Sasha and Mrs. Gavin's granddaughter, Lynette, were playing with the dolls. The two looked so much alike they could have been twins. Each wore their dark hair in pigtails. Today they wore nearly identical dresses in the same shade of blue. The Gavins had stocked a large quantity of that particular fabric, and most of the girls in town sported play dresses in royal blue.

"I'm so sorry for your loss, dearie," Mrs. Gavin said as she cut a length of ribbon sufficient to adorn Charlotte's hastily dyed bonnet. "At least you're still young." Mrs. Gavin tried to lift her spirits as she handed Charlotte the ribbon.

At thirty-one, Charlotte didn't feel terribly young. After a year or two of mourning, she'd have lost even more child-bearing years.

She dug in her bag for payment, but Mrs. Gavin refused to take her money.

Unbidden shame rose to Charlotte's cheeks. "Charles provided for me." Unlike her parents, he'd left her enough to last three or four years if she was frugal. And she would be. Thirteen years might have passed, but not the memory of the empty cupboards and gnawing hunger following her parents' deaths. Charles's proposal had filled her belly if not her heart, and for that she would always be grateful. It had taught her to fight for what she needed. Never again would she let herself become that destitute. Never would she let Sasha endure the pain and humiliation she'd faced. "I can pay."

The plump proprietress patted her hand. "It's something we do for all widows."

Widow. The word ricocheted through Charlotte's head. A widow had few options. If she wanted to provide for Sasha once Charles's money ran out, she must either work or marry. But what man would marry a woman who appeared unable to bear children? To any outsider, thirteen years of childless marriage meant she was barren.

Sooner rather than later she must find work. She couldn't run Charles's wheelwright shop. The flood had destroyed it. Charles's apprentice had rebuilt the forge portion, and she'd accepted his generous offer to assume Charles's debt in exchange for the business.

No, she must look elsewhere. Perhaps Mrs. Gavin needed help.

"I wonder if—" she began to ask, but the proprietress

had hurried off to help Holly Sanders, the schoolteacher and Charlotte's friend.

"Miss Sanders," Mrs. Gavin exclaimed. "I hear congratulations are in order."

"Congratulations?" Charlotte drew near her friend.

Holly blushed furiously. "Mason proposed."

"He did? Oh, Holly. How wonderful." Charlotte enveloped her friend in a hug. "I'm so happy for you." Truly, she was, though the irony of their situations didn't elude her. She, once married, was now a widow. Holly, who'd admired Sheriff Mason Wright for ages, would now be married.

Holly pulled away. "Enough about me. How are you doing?"

Charlotte couldn't believe Holly would think of her at such a time. "I'm doing better. Having Sasha to care for helps pass the time. She's such a dear."

"How is she handling it? She seemed so bewildered at first." Holly had gotten to know all the orphans in her role as part of the orphan selection committee responsible for placing the orphans with families. She'd grown very attached to the children since their arrival in town.

"The poor girl has seen so much death. Losing her parents, and then Charles." Charlotte shook her head. "I had no idea his heart had weakened."

"No one did."

Charlotte fought the rush of memories. "There's so much to take care of. I should go through his things, but I can't bring myself to do it."

"Would you like help?"

Charlotte couldn't believe Holly would consider helping her when she had a wedding to plan. "Aren't you busy with the wedding?"

Holly waved a hand. "It won't be anything fancy. Besides,

we haven't set a date yet. I can certainly manage an hour or two for a friend."

Then there was no escaping the task. Since Charles's death, Charlotte had avoided the loft, the place where he'd lived his life apart from her. She'd respected his privacy when he was alive, and now that he was dead, it felt like even more of an intrusion to set foot up there. Maybe Holly's presence would make it easier.

"Thank you," she murmured. "I don't know what to do with it all. Perhaps someone who lost their belongings in the flood could use the clothes, but who?"

"I'll ask around." Holly smiled encouragingly and again grasped her hand. "Shall we do it Saturday morning?"

So soon? Charlotte's heart sank. She didn't know if she could face the task, but it must be done. She stiffened her resolve. "Saturday."

"Anything else, Miss Sanders?" asked Mrs. Gavin as the busybody spinster Beatrice Ward stepped into the store.

Considering the glare Miss Ward cast at Holly, she'd heard the news of the engagement and disapproved. Charlotte wondered if she had any reason to dislike the match, or if she simply felt no one should make major decisions in town without consulting her.

"Not today." But Holly's gaze drifted toward the dress goods after Mrs. Gavin left to wait on Beatrice. "I must admit that rose-colored satin is pretty."

Holly's uncharacteristic interest in fabric caught Charlotte's attention. Of course! Holly needed a wedding dress, something that would show off the beauty she didn't realize she had.

"The color suits you," she urged. "It would make a lovely gown, wouldn't it? Oh, Holly, let me make it for you—as a gift."

Holly cast aside the idea. "No, no, it would be frivolous. I'll wear the dress I wore to Newfield."

Charlotte couldn't let her friend get married in a travel suit. Her vow of frugality evaporated in the face of a friend in need. She would make that dress, whether Holly approved or not. It was a gift, and gifts didn't require approval.

"I'll make it in the latest fashion," she insisted. "Mason's heart will stop when he sees you walk down the aisle."

"No, please," Holly said frantically as Beatrice Ward drifted closer. "Thank you, but no." Her gaze darted toward Beatrice. "I should get back to the schoolhouse. I have so much work to do before school tomorrow."

Work. If Charlotte was going to make Charles's money last more than a few years, she needed to ask Mrs. Gavin if the store was hiring, but she hesitated with Beatrice within earshot. The woman opposed letting any of the orphans stay in Evans Grove. Worse, she was on the orphan selection committee. According to Holly, the mayor had given Beatrice the position in an attempt to placate her, but the woman had done everything to thwart placements. If she thought Charlotte didn't have enough money to raise a child, then she'd scheme to take Sasha away. No, she'd have to ask Mrs. Gavin about work later.

"I'll see you Saturday," she said to Holly. "Eight o'clock?"

Holly nodded. "Saturday morning it is. Say hello to Sasha for me. I look forward to having her in school after summer."

She darted off, leaving Charlotte stunned. Sasha in school? So soon? The summer would flit by. Why, Charlotte had barely enjoyed two weeks with her.

She turned to retrieve Sasha from the toy display and saw the girl gazing at the expensive doll with the porcelain head and sky-blue dress. It was beautiful but far too dear. She'd make Sasha a pretty doll with black hair and big blue buttons for eyes. She had everything necessary in her sewing basket except the black hair. She eyed the ribbon. A much better use than on her bonnet.

Sasha stood on her tiptoes, her back to Charlotte, and reached for the doll. Her fingers grazed the doll's feet, and it teetered precariously on the shelf.

"No," Charlotte cried, running to save the doll from being shattered on the floor below.

The girl turned toward her, eyes wide.

It wasn't Sasha.

Charlotte's heart stopped. The doll toppled harmlessly onto the shelf, but Charlotte no longer cared about a doll. Her daughter was gone.

"Where's Sasha?"

Lynette backed away as tears rose in her eyes. "I dunno."

Charlotte's heart went out to her. "Oh, Lynette, it's not your fault." *It's mine.* A sickening feeling grew in the pit of her stomach. She should have watched Sasha more closely. She should have seen her daughter walk away from the toys. "I'm sure Sasha just went to look at something else. I'll find her." The words carried more confidence than she felt.

Charlotte swept around the barrels of flour, her black crepe dress rustling as she moved through the store, checking every aisle and corner. Not in the hardware section or meandering among the groceries. Perhaps she'd gone to the candy counter. Charlotte spun around and saw only Mrs. Gavin and Beatrice Ward. Oh, dear.

"Sasha?" Once again she swept the length of the store. Her panic escalated with every step.

Sasha wasn't anywhere.

Miss Ward looked up sharply, her pinched mouth gloating in triumph. "That's the way those filthy urchins are. It's bred into them. I could have told you she'd run off. You can't trust their type for an instant."

Charlotte blanched at the cruel words. "She's only four and doesn't know her way around town yet."

"Now, don't you worry, Mrs. Miller," Mrs. Gavin said calmly. "She can't have got far."

But worry was exactly what Charlotte felt, along with shame and fear that washed through her in ice-cold waves. Why hadn't she noticed that Sasha had left? She hadn't even realized the difference between Sasha and Lynette. What sort of mother was she? Now Beatrice Ward would tell everyone what had happened, and they'd say she was unfit to raise a child.

They wouldn't take Sasha away, would they? Charlotte's heart rattled against her rib cage. Sasha was all she had, her only family, the only person she had to love.

She raced from the store, her feet barely touching the three wooden steps. She looked left. Then right. Horses. Pedestrians. A stray dog. No little girl.

Where was Sasha?

She ran first one way and then the other. *Sasha. Sasha.* Her name beat into Charlotte's brain in time to her pounding footsteps.

Then she saw her. In the arms of a stranger. A tall, lean man with the piercing gaze of a hunter cradled Sasha with the gentleness of a father.

Her steps slowed, stopped.

Starkly handsome, the man's dark hair swept the collar of his buckskin jacket. Dark whiskers dusted his cheeks. His eyes, shadowed under the brim of his well-worn hat, stared straight at her. He did not smile. He looked like… Charlotte swallowed hard. He looked like an Indian. Or a gunslinger. An outlaw.

Yet Sasha clung to his neck with total trust, her head nestled on his shoulder.

"Sasha?" The word caught in her throat.

The man's stony gaze swept her from head to toe. He must not have found the assessment pleasing, for his stern expression never changed and he made no move to hand Sasha to her.

Her panic escalated.

Who was this man, and what was he doing with her daughter?

Wyatt couldn't stop staring at the woman. Sun-gold ringlets, touched with a hint of sunset, peeked from beneath the black bonnet. The heavy, black dress only made her porcelain skin look more fragile. Clearly, she was in mourning. Just as clearly, she was this girl's mother, though the two looked nothing alike.

"Sasha." Her gentle voice trembled.

Sasha? He stiffened at the peculiar name, but the girl stirred and turned to the familiar voice.

"Mama." The thin little arms reached for the porcelain-skinned woman, who rushed forward.

"Where have you been? Where did you go?" In seconds the girl was out of his arms and into her mother's. The woman kissed the girl's dirty face and hair. "Don't ever leave me again, understand? I was worried to death."

Instead of answering, the girl burrowed her head into her mother's perfectly formed shoulder.

The woman nodded at him, half in fear and half with gratitude. "Thank you. You have no idea how worried I…" She gulped and averted her gaze. "Thank you, truly."

"My pleasure, ma'am."

He wanted to tip that pretty face up so he could get a second look, but she kept her focus on her daughter.

"Yes, well, I should get home to fix supper." She backed away a step.

"My name's Wyatt Reed." Now, why in blazes had he

done that? He liked to keep contact with strangers to a minimum. *Get in, do the job and get out.* No emotional attachments.

"Charlotte Miller." Her gaze darted up for a moment, and her cheeks flushed a pretty shade of pink.

He wanted to touch that cheek to see if her skin was as soft as it looked, but beauties like her weren't meant for men like him. Still, he couldn't stop staring. A man didn't see all that many pretty women on the frontier. Who could blame him for taking an extra-long look?

"Like I said, I should go home," she murmured, again backing away.

He cleared his throat, reluctant to let her go. "I don't suppose you could tell me where to find the mayor." It was the only thing he could think to ask, even though he already knew where the town hall was located. "Evans, is it?"

"Yes, Mrs. Evans." Her pretty little chin thrust out with pride.

"Mrs.?" Baxter hadn't mentioned that little detail.

"Pauline Evans is a fine mayor, every bit as good as her late husband." She started out strong defending her mayor, but with every word her certainty faltered, as if she'd lost her nerve.

For some reason, he wanted to encourage her. He dug around for a suitable response and found none. "I have business to take care of. Don't suppose you'd know where I can find her?"

Again, she ducked her head. "You might try the town hall. If not there, then she'd be at home."

"Town hall?" He pretended he didn't know where it was to gain a few more seconds with her.

Her color deepened. "I'll show you there. It's on my way."

A peculiar thrill ran through him. She would willingly walk with him through town? It had been ages since any woman walked in daylight with Wyatt Reed. And this one was a beauty. She'd match up to any ballroom belle back in Illinois.

"Let's go home," she whispered to Sasha.

Home. The old ache came back, hard and furious. Wyatt Reed wouldn't find home until he set foot in San Francisco.

"Can you walk?" Charlotte murmured to Sasha, her face aglow with love for her daughter.

Sasha nodded solemnly and slid to the ground. "Go home."

For the first time, Wyatt noticed the girl's peculiar accent. Her voice had been too garbled by tears earlier, but now the foreign lilt was unmistakable. Sasha must not be Charlotte Miller's natural daughter. A knot formed in his gut. That meant she could be one of the orphans.

His simple job just got a whole lot more difficult.

Chapter Two

They found Mayor Pauline Evans huddled over the table at the front of the meeting hall with the Newfield banker, Curtis Brooks, at her side. Whatever they were discussing, it held their attention so thoroughly that they didn't hear Charlotte and Wyatt enter the room.

The mayor stabbed her finger at a piece of paper. "It's all detailed here, if you want to read it."

Mr. Brooks, his dark hair lightly salted with gray, struggled to hold back a grin. "Now, Mrs. Evans, I'm not questioning how the project is being handled. That's up to you. The bank sent me to supervise the distribution of your town's loan—nothing more. And from what I can see, you're doing a fine job with the chore groups and the distribution of the funds. The bank simply needs a report of expenditures, which I see you have right here." He slipped the paper away from the mayor. "Now, as to the matter of young Master Liam."

"I believe we're agreed on that."

Charlotte felt like she was intruding on private business. Yesterday, Liam McLoughlin, one of the orphans, had run away after Beatrice Ward called him a thief. The poor boy had hidden in a cave until Sheriff Wright found him. Since both the mayor and Mr. Brooks served on the orphan selection committee, they must be discussing what action to take against Beatrice for causing such a fracas.

She motioned to Wyatt that they should come back later. Instead, he rapped on the door frame.

Mayor Evans and Mr. Brooks looked up, startled.

"Charlotte." A smile sprang to Pauline's lips. "What can I do for you?" The auburn-haired mayor hurried toward her with genuine warmth. "And Sasha, too." The formidable woman's handclasp and smile conveyed sympathy and something else. Worry? No, pity.

Of course Pauline pitied her. She knew the pain of widowhood. Robert Evans had been a fine man, an excellent mayor and a loving husband. His death following the flood had been a harsh blow to the town. Everyone had expected him to take charge of the rebuilding. Only a woman with Pauline's will and determination could have fulfilled his dying request to take over as mayor.

"I'm not here for myself," Charlotte said softly as Sasha clung to her skirts. She glanced at Wyatt, who waited in the doorway, hat in hands. "This is Mr. Wyatt Reed. He said he has business to discuss with you."

Pauline looked genuinely surprised. Contrary to what Wyatt had implied, she must not have been expecting him. "Mr. Reed."

"Mrs. Evans." He stepped forward, his boots rapping on the plank floor. "I wonder if I might have a word with you." He glanced at Charlotte and Mr. Brooks. "Alone."

Though Charlotte understood that whatever he had to discuss was none of her affair, part of her hated to leave the man. He'd shown kindness to Sasha and had proven worthy of her daughter's trust.

Mr. Brooks, however, took umbrage. "What is your business, Mr. Reed?" He positioned himself beside Pauline, clearly ready to defend her.

Pauline saw it differently. "I am fully capable of handling city business on my own." Her curt response left no room for argument. "Your bank might have loaned us money to rebuild, but it does not have any place in council chambers."

Curtis Brooks, thoroughly chastened, left any protest unspoken. Bowing stiffly, he begged his leave and departed.

Charlotte had to go, too. She cast a shy smile at Wyatt and Pauline. "I should get Sasha's supper." Then she left the meeting room.

In the vestibule, she stopped to straighten Sasha's dress. Rising, she spotted a notice tacked to the wall. In the poor light she could just make out that the orphan selection committee was meeting tomorrow. Maybe someone had stepped forward to take one of the remaining four children. If Pauline removed Beatrice from the committee, more people might step forward. At least there wouldn't always be someone pointing out each child's flaws.

Just thinking of the way Beatrice had acted when families first came forward to take in the children made Charlotte fume. If only she could take in more children... But her resources were limited since Charles's death, and she doubted even a selection committee without Beatrice Ward would entrust another orphan to her.

"I've come from Greenville," she heard Wyatt Reed say.

Charlotte knew she shouldn't listen, but his voice carried so clearly that she could hardly avoid hearing what he said. She glanced at the door. To leave, she had to cross the entrance to the hall, which would make it clear she'd overheard them. Best to linger here until an opportune moment and then slip away.

"A prominent citizen hired me to find out why the orphans

didn't arrive there as promised." His words sent a prickle of unease up her spine.

She leaned a little forward for a better view and saw Pauline's elbow jerk in irritation.

Still, the mayor's response was calm and collected. "Which prominent citizen?"

Wyatt hesitated long enough that she wondered if he wasn't supposed to reveal the answer. "Mr. Felix Baxter, but he's just the one who hired me. He's acting on the town's behalf. They're wondering why the children have been delayed."

"I believe Miss Sterling wired Greenville about the situation immediately after arriving in Evans Grove. She needed to await instructions from the New York office after the train robbery forced them to stop here."

Charlotte pressed her hands to Sasha's ears at the mention of the train robbery. Holly had told Charlotte how the robbers waved guns and crowded aside Miss Sterling—one of the agents from the Orphan Salvation Society—and the orphans in their quest to steal the loan money Holly and Mr. Brooks had brought from Newfield to rebuild Evans Grove. Thanks to Holly's quick thinking and the orphan boy Liam's bravery, Sheriff Wright had been alerted in time to capture the robbers. Unfortunately, their victory had come at a terrible price.

"I wasn't told all the details, ma'am," Wyatt was saying, "but I understand the Orphan Salvation Society sends two agents with the children. If Miss Sterling was indisposed, couldn't the other agent have escorted the children to Greenville?"

"Unfortunately, Mr. Arlington was shot during the robbery and died before Doctor Simpson could treat him. Since he was the senior agent, Miss Sterling felt she couldn't in good conscience move forward without the Society's counsel." Mayor Evans wrapped up her argument. "As you can see, there was no one available to escort the children to Greenville."

"Maybe not at the time, but it's been two weeks," Wyatt pressed. "Surely Miss Sterling has recovered and gotten her orders from the Society by now."

"She has, and they accepted our offer to place the orphans here in Evans Grove. So you see, there's no need for an escort. The children will be staying."

"No, ma'am, I'm afraid they won't. The Orphan Salvation Society had a prior agreement with Greenville, and I aim to see that they deliver on the terms. They can't go changing their minds halfway through."

"The Orphan Salvation Society is the children's caretaker," the mayor reminded him.

"That is not my point. They already had an agreement. Those children are supposed to go to Greenville. Now, if there's no one to escort the orphans there, I'll take them myself. There are eight, I believe." Wyatt Reed's words shot through her.

All eight? Charlotte gasped and clutched Sasha to her side. He would take her daughter away from her?

Never!

Without the slightest concern of being overheard, she scooped up Sasha and fled the building.

Wyatt heard the gasp and turned in time to see a shadow of black flit across the doorway. Mrs. Miller. She must have heard every word.

If the mayor saw her, she gave no indication. "Several of the children have already been placed. Surely the citizens of Greenville would not want to tear children away from their new families." A triumphant smile slid into place. "For in-

stance, Mrs. Miller—the woman who brought you here—
took in Sasha Petrov."

So Sasha *was* one of the orphans. An icy finger of doubt
slid into his well-constructed plan. *Focus, Reed. You need
that money to get to San Francisco.* He took a deep breath.
The mayor said *several* of the children, not all.

"How many?" he said between his teeth.

"How many what?" she asked cheerfully.

So, she would play a game, would she? "How many of
the orphans are already taken?"

She hesitated, as if counting. "Four of the eight, but other
families are in the process of selecting children. One of the
boys was just claimed, pending the selection committee's
approval. I expect the rest will be placed soon."

Wyatt quickly calculated his options. If he insisted on
taking all eight, Evans Grove would fight him. The new
parents would fight him. That orphan society might fight
him. He could lose all eight and the rest of his fee. Better to
settle for something.

He stared down the mayor. "But only four are now
placed."

She drew in a sharp breath. "At this moment, but as I
said—"

"The four can stay."

Her eyes widened. "I beg your pardon?"

"The four children who've already been taken can stay,
but the rest go with me to Greenville tomorrow."

The mayor raised herself to her full height, completely in
control of her emotions, which at this moment indicated she
would not budge one bit on this subject. "It is late, Mr. Reed.
I suggest we continue this conversation tomorrow afternoon
with the entire selection committee present."

"I can't wait until tomorrow afternoon." The woman's
firm command was beginning to irritate him. "The train

passes the Evans Grove whistle-stop at noon. I'll need to arrange in advance for the train to stop. Let's make it a morning meeting. Say nine o'clock."

Her smile faded, but just for an instant. "The committee members do have businesses to operate. One of the members, our schoolteacher Miss Sanders, will need to arrange for someone to watch her class. In truth, Mr. Reed, tomorrow evening would be best."

He had to give her credit for quick thinking. She'd managed to push the time even later. At this rate, he wouldn't be out of Evans Grove until Saturday.

He pushed back. "Ten o'clock, Mayor. In the *morning*. No later. I expect to put those children on the noon train to Greenville tomorrow. Miss Sterling may accompany them if she wishes." It seemed a generous concession at this point.

"That is up to her," the mayor said stiffly, "but I will convey your demands—and your offer—at once."

He nodded, and picked up his hat. "Pleasure doing business with you, Mayor."

"Ten o'clock, Mr. Reed." Her words were tough, but she looked worried.

She should be. Wyatt Reed always got his man.

Even after feeding Sasha, Charlotte still quaked with fear. What could she do? Where could she go? Who would help her? Since Charles's death, life had been filled with uncertainty, but never as much as right now.

She couldn't lose Sasha. The little girl meant everything to her. But now Wyatt Reed was trying to take her away. She had to do something.

The sun's waning rays illuminated the Bible sitting on the trestle table. Charlotte ran her fingers over the leather binding. God's Word had brought her comfort in the past. It helped her understand the loss of her parents and Charles, but could it gird her for the loss of her daughter, too?

"Mama?" Sasha's voice trembled, and Charlotte realized the little girl had seen her tears and was frightened.

She blinked away the moisture and folded her arms around Sasha. "It's all right. Everything will be all right."

Still, the girl shook, and a sob wrenched out.

Charlotte smoothed her hair. "Look at me, dearest." When the girl finally lifted liquid eyes to her, she smiled with more confidence than she felt. "Everything will be fine. Understand? I love you, and I will always love you. You're my little girl, my forever little girl."

Unable to hold back the tears any longer, Charlotte hugged Sasha close and kissed her repeatedly until the trembling passed. She must do something to cheer Sasha.

Holding her at arm's length, Charlotte asked, "Would you like a new doll?"

Sasha's eyes brightened. Clearly, the promise of a doll had distracted the little girl. Charlotte pulled some blue muslin from the bottom of her trunk. "Won't this make a pretty dress for her? She'll have black hair, like you, and blue eyes. Would you like that?"

Sasha nodded vigorously and stretched out her hand for the fabric.

Charlotte almost told her to wait, but Sasha had waited for so much already—parents and love and a real family. And it could all be taken away tomorrow. Why make her wait for anything more?

She dug some more in the trunk and found her tattered old rag doll. "This is the doll I had when I was your age. You can play with her while I make your new one."

Sasha hugged the ragged old doll.

Charlotte smiled to think Sasha could like something so misshapen. "Let's think of a name for your new doll."

"Katya."

Charlotte wished she would have chosen a more common name like Katy or Katherine, but she supposed the girl couldn't help but hang on to her Russian roots. Unfortunately, people like Beatrice Ward would frown on the foreign name and hold it against Sasha. But for now, it was better to please a little girl than a bitter old woman.

"What a pretty name. Katya it is."

If only keeping Sasha could be handled so easily, but that man, Wyatt Reed, wanted to take her away. Moreover, she'd trusted him! How foolish. She should have known he was trouble from the start, but she'd been misled by his tenderness toward Sasha. How could a man who'd held Sasha so gently turn around and tear her and the other children from their homes?

A rap on the door startled her from her thoughts. Even Sasha swiveled in her chair, worry creasing her little brow.

"I'm sure it's nothing," Charlotte said, forcing a smile, but all she could think about were Wyatt's words. He'd come to take away the children. Was he here now?

Her heart pounded as she grasped the door handle. What could she say to persuade him to leave Sasha with her?

"Charlotte, it's me," said a female voice on the other side of the door. "Holly."

Holly? Relief coursed through her until she remembered that Holly should be with Mason tonight. Something must have come up. Maybe she wanted to help Charlotte tonight instead of Saturday.

She opened the door. "I can't sort through Charles's things tonight."

Holly shook her head and motioned for Charlotte to step outside. "There's news."

Judging from the distress on her face, Charlotte knew what that news was. She closed the door behind her.

"This man came from Greenville to take away the orphans," Holly said breathlessly.

"I know."

"You know?"

"We met already." Charlotte swallowed hard. How could she have misjudged the man so badly? Worse, she'd led him straight to the mayor. "I overheard him talking to Pauline."

Holly drew in a shaky breath. "Then you know that Liam would have to leave." She choked. "Oh, Charlotte, I can't lose him. Mason can't lose him. We…we love him."

Charlotte wrapped her arms around her friend, marveling that they found themselves in a similar situation. In the past couple weeks, they'd both come to love a child. Holly adored Liam, and Sasha had claimed Charlotte's heart.

"I know, I know. I can't bear to lose Sasha, either." Charlotte fought back tears of her own. "What will we do?"

"We'll fight." Determination fired Holly. "The mayor had Rebecca cable the Orphan Salvation Society office. Then she called an emergency town meeting for first thing in the morning. Nine o'clock. She told the Greenville man to come at ten o'clock. By then we'll have figured out what to do." She squeezed Charlotte's hands. "Pauline is on our side. She won't let anyone take away our children."

That *anyone* meant Wyatt Reed. Charlotte felt sick that she'd trusted him.

Holly let go of Charlotte's hands and dashed toward the street. "I have to tell the Hutchinsons, the Hollands and the Regans. We'll win this, Charlotte. With Mayor Evans in the lead, we're bound to win."

As Holly flew off into the night, Charlotte hugged her arms against the chill wind. She hoped Holly was right, but hope alone wouldn't do it.

She cast a prayer high into the star-filled sky. *Lord, You love all Your children. Be with us tomorrow. Show us the way to keep Sasha and Liam and all the children here where they're loved. We're counting on You.*

In the meantime, Charlotte would do all she could to stop Wyatt Reed.

Chapter Three

The next morning, Wyatt sat in the hotel dining room eating breakfast and waiting for the ten o'clock meeting. From his seat at the window, he could see people scurrying through the grove of hackberry trees toward the town hall. He checked his pocket watch. A quarter to nine. Something was afoot, and he wouldn't put it past Madam Mayor to work some shenanigans ahead of the scheduled meeting.

He left enough money on the table to cover his meal and strode out onto the porch, where he put on his hat. When he saw Charlotte Miller hurry from the general store toward the town hall, he knew he'd guessed right.

It took less than a minute to catch up to her. "Good day, Mrs. Miller."

She jumped but didn't slow.

He matched her stride. "How is Sasha this morning? Any ill effects?"

She shook her head, but her shoulders squared defensively. "She's visiting her friend, Lynette Gavin."

He hadn't accused Charlotte of losing the girl, but she'd clearly taken it that way. He tried again. "You're sure in a hurry this morning. Anything I can help you with?"

"No." Her reddened cheeks said otherwise.

The rosy tinge became her, and again, Wyatt fought the urge to touch her cheek. "I'd gladly help."

"You've done quite enough already."

Her sharp words caught him in the gut. She wasn't embarrassed. Those flushed cheeks came from anger. Why? He wasn't going to take her daughter away from her. But had she heard that part? He thought back to yesterday. The gasp. The slamming of the door. Had it come before or after he'd agreed to let Sasha and the other placed children stay?

Charlotte accelerated her pace.

He chased after her. "Let me explain."

"There is nothing you can say to me," she choked out.

"But I—"

"Y-y-you heartless man." She halted and faced him, her fists balled and her eyes blazing. "How could you?"

"I—"

"Innocent children." She shook a fist at him. "You're taking innocent children from their homes. What sort of man are you?"

Wyatt's temper piqued. He'd done plenty that he wasn't proud of, but not this time. He wasn't taking any children from their homes. He was trying to *give* homes to the orphans who hadn't been selected. But Charlotte got him so addle-brained that he couldn't piece together the words.

He settled for pointing out the facts. "I'm a man doing a job."

"A job." She trembled with emotion, which only made her prettier. "You're ruining children's lives for *money?*"

She said the last word with so much distaste that he couldn't keep back a smile. If she'd just give him a chance to explain, most of that anger would go away. "First of all, I'm not ruining children's lives. Second, if I didn't do it, someone else would. But you need to understand—"

"Oh, I understand perfectly." She lifted that gorgeous

little chin, her eyes afire. "The only thing you care about is money. Well, if that's all you want, then maybe we can work something out. How much are you getting paid?"

He stared at her. She was offering to top Baxter's fee? He wouldn't take money from a widow, especially when it wasn't necessary. "More than you can afford."

Her cheeks darkened, and her spine straightened. "I see."

But he could tell she was struggling to hold back tears. "Let me explain."

"I don't want your explanations, Mr. Reed." Without waiting for a reply, she stormed off toward the town hall, where quite a crowd was forming.

He started after her, but she quickly fell in with a pale, somewhat plump woman. Wyatt rubbed his chin, half frustrated by Charlotte Miller and half intrigued by what was going on. Once the last person entered the hall, he made his way to the wooden steps and carefully cracked open the door. A gavel pounded on a tabletop, and the murmur of voices hushed.

Ten o'clock meeting, eh? According to his watch, it was nine o'clock. He slipped inside and let the door glide shut. Mayor Evans wasn't going to surprise him with this little early meeting. He'd hear every word.

Charlotte tugged at her bonnet strings as she settled onto a seat in the crowded room. Even at this cool hour, the hall was hot and her old wool mourning dress pinched at the waist so she could barely breathe. So much had happened since Charles's death that she hadn't found time to dye one of her everyday dresses. She'd have to do that soon or suffer through the heat of summer in thirteen-year-old dresses that had been made for wintertime. Still, that prospect, miserable as it would be, couldn't top her distress today.

That man, Wyatt Reed, had made her lose her temper,

something she never did. But how could she remain calm when he was going to take Sasha away? For money, no less. Tears stung her eyelids. She'd thought he was a good man. He'd held Sasha so tenderly. He'd rescued her. Or had he? Maybe he'd been whisking her off when Charlotte saw him carrying Sasha down the street. Anger welled up again. He'd dismissed her offer to pay him to keep the children in Evans Grove without even hearing her out. Men like him had no heart.

Mayor Evans called the meeting to order with a rapping of the gavel. "Good morning." Her strong voice carried above the chatter, and talk ceased in seconds. "I'm pleased to see so many of you here at this early hour."

Theodore Regan stood. He and his wife had taken in one of the orphan girls. With three boys already, Helen Regan had wanted a girl, and snapped up little Galina Denikin at once.

Mr. Regan's thick shoulders and arms gave him an imposing figure. "We heard Greenville's tryin' to take away our children."

A murmur of protest rose until Mayor Evans put it to a stop with an upraised hand.

"They did send a Mr. Wyatt Reed to request the orphans continue on to Greenville as originally scheduled."

"Well, Reed can't have 'em," Regan said.

A jolt of emotion shot through Charlotte. Could the town succeed where she'd failed? Could they convince Mr. Reed to leave without the children? She started to tell them he'd refused her offer to pay him, but the grumbles made her realize they were already angry enough to run Wyatt out of town, perhaps at the end of a pitchfork. She didn't need to do a thing.

Mayor Evans calmly regained control. "Let's not act in haste. Even though the Orphan Salvation Society office in

New York confirmed the agreement with Greenville, Mr. Reed agreed that those children already placed in homes could stay."

Charlotte's jaw dropped. Had she heard correctly? Considering the nods of approval and diminishing anger in the room, she had. Wyatt wasn't going to take Sasha away. She could keep her daughter. Was that what he'd been trying to tell her outside when she kept interrupting?

She bit her lip. Maybe she should have listened. She should have given him a chance. He had arranged for her to keep Sasha. She felt like crying out in joy, but not everyone was pleased.

Holly looked stricken. "That solves part of the problem, but it doesn't help the children who haven't been approved for selection yet."

The crowd shouted in agreement.

Charlotte battled despair as she recalled how much Holly and Mason adored Liam. Of course they would want to take the boy in once they married. She pressed a hand to her mouth. Poor Holly. Poor Mason. Poor Liam.

"They have been through so much," Holly continued, battling her own fears with such bravery that Charlotte marveled at her fortitude. "I'm positive homes can be found for every one of them right here in Evans Grove. Why should they be wrenched away when they've just started to hope?"

"Because they don't belong here." Beatrice Ward stood to make her point. "The Orphan Salvation Society's agreement with the town of Greenville came first, did it not, Miss Sterling?" She briefly glanced toward the elegant orphan agent and gave her only time to nod before continuing. "It would not only be morally wrong to deny Greenville the children they desperately want, but it would be illegal to break the agreement. The children—*all eight* children—must go to

Greenville." With a look of smug triumph, she settled back into her seat.

The crowd erupted, mainly in protest, but Charlotte saw a couple of people nod in agreement with Beatrice. Her stomach knotted yet again. Beatrice couldn't win, could she? She anxiously looked toward the doorway, hoping Wyatt would appear and counter Beatrice's claims. The opposition came from another quarter.

"That's not quite correct, Miss Ward." Curtis Brooks, the dapper banker from Newfield, faced the crowd. He exuded such confidence that people instantly quieted.

After safely delivering his bank's loan to Evans Grove despite the attempted robbery, Mr. Brooks had garnered a lot of respect in tōwn. Then he'd insisted on staying to oversee the loan distribution, and Mayor Evans had asked him to serve on the Orphan Selection Committee. His dedication in the following weeks had led people to trust his opinion. He'd struck Charlotte as a thoughtful, perceptive man. Perhaps he had the answer to this mess.

"From what I've seen of the paperwork Miss Sterling showed me," he said, "I'd say Greenville's legal claim might be on shaky ground."

Charlotte's stomach unknotted a little as the crowd cheered. They seemed to take his words as proof Evans Grove would win this dispute, but Mr. Brooks had said the claim *might* not hold up to scrutiny. He didn't say it definitely wouldn't.

Beatrice Ward must have heard what the crowd did, but she didn't have the same reaction. Not at all. Her eyes practically bulged from her head, as if her tightly bound gray hair had stretched even tighter. Her lips pressed into a thin, straight line, but she rallied quickly. "If you're going to challenge Greenville's claim, shouldn't you address their representative?"

Mayor Evans sighed as the crowd focused on her. "Miss Ward is right." She looked at Sheriff Wright. "Please summon Mr. Reed. I believe he is staying at the hotel."

Charlotte felt sick. What would Wyatt say? What would he do? Would Beatrice convince him to take Sasha away? She tried to pray but couldn't find the words. Surely God understood. Surely He would protect the innocent.

She didn't have long to wait. Wyatt Reed must have stayed near the town hall, because he arrived almost at once.

Every head turned when Wyatt strode into the room. He stood taller than any other man in town, and his hardened yet startlingly handsome face sent whispers through the women present. She hadn't noticed earlier, but he'd shaved off the stubble of yesterday, revealing cheeks honed to a hard plane and tanned by the sun.

He addressed himself to the mayor. "Ma'am." He removed his hat and held it in both hands.

"Mr. Reed." Mayor Evans showed not one ounce of discomfort before the intimidating man. Though considerably shorter in stature, she stood equally confident. "There is some debate over the legality of your claim."

Mr. Brooks rose beside her, creating a strong and united front. "As I understand the agreement, which Miss Sterling graciously allowed me to peruse, Greenville will have the opportunity to select any of the children that have not yet been taken by the time the Orphan Salvation Society agent reaches their town. It stands to reason that if all the children have been claimed before Greenville, none will be available for selection. There was never a guarantee that any of the children would come to Greenville. Thus, the agreement has not been violated."

Wyatt's jaw tensed as he pondered Mr. Brooks's words. The tiniest flicker of a smile indicated he'd found a crack in that argument. "The way I see it, you've forgotten two points. One, the Orphan Salvation Society doesn't have a formal agreement with Evans Grove. That means this town never had a right to the children in the first place."

The crowd murmured, but Mayor Evans wasn't daunted. "We received approval from the Society to form the selection committee and hold a distribution."

The murmurs turned to cries of agreement, especially when Rebecca Sterling confirmed everything the mayor had said.

Wyatt showed no sign of retreat. "Second." He waited for the crowd to quiet down. "As I said, I have two points. The second is that all the orphans haven't been picked yet. Even though Evans Grove got approval to take some of the orphans, you still have to follow the rules. I understand that the standard procedure is that any children who weren't claimed after a town's distribution have to get back on the train and go to the next town. That means those orphans that weren't taken at the distribution here must go to Greenville."

Holly's face fell. Liam hadn't been officially placed yet. In fact, only Sasha, Lizzie and Galina had been selected at the distribution. Friedrich had gone to the Hollands later.

Pauline rapped her gavel. Judging from the set of her jaw, she wasn't giving in, either. "All the children might not be placed in families yet, but they've been claimed by the town. We're committed to finding homes for every one of them, right here in Evans Grove."

Wyatt had to wait for the cheering to die down. "With all due respect, ma'am, I don't imagine a town has ever been approved to claim the children. Have they, Miss Sterling?"

Rebecca Sterling had grown pale as ash. "N-n-no," she finally conceded.

"But there's nothing that specifically forbids it?" Mr. Brooks asked her with a gleam in his eye.

A little of Rebecca's color returned. "No. No, there isn't."

"In that case," Mr. Brooks said smoothly, "I'd say the agreement is officially in dispute. The only resolution I can see would be to bring the matter before a judge. Wouldn't you agree, Madam Mayor?"

Pauline gave him a stiff yet clearly grateful nod in return. The mayor might chafe at Mr. Brooks's oversight of the loan, but his handling of this incident had apparently raised him a few notches in her estimation.

"Yes, Mr. Brooks, that is the clear course of action." Pauline turned back to Wyatt. "Mr. Reed, I believe I speak for the town when I say that you must make your case before Judge Broadside."

Again, Wyatt didn't show any emotion at her decision, but his question came out clipped. "Where can I find the judge?"

Pauline offered a dismissive smile. "He is currently on circuit and is next due in Evans Grove on Monday. That gives you the weekend to prepare your argument."

He barely flinched, but Charlotte saw it. "Greenville won't be pleased. They're expecting the children to arrive on this afternoon's train."

Mayor Evans didn't blink. "The town, and Mr. Baxter, may react however they wish, Mr. Reed, but the law will decide this matter."

He must have known he'd been bested, for he nodded curtly and strode out of the room, his eyes dark and unreadable. Was he upset? Would he fight them? No small part of Charlotte hoped he would reconsider and end this before the judge ever showed. He had already agreed that Sasha and the other placed children could stay. Surely it would only take a little more persuasion to get him to spare all the children.

But who could convince him? Wyatt had disregarded her plea. Perhaps Mr. Brooks had the answer.

She watched Brooks join Mayor Evans, Holly, Beatrice and Sheriff Wright at the front table. The Orphan Selection

Committee. Of course. They were supposed to meet today. Perhaps more children had been selected. Maybe the committee would have even let Holly and Mason take in Liam before they wed, but now, with this mess, the prospective parents would have to wait for the judge's ruling. Charlotte ached for them, but at least they had hope. And she had Sasha. She breathed in that single wonderful fact.

Curtis Brooks stood, and the room quieted. The man exuded genteel authority, and given that he had been the one to suggest Greenville had no case, everyone wanted to hear what he would say next.

"If we want to see the orphans stay here, we can help our case by ensuring the remaining children have good homes. If we can demonstrate to the judge that the town is capable of taking in all the orphans, he may look more favorably upon our position."

"Let's do it," cried more than one person.

Holly and Mason Wright nodded, as did Mayor Evans. Only Beatrice didn't.

In fact, she glared at Mr. Brooks. "As Mr. Reed clearly stated, any children who weren't chosen at the distribution should have been put *immediately* on the train to Greenville. We can't continue to break the rules by letting people claim children now."

Charlotte's heart sank for Holly and Mason's sake. The rest of the committee wouldn't listen to her, would they?

Beatrice pressed on. "And that's assuming that the distribution we held here was even legal. According to the original agreement, *all* the children should go to Greenville."

"No one is going to Greenville until after the hearing before the judge," Pauline Evans insisted.

Beatrice shot her a scathing look, but Mayor Evans backed down to no one.

"We will let the judge decide the case."

Beatrice clearly struggled with the possibility that the judge might rule against her. "But whatever he decides must apply to all of them, correct?"

Charlotte held her breath.

"Not to my girl." Theodore Regan stood, looking like he would take off Beatrice's head if she so much as threatened to come near his farm. "We followed all the rules and got her fair and square. Lina stays with Helen and me."

Mel Hutchinson, Charles's apprentice, chimed in, "And Lizzie isn't going anywhere, either. Marie won't stand for it."

Beatrice frowned, but even she saw the wisdom in avoiding conflict with the burly men. She opened her mouth and snapped it shut again until her gaze landed on Charlotte.

Panic beat hard against Charlotte's rib cage, but what could Beatrice do? She alone couldn't take Sasha away.

"Perhaps you have a case for your two families," Beatrice said coyly, her lips curving into an ugly smile, "however, Mrs. Miller is now a widow. If I recall the rules correctly, an unmarried person cannot have an orphan."

Charlotte felt all eyes turn to her. She couldn't breathe, couldn't move, couldn't stop shaking. This couldn't be happening.

"The placement must be revoked," Beatrice crowed, fixing her gaze on each of the committee members in turn. "If the judge rules that only the unplaced children must go on to Greenville, then Sasha must go with them."

Charlotte looked hopefully to the committee. Surely they would disagree. But Curtis Brooks frowned. Sheriff Wright took a deep breath. Mayor Evans cast her eyes downward. Charlotte looked to Holly. Surely her friend would stand up for her. Yet even Holly stayed silent, though stricken.

The room buzzed, narrowing as Charlotte's head began to spin.

"Give her air," someone said, and Charlotte sensed the

people around her moving. Someone instructed her to breathe deeply. Another person fanned air toward her. The window squeaked as it was raised.

Gradually, Charlotte came to her senses, but nothing had changed. The selection committee still sat in front. Curtis Brooks was whispering something to the mayor, who rapped on the table to recall everyone's attention.

"I'm sorry, Widow Miller," she began.

Charlotte knew what that meant. She knotted her hands together until her knuckles turned white. She bit the inside of her lip until it bled, but physical pain could not dull the pain of her heart. Tears streamed unhindered down her face.

Pauline Evans gave her a look of sympathy, but her words still hurt. "I'm sorry, but Miss Sterling confirmed that the Orphan Salvation Society makes no allowance for widows or widowers. You must be married to take in an orphan."

"But Sasha," Charlotte squeaked, her heart breaking more than she thought possible. "She's talking and playing like normal now. She calls me Mama." She choked, unable to continue. How could they do this? She fought to regain enough composure to speak. "I've just lost my husband. Now you're taking away my daughter?"

Not Sasha. Please, not Sasha.

"There is one solution," Curtis Brooks said calmly. "You could marry."

Virtually everyone gasped at the scandalous suggestion.

"Marry just days after she buried her husband?" Beatrice practically shouted. "She's in mourning. If she married now, she'd dishonor her husband's name. You can't be serious."

"I'm completely serious." Mr. Brooks fixed his gaze on Charlotte alone. "In difficult times, convention must be set aside in favor of the greater good. Jesus himself ignored the rules when the situation demanded it. On more than one occasion he worked miracles on the Sabbath to heal those in need. If Widow Miller is inclined to wed, we shouldn't forbid it, lest we be like the Pharisees."

That quieted Beatrice, though she looked none too pleased. But Charlotte couldn't see how this helped. Who would marry her so quickly? Who would make Sasha a good father? She glanced around the room and saw only husbands and men too young or too elderly to take on a thirty-one-year-old wife.

She drew in her breath. "How long?" The question trembled in the warm air like a butterfly just emerging from the cocoon, weak and unable to fly.

Somehow the committee knew what she meant. Mayor Evans glanced at Mr. Brooks for confirmation before she spoke. "Three days. You would need to marry before the judge hears Greenville's case."

Three days? How could she find a husband in three days?

Chapter Four

The meeting ended, and many of the women gathered around Charlotte in support. She struggled to regain her composure, but Mayor Evans's words echoed in her head.

Three days.

Marry in three days.

"It isn't right," one woman said.

Others echoed the same sentiment. Amelia Hicks squeezed Charlotte's arm in sympathy.

Charlotte could only nod. Her eyes were so blurred she couldn't tell one woman from another, but she did know that none was Holly. She desperately wanted to talk to her friend. Holly would know what to do. She had a cartload of smarts, sky-high faith and bone-deep courage.

Unfortunately, Holly had darted out of the room as soon as the meeting ended. Mason was gone, too. They were probably discussing what to do about Liam. Then Holly had to return to the schoolhouse to relieve whoever was watching the children. Charlotte would have to wait until after school to talk to her friend.

"Poor dear." Mrs. Ingersman, one of Beatrice's cronies, hovered over her. "Such a ridiculous idea. Remarry when you've barely begun to mourn." She clucked her tongue.

"I can't believe that banker would even suggest it. It'll be hard at first to say goodbye to the girl, but it's for the best. How could you ever hope to support a child all by yourself? Whatever Charles left you won't last forever, you know, and you're not a young woman anymore."

Amelia Hicks paled, but Charlotte's hackles rose with every word. How dare anyone think she would give up Sasha? She wouldn't. She'd do anything to keep her.

Even marry. Marry! And she had to do it within three days. The only question was who. Who would be brave enough to step forward? She again scanned the men in the room. Every one of them had gathered across the room around Curtis Brooks. Not one looked in her direction.

No wonder. They were all married.

"It'll be easier to find a husband without a child," offered another of Beatrice's cohorts. "Men don't like to take on someone else's family. They want their own children. They sure don't want some hand-me-down foreigner."

Charlotte's ears rang. The insufferable comments, the women pressing around her and the mock sympathy left her light-headed. "I think I need some air."

"Of course you do." Mayor Evans cut through the crowd and steered her out of the hall and into the sunshine and fresh air.

Charlotte gulped but still fought the light-headedness. Though still morning, the day promised to be a warm one, and the muggy air closed around her. Only a faint breeze tickled the bright green spring leaves.

"Now take a deep breath," Pauline said firmly, "and keep breathing slowly until your head clears."

Charlotte fought the swirl of fear, anger and tears as she took her breaths. What was she to do? Her head cleared, but not her distress. "I can't lose Sasha. Please help me find a way to keep her."

Pauline patted her back the way a mother would console a daughter before pushing her out to face her fears. "I wish I had a better answer for you, but Mr. Brooks's suggestion is the only option we could find."

"But how can I marry? Who?"

Giles DeGraw ambled down the street in their direction. He was helping rebuild the mill and was probably on his way to the general store. The twenty-two-year-old bachelor halted the minute he saw Charlotte and did an about-face, hustling away at double speed.

"Oh, dear," Charlotte said. "Is that how every bachelor is going to react when he sees me?"

"Maybe for a day or two, but they'll get over it."

Pauline's encouragement didn't help. A day or two was all Charlotte had. Clearly no man would step forward of his own account. That meant she had to convince someone to marry her. But how? Beatrice was right about one thing. A lifetime commitment shouldn't be entered into casually. Yet, for Sasha's sake, Charlotte must find a man willing to marry her.

"Ah, good. Miss Sterling." Pauline withdrew her comforting arm to wave down Rebecca. "Perhaps you can see to Charlotte. I need to speak with Mr. Brooks."

As Pauline left, the Orphan Salvation Society agent approached with Amelia Hicks trailing behind her. Rebecca looked just as stricken as Holly. It took a second for Charlotte to realize why. Rebecca would have to take Sasha away from her and return the little girl to the schoolhouse, where the unclaimed orphans were staying. Charlotte's heart pounded. Rebecca wouldn't take her daughter away today, would she?

Rebecca wrung her hands, elegantly covered in white lace gloves. "Charlotte?"

Charlotte felt the blood drain from her face.

Rebecca averted her gaze and took a deep breath. "I

wanted to tell you how sorry I am." She nibbled her lower lip. "Mr. Armstrong—he's the head of the Society—insists we adhere to the rules."

Charlotte waited for the rest to fall.

Rebecca hesitated. "I—I just wanted you to know. If it were up to me, I'd let you keep Sasha. She clearly adores you."

Tears misted Charlotte's eyes as the lump in her throat grew. "I can't lose her," she choked out. "Is there any other way?"

Rebecca slowly shook her head.

Charlotte held her breath, waiting for the woman to ask her to bring Sasha to the schoolhouse, where the unclaimed orphans were staying.

At last, Rebecca lifted her gaze and squared her shoulders. "The rules don't say when I must take Sasha back. I don't see why it wouldn't be all right for Sasha to stay with you until Monday, until everything's settled with the judge and…and…well, maybe you'll find someone."

She gave Charlotte a hopeful smile, but Charlotte felt only the rush of relief. She could keep Sasha for three more days. And then… The pain came back, even worse.

"That was all I wanted to say." Rebecca edged away. "I should see to the children." She hurried off, leaving Charlotte in despair.

"What am I going to do?" She clutched her arms around her midsection.

Amelia gently laid a hand on Charlotte's clenched arms. She'd been so quiet that Charlotte had forgotten she was there. The petite woman lifted liquid eyes. The depth of sorrow and pain in her expression stunned Charlotte. Amelia wasn't the prettiest woman in town, nor the most talkative. She tended to keep to herself and skitter off nervously whenever her husband drew near. Who could blame her? She'd married the most obnoxious drunken fool in town. But she was a good woman, who had been very kind to the orphans since their arrival in town. Charlotte, who had barely known her before that, was starting to consider her a friend.

"There are worse things than being alone." Amelia's voice was so soft that Charlotte had to listen carefully to hear her.

Such as marrying the wrong man.

"I know. But Sasha…" Charlotte's throat clotted again. "She's my little girl."

Amelia's tears threatened to overflow. "I hope you can keep her." She sniffled and pulled out a worn handkerchief. "It's not fair that we have to marry to…to…" She never managed to finish her sentence, but Charlotte knew what she meant. *To have a family.*

It wasn't fair, but she still had to do it. Somehow. Whoever she could get to agree to marry her, she prayed he wouldn't turn out to be a drunkard or a wife beater.

Wyatt held his temper in check until he'd left the town hall. Bring his case before the judge? Madam Mayor had some nerve. No doubt she and that Mr. Brooks had concocted this plan overnight. From what Wyatt had learned, the banker wasn't even from Evans Grove. He also didn't doubt that the pretty mayor was the source of Brooks's interest in the matter. He'd seen the way the man looked at her the first time he'd talked to Mayor Evans. Protective. Defending her against all attacks.

The way Wyatt had protected Charlotte Miller by letting her keep Sasha. He'd had to force himself not to look in her direction or risk losing his focus.

What good had that focus done? Thanks to Madam Mayor and her conniving banker friend, he had to convince a judge on Monday that he was right or lose every penny of his fee.

How could he sway a judge? He wasn't a lawyer nor could he afford to hire one.

Wyatt stormed toward the livery. Whenever he had to think things through, he saddled up Dusty and headed for open country. The endless sky and untamed land helped clear his head, and after this little fiasco, he sure needed to do some clearing.

Sweet stars, he'd already made an enormous concession by letting Sasha and three other orphans stay. Baxter would never have agreed to that. The man told him the town wanted all eight. *Bring them all,* the man had said. What was so special about these eight orphans that two towns were fighting over them?

He rubbed his clean-shaven jaw. He'd thought the town would give him more respect if he shaved. Clearly not. They were set on keeping those kids. Greenville was equally determined to get them. Wyatt shook his head. Who knew how long those kids had gone unwanted. Now everyone wanted them. Life was sure full of mysteries, but he suspected the answer to this one could be rooted out with a little effort.

The woman sweeping the porch of the general store shouted out a greeting, jolting him from his thoughts. He mumbled a response and tugged the brim of his hat lower before continuing on to the livery. By the end of the day, he would become the town enemy, and no one would speak to him, not even pretty Charlotte Miller.

His gut knotted a little at the thought of disappointing her. Like the rest of the town, she wanted all the orphans to stay. The best he could do was let her keep her daughter. Sasha's wide blue eyes danced into his head. He could still feel her trusting arms around his neck. Her trust had felt good, really good.

He found the stable boy dozing on a pile of straw in an empty stall, pitchfork cast aside. Wyatt smiled. No doubt the lad had been up since dawn mucking out the stable. Wyatt's father had worked him just as hard. *A farmer's work is never done,* his pa had told him more times than Wyatt could remember. But Wyatt didn't love the Illinois farm the way his father had. For as long as he could remember, he'd dreamed of adventure. When the war started, he'd enlisted and never went back. Now it was too late; too late to make amends, too late to explain, too late to tell his father that he'd made the wrong choice. *If only they'd reconciled before Pa died.*

Life was littered with regrets. Wyatt let the stable boy sleep. He could saddle his own horse.

Dusty snorted when Wyatt drew near, as if to say he didn't think much of being stuck in a stable. Like Wyatt, his horse spent most days out in the open. They'd traveled across the country together and slept under the stars at night. Dusty had been his only friend. He was also just as stubborn and ornery.

Wyatt flung the saddle blanket on Dusty's back, and the horse's ears pricked in anticipation.

"That's right, boy. We're heading out onto the prairie." He patted Dusty's flank. "A little air'll do us both good."

"Leavin' town?"

Wyatt whirled around to see Sheriff Mason Wright standing outside the stall. "You'd like that, wouldn't you?"

The sheriff didn't betray an ounce of emotion. "We all got a job to do." His hard blue eyes pierced through Wyatt, as if trying to read his motives, but Wyatt was good at masking his intentions.

He turned back to saddling Dusty. "You're right about that. It's a job."

"Must pay right fine to work for someone like Baxter."

Wyatt narrowed his eyes. His gut had warned him not to trust Baxter, and now the sheriff had seconded it. He wasn't about to tip his hand, though. "Well enough." He hefted his saddle off the rail.

"Then you are going before the judge."

"I was hired to bring the orphans to Greenville. Your mayor can drag her heels all she wants, but in the end, they're going where they belong."

The sheriff didn't argue that they should stay in Evans Grove like pretty near everyone else here. Instead, he stroked his mouth, deep in thought. "I see you're a man of conviction. Probably no use trying to change your mind."

"That's right." Wyatt set the saddle on Dusty's back. "I trust you'll uphold the judge's decision."

"That's my job." But he didn't sound pleased. A slight tick at the corner of Wright's mouth betrayed more than passing interest in the outcome of that decision.

Wyatt had no idea what that interest might be, nor did he want to know. A tracker did not get personally involved in others' lives. "Glad to hear it."

He hoped their conversation was over, but the sheriff showed no sign of leaving. "Thought you might give up."

"I never give up."

"That's what I heard."

Ordinarily, that would be a compliment, but Wright said it like he was condemning Wyatt for being inflexible.

"You of all people must understand the law can't be broken."

The sheriff had a casual manner about him that belied his true intensity. "It can be changed, though."

"Too late for that." Wyatt was getting tired of this conversation. He wished Wright would either get to the point or leave him alone. He cinched the saddle. "I'm not trying to hurt anyone."

"Now, that's going to be tough, isn't it? Take Widow Miller, for one."

"Mrs. Miller?" Wyatt's hands stilled as the pretty woman's face floated into his head. Something about her drew him like iron to a magnet. "I said the orphans already taken could stay."

"But she's a widow now, and only married couples can take in an orphan. Sounds to me like you'll be taking Sasha with you."

Wyatt stiffened. Sasha was the whole reason he'd agreed to let the already-placed orphans stay. He couldn't rip the little girl from Charlotte's arms. Never in a million years. He couldn't take Sasha, who had trusted him wholly, to Greenville to be given to another family, end up in Baxter's orphanage or go back to New York. The whole idea made him sick.

The sheriff drove his point home. "How's that going to feel, knowing you took a four-year-old girl from her loving mother?"

Wyatt steeled himself. *Get in, do the job and get out.* No emotional attachments. He couldn't afford them if he was ever going to get to San Francisco. "That's not my problem. I'm just upholding the law, the same as you."

The sheriff grunted. "Guess that's one way of looking at it."

"Do you have another way?" Wyatt snapped.

"Like I said, only married couples can take in orphans."

Wyatt didn't miss the emphasis on *married*. The man must be out of his mind. "What do you expect me to do about that?"

Wright tapped his fingers on the stall door. "I wouldn't know."

"Neither would I."

Still, Wright didn't leave. "You could help the other families. If those kids have to go to Greenville, there'll be more broken hearts."

"That's not my problem, Sheriff. I'm here to do a job. Nothing more, nothing less."

"Too bad." The sheriff paused before backing away. "Just want you to know that I'll be keeping an eye on you, Reed."

Now, that sounded like a warning.

Chapter Five

As soon as Charlotte heard the bell signaling the end of the school day, she hurried to the schoolhouse, Sasha in hand. The exertion and the sun beating down on her black dress made her perspire terribly, but she had to see if Holly had any ideas.

Students hurried away, some to chores and others to play together. Two girls skipped on a hopscotch board drawn in the dirt. Sasha looked longingly in their direction, but the older girls probably wouldn't welcome the company. Charlotte hurried her up the steps and opened the door.

Holly, Rebecca and Heidi, the last orphan girl still unplaced, were washing slates while Patrick and Tommy, two of the remaining orphan boys, whined to go outside. Liam paced behind Holly, clearly trying to get her permission to do something. Charlotte halted. She'd forgotten that the orphans and Rebecca stayed in the schoolhouse and would be there after school.

The orphan agent looked up at Charlotte and Sasha, who begged to join Heidi.

"Charlotte." Her eyes instantly averted and her cheeks flushed.

Charlotte had the distinct impression she'd interrupted something, but Holly motioned her to come in.

"I hoped we might talk," Charlotte said to Holly, then glanced at Rebecca. The woman took the hint with grace.

"Very well, boys. The rest of your chores can wait. We'll go outside for a little while."

The boys whooped their approval and scrambled out of the schoolhouse in record time.

Rebecca smiled at their exuberance. "Sasha may join us, if you approve."

Charlotte let her daughter run to Heidi. Bless Sasha for her eagerness to play with the disfigured girl that most people avoided. To four-year-old eyes, Heidi Strauss was simply a friend. The burn scars on her face from the fire that killed her parents were no more unusual than different-colored eyes or hair.

Rebecca rose but before taking the girls outside, thanked Holly. "It's an honor. Truly."

As she passed, Charlotte saw that flush in her cheeks again. What had Holly done that both embarrassed and honored Rebecca?

She didn't have a chance to ask, for Holly, who looked a bit anxious, brought her straight to the task at hand. "What will you do?"

Charlotte sank into the chair Rebecca had vacated. "I was hoping you would have an idea."

Holly dipped her rag into a bucket of water and then wrung it. "I usually have the students wipe the slates," Holly said, "but they're restless with spring in the air. It happens every year around this time. They can't sit still for a moment."

Charlotte picked up Rebecca's rag and swiped one of the slates. "Two pairs of hands make for light work." Only that made her think of how she'd soon have only one set of hands in her house if she couldn't find a husband. "Oh, Holly, I don't know what to do. Every bachelor in town avoids me like poison ivy."

Holly chuckled. "They're just a bit skittish."

"Skittish? They're terrified. But I only have tomorrow and Sunday, and I'd have to do the asking." Charlotte's hand paused midswipe. "How does a woman ask a man to marry her? What man would agree to such a thing?"

"I don't know." Holly shrugged. "You can only try."

"But who would I ask? I've tried to think of someone, anyone, and I come up empty."

Holly scrunched her face, deep in thought. "There's Giles DeGraw."

"You should have seen him run away the moment he saw me looking at him."

Holly snorted with laughter and then covered her mouth. "I'm sorry."

"It is funny, or it would be if I wasn't in such a desperate situation."

Holly leaned both elbows on her desk and propped her head in her hands. "Then Giles is out."

"He's also too young. A man in his early twenties isn't going to marry a thirty-one-year-old woman."

"But you're so beautiful." Holly sighed. "You look years younger."

Charlotte could never reconcile Holly's insistence that she was beautiful with the image that reflected back at her in the mirror. "I'm not young, and everyone knows it. I think we need to confine ourselves to the older bachelors and widowers."

"Widowers? Well, there's Elmer Droll. He lost his wife last year."

"Elmer Droll!" Charlotte stared at her friend. "He must be sixty-five years old."

Holly shrugged. "It is a last resort."

"It's no resort at all." Still, Charlotte was ashamed that the thought had already occurred to her, along with the even more shameful thought that he wouldn't live that long after they wed. "I can't imagine…you know…if he…" She couldn't bring herself to say aloud that she couldn't bear to perform her wifely duties in such a marriage. She choked back rising bile. "But I suppose I might have to."

Holly took her hand. "No, no. Don't even think it. There are lots of other prospects. Take Colton Hayes, for instance. Now, there's a handsome man."

Charlotte couldn't disagree with that. The tall rancher had made many a heart flutter, just not hers. "But he's so dedicated to taking care of his parents and the ranch. He hasn't seen anyone since his father's injury and his mother took ill, has he?"

Holly shook her head.

"Poor man. He has so many responsibilities. I couldn't ask him to take on a wife and child, too, not with his parents in such ill health." Charlotte pressed her fingers against the cool slate. It reminded her of childhood, when she'd dreamed of finding her prince and living happily ever after.

Holly sighed. "I can't think of anyone else. There's not another man in town who meets your criteria." She glanced at the schoolhouse clock. "I'm sorry, but I need to meet Mason. If I think of anyone, I'll let you know right away."

Charlotte's heart sank. Holly and Mason would soon marry. They would have the family she so desired. Her shoulders slumped. "I understand."

Suddenly, a glint of excitement lit Holly's eyes. "There is one other possibility. Wyatt Reed."

Her words knifed through Charlotte.

"Mr. Reed?" She could barely choke out his name.

"He is handsome."

"He's the enemy."

Holly's expression drooped for a second before her innate optimism returned. "Perhaps to some people, but not for you. He said that the orphans who were already placed could stay. I'm sure that's because of you and Sasha."

"I don't think so."

"I do. I noticed he avoided looking at you during the meeting."

"That only proves he feels nothing for me."

Holly smiled coyly. "Except that he sneaked a glimpse when he thought no one was looking."

Charlotte felt the heat in her cheeks. "I'm sure you're mistaken. He was probably looking at…at…" She searched her mind for who was seated near her. "Amelia."

Holly laughed. "I don't think he could even see her, nor would he care. I'm sure he was looking at you."

Charlotte had to cut this off at once. She pressed her hands to her ears. "Please stop. Wyatt Reed would never marry me or any other woman. He's a hired tracker, a loner. He has no heart for anyone but himself."

"He's honorable enough to agree to leave the children with families here."

"H-he's obstinate. And loves money."

"We all need money to survive."

Charlotte knew that, but Wyatt was different. He would take children from the chance to find good homes just for money. But she couldn't tell Holly what he'd said to her, not when Holly and Mason loved Liam so. So she settled for complete denial. "It's a ridiculous thought."

"Perhaps. But he'd be a lot nicer to kiss than Elmer Droll."

Charlotte couldn't argue with that.

"Think about it overnight, and we'll talk again in the morning. I think I can spare an hour early. We did say eight o'clock?"

Charlotte's eyes shot open. "Tomorrow morning? Oh, dear, with everything that happened, I forgot about cleaning out Charles's things." She bit her lip. "I—I don't know. Maybe now isn't such a good time. I should, well, think on other things."

They both knew what those "other things" were.

Oddly enough, Holly looked relieved. "You will at least need to crate up Charles's things before you bring another man into the house."

Another man. Such as Wyatt Reed. Waves of heat rolled through Charlotte as she imagined him sitting at the trestle table or carrying in water for her or sleeping beside—

She shook herself. "We'll deal with that if it happens."

"*When* it happens," Holly stated with dead certainty, as if finding a husband in less than three full days happened all the time.

"When what happens?" The schoolhouse door banged open, and Sheriff Mason Wright entered. "What's going on here?"

Holly rose, her face flushed with pleasure. "Nothing important. Is Liam still playing with the boys?"

He nodded and glanced at Charlotte, who suddenly felt out of place. Holly positively glowed as she glided over to greet him. His gaze riveted on Holly's face, shutting out everything else. He took her hands so tenderly that it made Charlotte's heart ache.

This was a private moment, one Charlotte couldn't bear to witness. She slipped silently past them and out the door. Before fetching Sasha, she took a breath to calm herself. Mason and Holly were truly in love, something she would never have.

The ride wasn't clearing Wyatt's head. Moreover, everyone in town glared at him as if he was a murderer. He was used to being disliked by civilians, but for the most part the lawmen tolerated him. Based on the encounter with Sheriff Wright in the stable, this one wanted him out of town now, too.

He kept his gaze fixed forward and put blinders on his peripheral vision. Some peculiar job this was. Usually he had to use all his senses to track down the fugitive and save his own hide. Now here he was trying to block out the voices and the people around him.

He headed to the outlying farms and ranches west of town, those in the direction of Greenville. Between the nagging in his gut and the sheriff's obvious dislike of Baxter, he wanted to see if anyone else here had dealings with the man. If he found anything against Baxter, he might reconsider taking the case to the judge.

He would not reconsider the sheriff's not-so-veiled suggestion. Wyatt was not a marrying man. Period.

The first two farms yielded nothing, but the Hayes ranch was a different story.

The tall rancher eyed him solemnly, his strong jaw taut. "We don't do business with men like Baxter."

Though Wyatt pressed, Colton Hayes refused to elaborate.

What sort of business? As near as Wyatt could tell, Baxter made his money in trade. He shipped supplies out to the mines in Colorado and the big farms in his area. His storefront was small but well stocked. At first glance, Greenville seemed an odd place to plant such a business, but it was the last large town on the rail line. Baxter must be using that to his advantage. Maybe he overcharged. That would explain the rancher's disdain.

Baxter's orphanage also seemed to pass muster. From what Wyatt heard, it handled cases of children in Greenville and the surrounding area who became orphans, and also took in almost all the orphans the Orphan Salvation Society brought through that didn't find homes. Greenville's mayor spoke glowingly of it and of Baxter. "A first-rate philanthropist." "Above reproach." Over and over he heard the same words. Everything had checked out, or he wouldn't have taken the job.

When Wyatt had stopped by the orphanage, it was empty. Baxter had taken considerable pride in his ability to place the children. That hadn't struck Wyatt as odd at the time, but now he wondered how Baxter succeeded when the orphan society couldn't.

He shook his head. None of this explained Greenville's determination to get the orphans and Evans Grove's equal insistence on keeping them.

Frustrated, he rode Dusty hard on the return. The steed appreciated the gallop, but Wyatt hadn't gotten any answers. He had pieces to a puzzle, but none of them fit together. Mayor Evans standing oh so confident next to that distinguished banker fellow, sure she'd find a way to thwart him. The sheriff out-and-out suggesting he hightail it back to Greenville and give up a lucrative job. Charlotte Miller.

His heart caught in his throat. He had no idea the orphan society would take away Sasha. It wasn't fair. Making her marry to keep her daughter? Ridiculous. The whole thing made him so angry that he wanted to walk into that town and shake some sense into those orphan society rule makers. And that was the trouble. He couldn't get involved. He couldn't let emotion get hold of him, or he would ruin yet more lives.

He unclenched his fist and flexed his hand. He'd been holding the reins too tightly. That was the trouble with emotion. It hurt. And Wyatt couldn't risk hurting any more women and children.

The faces in the fires still haunted his dreams. Atlanta burning. The march to the sea. The echoes of cannon and crackle of flames. His hand on the torch, anger seething until it overflowed. Houses burning. Screams. Cries for mercy.

He drew in a rattling breath. Wyatt Reed couldn't be trusted around women and children. Ever.

Marry Wyatt Reed?

The thought niggled at Charlotte's mind as she walked Sasha home. The man kept his emotions in check, much like Charles. The only hint of feeling came when he held Sasha, but did he care enough for the little girl to tie himself to a woman he didn't know? It was a preposterous idea. She couldn't believe Holly had suggested it. Worse, her friend insisted Wyatt had looked at her in a special way, the same way Mason looked at Holly.

Impossible.

She'd never seen it.

Yet what choice did she have? Elmer Droll?

Sasha slipped from Charlotte's grasp to greet the Hutchinsons' dog Sparky, like she always did when they passed. The beagle mix had started to wait expectantly each day for his hug and kisses. Sasha squealed with laughter as the dog lapped her face.

The little girl was starting to fit into the community. To Charlotte, she'd become dearer than life. Charlotte would do anything for her—even marry. Thirteen years ago she'd wed Charles Miller out of necessity. She could do it again. Given the slim selection of available men, she preferred Wyatt by far.

But how could she convince him to marry her? The brides of old used a dowry to lure an eligible husband. Her parents had left her nothing, but Charles had. That was it! She'd offer him money.

Wyatt Reed would take any job for money. Hopefully, the sum she had would be enough. She felt a flash of panic at the thought of giving up the money—her security to take care of herself and Sasha—but she pushed it away. Sasha was worth it. At first, Charlotte would offer only part of the total amount of money she had, but even if Wyatt demanded every last dollar, Sasha was worth the price. When all this was over and the little girl was truly hers, Charlotte would do anything—even scrub floors—to put food on the table. Whatever it took, she'd do it to keep her daughter.

Charlotte gathered Sasha and marched toward the hotel. If she was going to do this, she'd do it now, before Wyatt Reed had time to run and she lost her nerve.

The distance had never seemed so short. Before she had time to formulate how to broach the subject, the hotel porch came into view. What on earth would she say to him? *Good evening, Mr. Reed, would you be looking for a wife?* Or perhaps, *Mr. Reed, perhaps you would prefer not to eat alone each night.* Or even outright begging.

Every approach made her blush madly.

When Mrs. Regan stopped to console her, she fanned her face and made up excuses. "This mourning dress is so hot and heavy."

If the woman recognized the true source of Charlotte's discomfort, she had the grace not to point it out. "I'm so glad we get to keep Lina. Teddy and I were beside ourselves over this whole mess. Why, that Mr. Reed should go back to Greenville where he belongs and leave us alone. I say if the Orphan Salvation Society agreed to keep the children in Evans Grove, then that's where they should stay."

As she rattled on with her condemnation of Wyatt, it took all Charlotte's strength not to walk away. If even those who'd benefited from his concession despised him, how would they feel if she married him? Would they hate her, too? Would they spurn Sasha?

She glanced at her daughter, hoping she didn't understand all that was swirling around her.

"I'm sorry to hurry away, but we have business." Charlotte couldn't listen to another word. "Urgent business that can't wait."

Taking Sasha's hand, she hurried toward the hotel. The little girl appeared not to have understood what Mrs. Regan had said. But Charlotte wondered how to break the news to Sasha if she couldn't find a husband.

Her stomach churned as she envisioned handing Sasha to Rebecca to take on the train to Greenville. The little girl wouldn't understand. She'd cry and wail. She'd reach for Charlotte and wonder why her mama was abandoning her. And then to board a train again after the horrible robbery and shooting that had occurred on Sasha's last train ride. Charlotte couldn't bear to think of her little girl scared and alone, without her mama to comfort her. She stumbled and had to stifle a sob. No one could take away her daughter. She'd do anything, marry anyone to prevent it. Even Wyatt Reed.

Please, Lord.

They'd reached the hotel with its broad veranda. Charlotte stood before the steps. She'd never realized how many there were. Six in all. Was Wyatt there? She looked toward the front windows, but they reflected the late-day sun, and she couldn't tell if he was dining. Through the door spilled a jumble of conversation and the clinking of glass and flatware.

The time had arrived. She must do it. For Sasha's sake.

She took a deep breath. "Come, Sasha, let's see if Mr. Reed is here."

They climbed the six steps. Charlotte waited for Sasha on each while the men chewing tobacco on the porch watched her progress. With each step, her heart pounded harder.

Good evening, Mr. Reed. Could I have a moment of your time?

Perspiration trickled between her shoulder blades.

I would like to propose a business transaction.

Her knees threatened to give out.

A marriage in name alone, so I can keep Sasha.

Bile rose up her throat.

You may come and go as you please.

She couldn't catch her breath.

And will be handsomely paid.

Dear Lord, what am I thinking?

They'd reached the porch. One of the men spat into an old chamber pot and grinned at her. Would he offer himself as a husband? His gapped yellow teeth made her queasy.

"Papa!" Sasha cried and, in an instant, slipped from her grasp.

Papa? Charlotte stumbled after her. She was an orphan, wasn't she? How could her father be here?

Sasha raced into the hotel and through the dining room door. Charlotte strode as quickly as she could in the heavy skirts but couldn't catch up. When she reached the hotel dining room, she halted, stunned.

The man she'd called papa was none other than Wyatt Reed.

Wyatt hated needless waiting. Stalking a fugitive was one thing. In those cases he was on the move, using his senses and his wit to outfox the criminal. Waiting for a judge was another thing altogether. He had to do something, find some way to fill his time. He couldn't just sit around the hotel.

He'd figure out why these orphans mattered so much to the folks here. He could understand the ones that had been taken into homes already, but the unclaimed? It made no sense.

He picked at his heaping plate of roast beef and potatoes slathered in gravy and then reached for the cup of coffee. Ordinarily Wyatt wouldn't drink coffee so late in the day, but he wanted to see what went on in Evans Grove after dark. Who visited whom, who took care of the orphans and where. Few houses had curtains, and much as it galled him to look in on unsuspecting people, many a parlor became visible after dark.

While eating, Wyatt pondered the banker. Brooks was an interesting part of the puzzle. Wyatt had never known a banker to get personally involved in a project like this, particularly in a town where he didn't reside, yet Brooks had sat right there beside the mayor making policy decisions. Odder yet, everyone approved his interference.

Maybe that could be used against the town. If he could get the man tossed off that council, then maybe he could win over enough remaining members to finish up this job. Miss Ward was certainly on his side. He might be able to sway that petite schoolteacher gal, too. That left the preacher, the sheriff and the mayor. He'd have to work hard to make inroads with any of them.

"Papa!" a young girl squealed.

Moments later, that girl launched herself at him. Wyatt dropped his fork and put his hands up. What on earth? The girl's raven hair and pigtails betrayed her identity. Sasha. Her thin arms wrapped around his waist. Why would she call him papa?

Everyone in the dining room was staring at him. Apparently, they had the exact same question.

"She's not mine." He awkwardly patted Sasha's back and gave the staring diners a half smile. "She must be confused. Maybe I look like her pa."

"Not at all," chuckled an overweight woman with a splotchy yet kind face. "Charles Miller was a big man."

"I meant her—" How could he say it? *Real* father sounded cruel and might remind the girl of the parents she'd lost.

Miss Ward, who was eating across the room, saved him from finishing. "Nettie, you know as well as I do that the creature has no parents. She's one of those orphans. She can't even speak proper English. Charles Miller was bamboozled by that wife of his into taking her in."

Her strident denunciation chilled Wyatt. Didn't she care what Sasha heard? He covered the girl's ears as the debate heated up.

"She's a darling little girl," Nettie protested, "and Charlotte loves her dearly. I for one hope she gets to keep her."

Miss Ward's already taut expression got even tighter. "No one will keep any of the lot. They're dirty little urchins." She lifted a handkerchief to her nose as if the stench overwhelmed her.

"They're just children who need to be loved. Why, if our house wasn't in such disrepair, we'd take one of them."

Miss Ward looked aghast. "None of them are staying. If not for that nonsense this morning, good Mr. Reed would have the lot of them out of here already."

All eyes turned back to him.

Wyatt cringed. If that's how good was measured, he wanted no part of it. He pressed his hands more tightly over Sasha's ears. "Now is not the time to discuss this."

"Sasha, what are you doing?" Charlotte Miller ran into the dining room, and he could tell by the look on her face that she'd heard every appalling word that Miss Ward had uttered. He also saw gratitude there. For him.

The thought strangely warmed him.

She moved close to the table, her cheeks flushed and her light hazel eyes shining. "Thank you." It came out in a whisper.

My, she was beautiful. He couldn't take his gaze off

her perfectly proportioned features. The brows that arched in exact crescents. Her dainty nose and rosy, full lips. He couldn't help noticing how soft they looked, just like her skin. The curls peeking from her bonnet promised a stunning cascade of reddish-blond hair. Even in the stiff, black mourning dress, she shone. Her delicate hands and graceful arms fluttered to her neck in a gesture of self-consciousness and humility.

He forgot to breathe.

Then her brow puckered, and he looked down to see he still covered Sasha's ears. He quickly removed his hands. "I don't know why she ran to me."

Charlotte touched her daughter's back. "Sasha, Mr. Reed doesn't need you on his lap when he's trying to eat his supper."

"It's all right." And truthfully it was. The little girl's embrace did something to him. He felt alive, like he'd slept for the fourteen years since joining the army, and finally woke up. He didn't want her to move away. And considering the way the girl burrowed deeper into his lap, there wasn't much he could do to dislodge her, anyway.

"I'm sorry." The color rose again in Charlotte's cheeks. "I don't know what's gotten into her."

She glanced around the room, and he realized everyone was still watching the scene. He nodded toward the chair across the table. "Please sit."

She wrung her hands, alternately looking at the chair and the other diners, as if afraid sitting with him would damage her reputation forever.

"I promise not to bite." He let his lips quirk into a smile for her sake, and, if he was honest, because he wanted her to stay. Her and Sasha, who'd nestled on his lap and was playing with the fringe on his buckskin jacket.

Apparently convinced, Charlotte sank into the chair. "I

don't know what got into her. Maybe you look like her father. Does he, Sasha?"

The little girl looked up at him but didn't answer.

Charlotte didn't know quite what to say. Here she was, in the perfect position to lay out her proposition, and her heart was pounding through her rib cage. Of all things, Sasha had opened the door by calling him papa. How easy it would be to ask if he was willing to really be Sasha's papa, but the words stuck in her throat.

Instead, she croaked out insignificant chatter. "I understand her parents were Russian."

His brow furrowed. "Russian? That's unusual, but it explains the accent."

"And her limited vocabulary. But she's learning new words every day. Aren't you, Sasha?"

Naturally, the girl didn't fully understand what she was asking, but she would. Holly had told Charlotte to read to Sasha, so that the girl would pick up the language quickly.

"I read to her each night." Charlotte's constricted throat began to open. It was so much easier talking about Sasha. "Maybe I should read in the morning, too, but there are so many things to do. Breakfast to fix, water to pump, coal to haul inside—" She halted, realizing she was blathering.

"You haul coal?" Wyatt looked outraged.

"Well, Charles did, but since he—" She couldn't bring herself to say *died* in front of Sasha. "Well, I have to do it now."

His gaze narrowed. "No one helps you out?"

"When they can." She fussed with her gloves rather than look him in the eye. "But I hate to ask them to take time out of their busy days."

He barely hesitated. "I can help."

She stared at him, shocked.

"While I'm here," he amended. "I'll make sure your scuttle is full."

"Thank you." She ducked her head. Again, the perfect opportunity. Again, her heart pounded through her chest. She licked her lips. "I wonder if…"

"If what?"

The words caught in her throat. "If…if…"

A commotion at the door halted conversations and drew everyone's attention.

"Charlotte! I'm so glad you're here." Holly burst into the room with Mason right behind her. "I have something wonderful to tell you, to tell everyone."

"That's right," boomed Mason with the broadest grin she'd ever seen cross that man's face.

Holly fairly bounced, her smile so wide it would light up the night sky. "We're getting married tomorrow morning." She pressed her hands to her face as if in disbelief.

"You heard the lady." Mason pulled her closer, if that was possible. "We're getting hitched at ten o'clock, and you're all invited."

The room erupted into congratulations, and everyone except Beatrice converged on the couple. The men shook Mason's hand roundly. The women hugged Holly and said they'd known all along that Mason would come to his senses. Sasha squealed and slid off Wyatt's lap to hand Holly the bedraggled forget-me-not that she'd plucked on the way to the hotel. "For you, Miffanders." Sasha couldn't quite pronounce Miss Sanders.

Charlotte wiped away a tear and struggled to hide the terrible envy that swelled inside her. Holly was her friend. She should be happy for her. She'd known this day was coming. They were perfect for each other. Then why this horrible feeling? It wasn't right or good.

"Oh, Holly, I'm so happy for you." She hugged her friend

and managed a wide, tearful smile that she hoped would pass for joy.

Holly squeezed her tightly before stepping back with a grin. "Your turn will come. Have faith."

Except that sometime during the confusion, Wyatt had slipped out of the room.

Charlotte panicked and grabbed Sasha's hand. She needed to catch him before he disappeared upstairs, but Holly wasn't finished.

"And, well…" Holly bit her lip. "I hope you don't mind that I asked Rebecca to stand up with me. I didn't want to keep you from Sasha."

Charlotte's mind whirled. That was the least of her concerns. She reassured Holly that she was delighted Rebecca would do the honor, all the while looking for Wyatt.

"Speaking of children…" Holly tugged on Mason's arm. "We should tell them the rest of the news."

Mason grinned and asked the well-wishers for silence, which they roundly ignored. Holly then clapped her hands three times, and the crowd instantly hushed. She then deferred to her husband-to-be.

"As you know, I've taken a shine to Liam. That is, we have. Well, we thought, that is, we talked it over, and, you see—"

Holly rolled her eyes. "What Mason's trying to say is that we're going to take in Liam as soon as we're married. The selection committee approved it. Now we just have to pray that the judge rules in our favor."

Charlotte hoped Holly's prayers came true. The spunky lad had been Mason's sidekick since the day he arrived in town to warn the sheriff about the train robbery. Liam belonged with Holly and Mason.

The congratulations erupted anew, though Beatrice's

frown only deepened. Without a word, she stalked out of the dining room, just like Wyatt.

Wyatt. Charlotte had never asked him if he would marry her, and now he was gone. She had to hurry to catch him.

"Please excuse me," she said to Holly, but it wasn't necessary since the couple was overwhelmed with well-wishers.

Charlotte hurried into the lobby, vacant except for Ned Minor, who manned the registration desk. Frantically, she looked at the porch and then the stairs.

"If you're lookin' for Mr. Reed," Ned drawled, "he retired for the night."

Her chance was gone. In just days, Sasha would be taken from her. Sobs rose in her throat while laughter rang from the dining room.

Holly was getting married.

Charlotte choked down the tears. It needed to be her.

Chapter Six

The ringing of church bells hurried Charlotte's preparations. She'd dressed Sasha in her Sunday best but was having a hard time getting the girl to sit still so she could braid her hair.

"All right, we'll leave it loose," she finally conceded.

At least she'd managed to brush Sasha's dark locks until they shone. A ribbon would have looked so pretty, but the little girl was having none of it.

"Miss Sanders is getting married today," she reminded Sasha, "and we want to look our best."

Too bad Charlotte had to wear that horrid black. She'd much rather don her emerald-green taffeta gown—an enormous indulgence that had brought a smile to Charles's lips and hope to her heart.

"Miffanders get marry?"

"Yes, to Sheriff Wright." Charlotte had no idea if Sasha understood, but she did sit still long enough for Charlotte to tie the ribbon in her hair.

"Katya come?"

"Yes, Katya may join us. In fact, I think Miss Sanders would insist."

Sasha squealed with joy and jumped up and down, making her doll flop this way and that.

Charlotte slid open the front of Charles's desk and pulled out the tray that concealed the money compartment. The leather wallet contained everything Charles had left her, enough for three or four years. She would give it all to Wyatt to keep her daughter. She prayed he would accept.

Lord, soften his heart so he will agree to my proposal. Help him to see the good he can bring to this little girl and give me the strength to follow through.

After putting the wallet into her purse, she reached for Sasha's hand. "Let's go."

The little girl willingly took her hand. So trusting. So loving. Yes, no matter the cost, Sasha must stay.

They stepped into the morning sun. The early streaks of crimson had vanished, leaving a brilliant blue sky. Thank goodness! Holly and Mason would have a beautiful wedding day.

It seemed the entire town streamed toward the church. By the time she arrived, the pews were jammed. She looked around the small sanctuary but didn't see Wyatt. Everyone had been invited, but he must not have thought that included him.

Unable to find a place to sit, she sought an empty spot along the side.

"Please, Widow Miller, take my seat." Mr. Brooks stood and motioned her to a small spot at the end of a pew.

Pauline Evans slid over a bit to make enough room for Charlotte and Sasha. Charlotte smiled her thanks as the pianist played the "Bridal Chorus" and managed to get seated before the wedding party appeared.

Mason walked in with his friend, Bucky Wyler. Both men looked nervous. Then Heidi walked solemnly down the aisle, every step measured. Liam followed a bit behind her, head held high but hands in his trouser pockets. Charlotte stifled a grin. The lad clearly wanted to impress Mason while not acting too fancified.

Rebecca, in a fashionable yet surprisingly subdued gown, followed next. Seconds later, Charlotte understood her thoughtful choice, for Holly wore her best suit, the one she'd worn to Newfield to apply for the loan. Charlotte regretted not having time to sew the wedding gown for Holly. The ever-sensible schoolteacher had simply worn her best. She carried an equally simple bouquet of wildflowers.

Judging by the dumbstruck grin on Mason's face, it didn't matter one bit. He saw Holly's true beauty. Every ounce of it. The pride and joy on his face brought tears to Charlotte's eyes. Holly positively glowed. Her feet floated down the aisle. She saw only Mason. The love they felt for each other was palpable.

If only…

Charlotte wiped away a tear. That's the kind of marriage she'd wanted her entire life, but if her plan succeeded today, she would never have it.

Wyatt had no interest in seeing the sheriff married off. He didn't, as a rule, attend weddings. They only reminded him of all he'd lost. Moreover, they took place in a church, and Wyatt hadn't crossed one of those thresholds since the war.

Still, from the hotel porch he couldn't help noticing the stream of people going to the ceremony. He saw Charlotte arrive late with Sasha in tow. The little girl looked his way and smiled before Charlotte tugged her into the church.

Since the church was just down the street from the hotel, he ambled closer. Mason waited outside with a nervous fellow who must be standing up with him. The two laughed and joked, but the sheriff kept checking his pocket watch.

Anxious fellow, in a hurry to get hitched. Wyatt supposed he would be, too, if he was marrying a woman he loved.

Charlotte's face drifted to mind, but he tossed away the thought. Wyatt Reed did not get involved. *Get in, do the job and get out.* Nothing more.

After the last guest arrived, a redheaded lad shuffled toward the sheriff. Wright clapped the boy on the back before entering the church with his friend. Moments later, Miss Sanders and Miss Sterling walked down the street from the direction of the school. The orphan girl with the disfigured face followed, holding a bouquet of wildflowers. The redheaded boy hung back and kicked at the dirt before the schoolteacher rounded him up and pushed him into the church.

Wyatt stifled a grin as he watched from the village green, where tables were being set up for the luncheon. A wedding brought people together. The luncheon afterward would give them opportunity to talk. Maybe someone would mention Baxter. A small segment of the population wanted the orphans to go to Greenville. Miss Ward appeared to be their leader. Was she in cahoots with Baxter? Maybe today he'd find out.

"If you ain't goin' to the wedding, make yourself useful." A domineering woman with a kind face shoved a tray of glasses into his hands. "Set 'em around the tables."

Set tables? Wyatt hadn't done that since he was a small child. On the farm, that was women's work, and once he was big enough to work in the barns and fields, he'd been excused from housework.

Exactly where was he supposed to put them? By the plates, certainly, but there weren't any plates on the tables. Linen tablecloths fluttered in the light breeze, weighted down by enormous vases of fragrant lilacs. The ladies were busy tying bows around the vases, which, now that he looked closer, were a mix of pitchers, mason jars and the occasional vase.

He decided to set a glass by each chair. It took forever. He counted a hundred chairs, and few glasses looked alike. Apparently, every woman in Evans Grove had emptied her cupboard for the wedding feast. Judging by the number of cakes on the dessert table, they'd also baked all night.

The community's affection for its sheriff and school-teacher put a smile on his face. That was the type of town that deserved to thrive. It was the type of town to raise a family in, good for children, good for orphans.

That last realization hit him hard. He'd known it deep down since yesterday but hadn't put it in so many words. Those children deserved to stay here, but his stubborn persistence had forced the town to a legal impasse that could send the children to Greenville.

After setting down the last glass, he rubbed the back of his neck.

If only he'd abandoned the job right away. Maybe then the kids could have stayed.

He shook his head, knowing that was wishful thinking. Baxter wanted those orphans badly. He wouldn't have let them go. To save the kids, Wyatt had to find out why.

"Well?" The woman who'd handed him the tray of glasses glared at him. "Go on back to the hotel and fetch another load."

Wyatt blinked. He hadn't been ordered around since the war, but that conflict had also taught him when to surrender. "Yes, ma'am."

He trudged back.

The stable boy strolled out of the livery, spotted him and grinned. "Got ya waitin' tables, don't they?"

Wyatt cringed. Sweet stars, he wasn't a table waiter. He was Wyatt Reed, expert tracker. Outlaws feared him. Lawmen respected him. Yet in no time at all he'd been reduced to a servant. That's what women did to a man. Even the stable boy snickered.

After looking each way, the lad sauntered closer. "Better you'n me. Ma'd have my hide if she knew I was hidin' in the stable instead a helpin' get those tables all prettied up. Don't let on you saw me, all right?"

Wyatt recalled his boyish days, when he'd run off with his friends rather than do his chores. "Sooner or later she'll catch up to you."

The boy's grin split his face. "Hasn't yet."

"Allen Edward!" The woman who'd ordered Wyatt around strode across the street. "Get into that kitchen and help Mr. Reed."

The stable boy's confident grin collapsed. "Yes'm."

Wyatt grinned as the boy trudged into the hotel.

The woman turned to him. "What you waitin' for?"

"Yes, ma'am." Wyatt scurried after the lad, strangely warmed and comforted that he'd been treated the same as everyone.

That's what community felt like. That's what he'd been missing since the war.

Where was Wyatt? Charlotte tried to put the urgency out of her mind, but as the minister spoke of commitment and how God had set aside marriage for the betterment of mankind, her mind drifted. Had Wyatt left town? Had he ridden to Greenville?

She nibbled her lip.

Pauline squeezed her hand. "I'm praying you find someone."

Charlotte was too.

The vows brought tears again. From the way Holly and

Mason looked at each other, it was clear that God had meant them to be together.

At last the ceremony ended, and everyone streamed out of the church to congratulate the couple. Charlotte let Sasha run off to play with Lynette with strict instructions to stay on the village green. Mrs. Gavin chuckled and said she'd keep an eye on them.

Charlotte waited for everyone else to congratulate the newlyweds. In truth, she was trying her best to still the butterflies in her stomach and figure out how to ask Wyatt. *Lord, give me the words.* She sure didn't have them.

When Holly was finally free of well-wishers, Charlotte embraced her friend. Words wouldn't come at first, though the emotion did.

"I'm so happy for you and Mason," she finally managed, blinking back yet more tears. "I'm still making you that dress. I wish I could have had it done for today."

"Nonsense." Holly pulled away. "I don't need a fancy dress."

Charlotte knew Holly would react that way. "You deserve it," she insisted. Holly was a dear, always sacrificing for the children. It was time she had something pretty of her own. "Mason will love it."

Holly blushed a color that would match the new dress and glanced toward her new husband, who was standing off to the side with Bucky Wyler and his wife.

"Go to him," Charlotte urged.

"Are you sure?" But her eyes sparked with desire.

Charlotte nodded.

Holly leaned close before darting off to join her husband. "There's someone waiting for you." She nodded toward the table closest to the road.

Wyatt Reed.

Charlotte felt all the blood drain from her face. The time had arrived. She must make her proposition.

Wyatt stood by the table closest to the road watching the newlyweds. Sheriff Wright looked at his new wife with such adoration that it tore Wyatt to pieces. When she returned the same look, he had to turn away. He wanted to feel that way, wanted that unspoken connection with another person. A connection that said she would stay by his side no matter what, and he would walk through fire to be there for her.

But it couldn't be. What woman would ever place trust in a man who'd burned and killed? None.

Keep control, Reed. He was here to learn something about Baxter. That meant positioning himself as close to Miss Ward as possible. He scanned the crowds around the tables looking for the diminutive gray-haired spinster. There she was, commanding the cake table. She gestured for first this cake and then that one to be moved to different locations. The women around her hovered like bees, ready to do her bidding.

He'd get nothing from her.

On the opposite side of the grove, the rancher, Hayes, led a frail elderly woman to a chair in the shade. An elderly man limped along beside them. Wyatt might be able to get more out of Hayes. He started forward and instantly felt resistance.

"Papa." Something, or rather, someone, tugged on his trouser leg.

Wyatt looked down to see Sasha, her face tilted back so she could see all the way to the top of his head.

"I'm not your papa."

Just like the first time, she looked at him without blinking or speaking. This time, her lips puckered into a frown. Tears wouldn't be far behind.

"Now, don't go crying," he urged. "We'll find your mama."

Charlotte wouldn't be Sasha's mother much longer, he couldn't help thinking, thanks to a ridiculous set of rules that couldn't bend when it was obvious they needed to. That's what had frustrated him about the army. Orders were given, and he had to obey, regardless of whose lives were affected.

Sasha's eyes welled with tears.

He crouched down to her level. "Don't cry." He looked frantically for Charlotte. What was with that woman, always losing track of her daughter?

"Lynette!" a woman called. "Lynette, show your face."

A hand, followed by a dark-haired little head, poked from under the edge of the tablecloth. The pigtailed girl grinned at Wyatt. "Don't tell her I'm here."

Wyatt lifted an eyebrow. "Hiding?"

The girl, perhaps a little older than Sasha, shrugged. "I'm s'posed to watch Sasha. We're playin' wagon train."

"Wagon train?"

She nodded solemnly. "We're hiding from Indians."

Wyatt lifted an eyebrow. "You're obviously hiding, but maybe Sasha's a little young to understand your game." He wasn't sure she should be wandering around by herself. Charlotte would be frantic.

The girl shrugged again and lifted the bottom of the tablecloth. "She can join me."

Sasha scooted under with a giggle.

As an afterthought, Lynette added, "You can too."

Wyatt stifled a laugh and said with exaggerated seriousness, "I think I'd better leave the wagon train in your capable hands."

After another grin, Lynette dropped the tablecloth, and the two girls giggled, probably at him.

Wyatt straightened and shook out his stiff knee. Once out from behind the cover of the table, he saw people were taking their places. The sheriff and his bride walked arm-in-arm toward the table farthest from him, but the prettiest woman of all headed straight for him, purpose in her steps. Charlotte Miller definitely had something to tell him. Remembering the last tongue-lashing he'd taken when she'd been in a temper, he gulped and wished he'd taken up Lynette's offer.

Swallowing her nerves, Charlotte strode toward Wyatt. At first his back was turned, and then he ducked down behind the table.

She hesitated. Did he know what she was going to ask? Of course he did. Everyone in town knew she had to find a husband. He knew, and he was hiding from her.

Humiliation heated her cheeks.

Then he stood and looked right at her. The brim of his hat shadowed his face, so she couldn't see his expression, but at least he didn't run.

She still had a chance.

She covered the distance between them in seconds. Her heart pounded so wildly that it threatened to break her ribs. Her entire future depended on this. Sasha's happiness depended on this.

She pressed a hand to her chest to still that out-of-control heart, and summoned her courage. "Mr. Reed."

"Mrs. Miller."

That was an awkward start.

She glanced around. The tables were starting to fill. People looked at her with curiosity. She didn't have much time before their conversation would be overheard.

"I didn't see you at the ceremony."

His lean, tanned face tightened. "I wasn't there."

"I'm sure you would have been welcomed."

One brow lifted. "There's no need to be polite, Mrs. Miller. I know how the town feels about me."

"Maybe they don't know you. If they'd seen what I had, they'd feel differently."

"And what exactly did you see?"

"That you care about the orphans. It was in your eyes and the set of your mouth when Pauline—the mayor—explained how much the town wants them."

His intense gaze didn't waver. "Anything you saw was an act."

She gasped. Why would he say such a thing? The one quality she'd sensed in him from the start was unwavering honesty. Cold and withdrawn, yes, but honest. "I don't believe you. You're saying that to frighten me. Well, I won't be frightened. I know you're a good man. I see how you are with Sasha."

At her daughter's name, she thought she heard a giggle from under the table. She reached for the table linen, but Wyatt snagged her hand and placed it on his arm.

"Maybe you're right. Let's take a stroll and discuss it."

He didn't even ask if she wanted to walk, but after he tugged her forward, she realized that a little privacy would be best. Mr. and Mrs. Gavin were headed for that very table.

Wyatt led her toward the general store, which was closed in honor of the wedding. That's where this whole ordeal had begun, where Sasha had vanished. When Charlotte ran outside to look for her daughter, she'd first seen Wyatt. Tall and strong, he'd looked every bit the hero. He still could be, if he would marry her. How to ask?

While she fumbled for words, Wyatt started the conversation. "Are you friends with the sheriff and his bride?"

Small talk. Perhaps a good way to begin. After all, she barely knew the man. "Holly is a dear friend, yes, but this is such a small town that one can't afford to make many enemies."

"Except Miss Ward."

Charlotte stifled a gasp. She'd tried her best to forgive Beatrice, but the woman's hateful attitude toward the orphans prevented reconciliation. If not for Beatrice, no one would have suggested taking Sasha away. "How did you know?"

"She's opposed to the orphans staying here, isn't she?"

Charlotte tried to keep the rancor from her voice. "I don't know why. Granted, she's an unhappy spinster, but there are worse things than being alone." The repetition of Amelia Hicks's words came with surprising ease.

Wyatt halted and faced her. "Did your husband beat you?"

"No, never." Charlotte couldn't get the words out fast enough. "Charles was a good man, decent and kind."

He looked like he didn't believe her. "But?"

She drew in a deep breath. No one knew the truth. They all thought she'd had the perfect marriage. Now Charles was dead. No one should speak ill of the dead, but if she expected Wyatt to marry her, she ought to be honest with him.

She lowered her gaze. "There are other ways to hurt a person's soul."

His hands gripped her shoulders. "No one should marry without love and respect."

Which is precisely what she intended to do.

"H-he never promised me love," she admitted. This was going very much awry, but she must tell the truth. "He told me from the start that he'd buried his heart with his first wife. The fault was mine for thinking he might change his mind. And for thinking that I would change, too—because I wasn't in love with him, either."

She heard his quick intake of air, but he didn't say anything.

"My parents had died," she continued, "one after the other. They'd spent everything planting the first year's seed." Her lip quivered at the memory. "The rains didn't come. The seedlings died before they had a chance to live. My mother got sick, and then my father. They died two months apart."

"I'm sorry."

She shook her head. "I had to get on. That's the way it is here on the prairie. Back East I could have waited out the mourning period, but here I had to find a way to live." She clutched her hands to her stomach at the memory of the gnawing hunger. "Charles offered to marry me. He never said he would love me." It felt good to say the words, to release them into the heavens.

"Then he died."

She nodded, keeping her eyes averted.

"And you're alone again."

"Except for Sasha." Her eyes burned as she lifted them to search his face. Would he accept her proposal? Or would he laugh in her face? "I can't lose her, too." The whisper bounced off him with more fierceness than she'd thought possible. "I won't lose my daughter. I'll do anything to keep her."

He flinched and looked away. "I'm sorry. I tried my best."

"I know." She boldly grasped his arm, forcing his gaze back to her. "Thank you." The time had come. "Will you help me again?"

Confusion clouded his expression. "How?"

She opened her bag and pulled out the wallet. "Charles left me some money. Whatever Mr. Baxter paid you, I'll pay double."

He pulled back. "It's not that simple."

"Of course it is."

"No, it's not. The Orphan Salvation Society has an agreement with Greenville. If the judge rules that the children must go to Greenville, then I have no choice but to take them."

Charlotte shook her head. He didn't understand. "I'm not talking about all the children. I'm talking about Sasha."

Instead of walking away or shouting at her, he spoke firmly. "There's nothing I can do to help you keep Sasha."

"Yes, there is."

He stared at her. "No, there's not."

"You can marry me." The words exploded down the street like gunfire.

He didn't blink. Not one muscle flinched except that tick below his eye. Dear Lord, he must think her mad.

"For money," she added, lifting up the wallet. "I'll pay you double, triple. I'll give you all I have." Tears threatened, but she refused to let them surface. "I don't want anything from you. You don't even have to live here. I just need to be married long enough to legally adopt Sasha. Once the adoption goes through, you can move on." She shoved the wallet at him.

He held up his hands and backed away.

"Please help me." The words came out strangled, and for a moment she feared he didn't understand. She held out the wallet again. "Please."

Instead of taking the money, he turned his back and strode away.

Chapter Seven

The woman was a lunatic.

Wyatt stormed down the middle of the street, not caring where he was going or who saw him as long as he got far away from Mrs. Charlotte Miller.

Marry her? Was she out of her mind?

Wyatt Reed was not the marrying type. He kept his emotions under lock and key. He preferred to be alone. He refused all friendships and attachments, at least until he reached San Francisco. There he could begin anew. There he'd make friends. But marry? Marriage would never work for a man like him.

Not that he didn't find Charlotte a sight to behold. She was that and more, but he couldn't settle here. Too many people knew him. Too many people already hated him. Surely she knew that, yet she'd still asked him to marry her.

She must be out of her mind.

Worse, she expected him to take her money. All of it. Wyatt Reed didn't hire out for this kind of job. He sure didn't take a widow's entire savings.

If not you, then someone else.

His steps slowed at the thought. The wrong man would take advantage of her. The wrong man would sense her desperation and steal both her savings and her heart. He shivered. The wrong man would leave her worse off than she was now. Didn't she realize the risk she was taking? She hardly knew him. She certainly didn't know what he'd done in the war. She couldn't know he would refuse to take all her money. She couldn't know if he would go back on his word and leave town before finishing the job. Yet she'd come to him rather than one of the local men.

What would drive a woman to do such a thing?

Sheriff Wright's words came to mind. The man had been trying to tell him that Charlotte needed help, but Wyatt hadn't listened.

But why him? Why not ask one of the men around here? She must know them better.

Unless she wanted a man who would leave.

He halted.

Of course. She didn't want a man who'd stick around. She wanted the child, not the husband. That left only him and that banker from Newfield, Curtis Brooks. From the gossip he'd heard around town, Wyatt knew that Brooks was the one who'd suggested Charlotte marry. Was he hoping to snare the lovely widow?

Wyatt's gut twisted at the thought of Charlotte with the impeccably dressed man, despite knowing that he would treat her far better than Wyatt ever could.

Wyatt shook his head. No, Brooks wasn't besotted with Charlotte. His gaze had barely left another widow—Mayor Evans. He wouldn't marry Charlotte. If he'd been willing, he would have offered already.

That left Wyatt. As a drifter and a loner, he fit her plan perfectly. She could count on him to disappear once Sasha was legally hers. He needed money, as his thin wallet testified. If the judge ruled against him, Baxter wouldn't pay, and he'd lose his chance for San Francisco.

But the price was steep. Wyatt hadn't planned to tie himself to any woman, especially not a kind and gentle one like Charlotte. Her soft voice and refined beauty reminded him far too much of the women he'd betrayed.

Wyatt's vision blurred. He couldn't marry. Ever.

The midday heat rose off the street in waves, but Wyatt felt the clammy grip of memories that refused to die. He wiped his forehead and replaced his hat.

He couldn't do it. No matter how great Charlotte's need. She'd have to look elsewhere. He squared his shoulders. She deserved a direct response, not a coward turning his back on her.

So he turned around, expecting to see Charlotte waiting for him, but she'd returned to the wedding celebration and was helping Sasha onto a chair. The sight sent a terrible feeling flooding into his heart. Affection.

He scowled. Wyatt Reed couldn't afford to care.

Charlotte struggled to contain her tears as she cut Sasha's chicken into tiny pieces. The look Wyatt had given her… She bit her lip. He thought her out of her mind. Any man would. She knew that, so why did it hurt so badly?

"Zee hor-sey," Sasha said between bites.

"Not today." Charlotte struggled to sound cheerful. "We're celebrating Miss Sanders's wedding to Sheriff Wright. When you go to school next year, you'll call her Mrs. Wright." She swiped away a tear, for Sasha would never have Holly for a teacher.

"Hor-sey," Sasha demanded.

Charlotte sighed. She'd kept Charles's pair at the livery, but they weren't getting a good workout since he'd died. She simply had no cause to hitch up the team to the wagon. Mel Hutchinson wanted to buy them. Maybe she should sell, but not just yet, not while Sasha was still here. She loved to pet the docile animals' noses.

"We'll go to the stables after we eat," she promised. It would take her mind off the bitter disappointment of Wyatt's rejection.

With a quivering lower lip, she surveyed the crowd. Nearly everyone was here. Colton Hayes assisted his parents. He was a good man, but she couldn't ask this of him, not when he had so many worries already. The other bachelors didn't even merit consideration. That left the elderly Elmer Droll. He'd marry her just to have someone cook and clean for him, but his pockmarked face and rotting teeth sickened her. If he would accept Sasha, however, she'd try to stomach her revulsion.

She couldn't be a true wife to him, however. He'd have to agree to a chaste marriage before they wed. Would he? It wasn't a question she'd even thought to ask of Wyatt. The prospect of his touch frightened her in a far different way. She could still feel where he'd gripped her shoulders, and she had to admit she'd hoped he would pull her closer, perhaps even claim a kiss.

Foolish woman! She sank to the chair beside Sasha, overwrought and overcome. *Dear Lord, what am I going to do?*

"May I join you?" The rumbling baritone sizzled down Charlotte's spine.

She stopped breathing, hardly daring to believe he'd changed his mind. Hadn't he walked away from her? Hadn't he looked at her with disgust? Yet hope made her raise her eyes until they met his steely gaze.

He didn't look pleased.

"Wyatt." Her voice came out all shaky. She swallowed and tried again. "Mr. Reed."

He looked to his left and right, but the table was empty

except for them. Everyone else had finished or drawn closer to the newlyweds. No one wanted to be near her.

"We need to talk." He pulled out the chair beside her, a child-size one from the schoolhouse, and folded his long, lean frame onto it. His knees stuck up like grasshopper legs.

Despite his comical appearance, a lump bigger than a boiled potato stuck in her throat. "I'm sorry. I shouldn't have…" But she couldn't finish. Saying the words once had been difficult enough. She couldn't do it again.

"And I shouldn't have walked off."

She stared at the table linen, at her empty plate, at anything but Wyatt Reed. "I understand." Even a fully cinched corset didn't squeeze her chest this painfully. Why did he have to rehash this?

"What have we here?" he said in a much softer tone, the voice he used with—

Charlotte whipped open her eyes to see Sasha squirming onto his lap, her hand outstretched.

"Sasha," she cried out, horrified, "Mr. Reed doesn't want your half-chewed chicken."

He chuckled, his attention wholly on Sasha. "Looks pretty good to a man who hasn't had a bite to eat." He took off his hat. "Why, thank you kindly, Miss Sasha." Then, to Charlotte's surprise, he took a piece of chicken from Sasha's hand and popped it into his mouth. "Mm-mm. That's some mighty fine eating."

Sasha squealed with delight, and the queasiness in Charlotte's stomach eased a little. She mouthed a thank-you at Wyatt, whose stormy eyes had softened to the color of spring rain. One arm circled little Sasha protectively. What a wonderful father he would make. She blinked back a tear.

That must have bothered him, for he looked away quickly, swallowed, so that his Adam's apple bobbed hard, and settled his attention on Sasha. He was fond of the girl, that was clear, but not fond enough to marry Charlotte.

She swallowed the faint hope that had arisen. Thirteen years ago, she'd buried her dreams of love to fill her stomach. That marriage had been loveless yet kind. Perhaps Mr. Droll wouldn't be that bad.

Sasha giggled and held up a handful of chicken bits. "Moh."

"I don't think Mr. Reed wants any more of your dinner," she chided, "when he can get his own."

This time when his gaze met hers it had gentled, and a smile teased his lips. "I think maybe you'd better call me Wyatt if we're going to get married."

It took a second for his words to register. She stared at him. She pressed a hand to her mouth to hold in the gasp of surprise, but nothing could stop the trembling that took over her limbs.

"M-m-m—" She couldn't even say it. "You will? We are?" Tears rose with the words, threatening to spill.

"That is what you wanted, isn't it?"

Seeing as her throat had completely closed, she nodded vigorously.

"Purely a business transaction. No sentiment."

Again, she nodded, relief pouring through her so much that she felt giddy.

His gaze sharpened. "One thing I want to make clear. I won't take a penny more than Baxter offered me, understand?"

She nodded, barely hearing his words. He would marry her. She could keep Sasha.

"And I'm free to leave once—" he glanced at Sasha "—once things are settled."

Inexplicably, Charlotte felt a sinking in her stomach. What had she expected? It was the deal she'd offered. Marriage in name alone, and he could leave the moment the adoption was final. Again, she nodded.

"Then the only question is when."

"Before Monday," she blurted out. "It has to be before the judge arrives."

The hard planes of his face didn't soften. "Then we'd best do it now."

"We want to get married," Charlotte blurted out to Reverend Turner. He and his wife sat at the bridal table with Mayor Evans and Mr. Brooks, to the left of Holly and Mason. Wyatt stood behind Charlotte, a strong, silent force that gave her strength.

"We?" The minister blinked as he attempted to grasp her statement.

"Wyatt—Mr. Reed—and I."

Jaws dropped. Reverend Turner frowned.

She felt foolish. *What woman approaches a minister with such an announcement?* Wyatt should have done the honors, but this was no ordinary wedding. She bit her lip and looked to Wyatt, hoping he would add his agreement.

The man stood silent except for a brief nod, Sasha in his arms.

"Papa." The dear girl giggled with delight, her hands cupping Wyatt's stubbled cheeks.

Though Holly had initially gasped and covered her mouth, she now found her voice. "Of course you do." She skirted the table to clasp Charlotte's hands. Her eyes shone with joy. "How perfect."

Mr. Brooks leaned back, his calm eye assessing Wyatt and her. "Well, well. I wouldn't have picked this one."

Reverend Turner's frown never eased. "Marriage is not to be entered into lightly, Widow Miller."

Charlotte hoped Beatrice Ward wasn't close enough to

hear his admonition, or the woman would find some way to sabotage this. Desperation squeezed her throat shut. She was so close to keeping Sasha. She couldn't lose her now.

"We're not taking this lightly, Reverend," Wyatt stated in his authoritative baritone.

Bless him, Lord. Charlotte cast Wyatt a smile of gratitude for stepping in when she couldn't. Her heart quickened at the sight of his strong features, the set of his jaw. My, he was handsome. She remembered the way the women had reacted to him the first time he walked into the town hall. She'd felt that, too, still felt it.

"We've discussed it and feel it's best for everyone." His statement left no room for questioning.

The man's focus impressed her. Once set on a course of action, he could not be easily moved from it. She was so thankful she'd been able to persuade him. Or maybe Sasha had done the persuading.

"We did suggest this solution," Mr. Brooks told the minister, "and it sounds to me that these two adults have discussed it thoroughly and soberly. I see no reason to impede their future." He smiled at Sasha. "They will be making their vows before God, after all."

Reverend Turner grudgingly allowed him that point, though he still looked skeptical. "When do you wish to marry, Mr. Reed?"

Charlotte felt a little disappointed that the minister spoke only to Wyatt, but she supposed that's the way it should be. Charles must have spoken to the minister before they married. She remembered nothing of the preparations beyond the overwhelming sense of dread. Odd that this time she didn't have the same cloying fear. Oh, her stomach fluttered with nerves and she couldn't keep the heat from her cheeks, but she definitely felt no dread.

"June is a lovely month," the minister continued. "I believe the church is available the second Saturday of the month."

"June!" Charlotte exclaimed. They couldn't wait until June.

But the minister didn't seem to hear her. His attention was focused on Wyatt. She held her breath, hoping Wyatt would remember the urgency.

"Today," he stated bluntly.

"Today?" Reverend Turner stared and then turned to Mayor Evans and Mr. Brooks for support. "No one marries that quickly."

"We came to you yesterday," Holly pointed out.

"But that was different," the reverend sputtered. "You and Mason were already engaged."

"Now, James." Mrs. Turner attempted to appeal to her husband's sympathy. "You know the situation."

Sheriff Mason Wright joined the growing chorus. "It's a reasonable solution in difficult times, Reverend." He nodded toward Sasha.

The minister's frown faded as he understood.

Wyatt's height cast a long shadow over Reverend Turner. "We only have today and tomorrow, and it wouldn't be right to marry on the Sabbath."

Brooks nodded thoughtfully. "The man has a point."

Once Mayor Evans added her blessing, Reverend Turner capitulated. "How much time do you need to prepare?"

"Let's do it now," Wyatt stated.

Charlotte agreed. She couldn't risk Wyatt backing out of the agreement.

"But you can't wear black for your wedding," Holly cried. "Even practical old me wouldn't stand for that. You should wear that pretty green dress of yours."

Charlotte adored that dress. She'd spent long hours stitching the slippery silk taffeta. Even Charles had approved of

the final gown and had taken her to Newfield to see a concert, an extremely rare treat.

She glanced at Wyatt and sensed impatience. "I don't
think what I wear matters."

Mayor Evans patted Charlotte on the arm. "Of course it
does. You want to look your best for your new husband."

Her words brought another flush of heat to Charlotte's
cheeks. Would Wyatt even notice her or would he be groaning with impatience, eager to see this job over and done?

As always, Pauline took charge. "If the new Mrs. Wright
can postpone her wedded life for an hour to help you dress,
I'll see to Sasha. Perhaps Mason can stand up with Mr.
Reed?"

Sheriff Wright and Holly readily agreed to their roles.
Hopefully, Wyatt accepted this change of plans. She glanced
at him and saw his expression had turned to stone. He hated
this. If she didn't do something now, he might back out of
the agreement.

Charlotte grasped the mayor's arm. "Please, we don't want
anything fancy. This is Mason and Holly's special day. They
deserve all the attention. Wyatt and I want a private wedding with no fuss."

She saw Wyatt's expression ease.

"But—" Pauline started to protest.

"We are adamant about this."

Seeing Charlotte's determination, Pauline relented. "How
generous of you to place Holly and Mason ahead of your-
selves. We'll keep this between us." A maternal smile curved
her lips. "But you do need to change your gown, dear. I agree
with Holly. That green one would turn any man's head."

Charlotte ducked her head to hide the blushes that
wouldn't stop. She doubted she could entice Wyatt Reed

with a mere dress. He'd made it quite clear that their marriage would be only a business transaction.

And nothing more.

Chapter Eight

"I hope you never have to wear mourning clothes again," Holly said as she buttoned Charlotte's emerald-green gown.

Charlotte had to admit it felt good to shed the dreary crepe in favor of the rustling silk taffeta, though she was unaccustomed to the bustle the dress required. She and Holly had struggled to get that on properly.

This green dress had been her one extravagance during her thirteen years of marriage, one that had managed to put a flicker of approval in Charles's eyes. He'd escorted her to the concert like a queen, eager to accept the admiring nods from the men of quality in Newfield. She'd been a prize that night, but once they returned home, nothing had changed. He still retreated to his sanctuary in the loft without giving her so much as a kiss.

How would Wyatt behave?

Charlotte gasped and put her hands to her cheeks as the full impact of her upcoming marriage hit her.

"What's wrong?" Holly asked. "Did I pinch you?"

"No. Not at all." But her cheeks blazed at the thought of the wedding night. What would Wyatt expect? Fear mingled with anticipation. How could she explain her feelings and her fears? Yet if anyone could understand, it would be Holly.

She looked around the house that Charles had built. "I—I hadn't quite realized Wyatt would live here."

Holly's fingers stilled as a nervous giggle escaped her. "That is what husbands and wives do."

"It's your wedding night, too. Are you afraid?"

"Not a bit." Holly quickly finished the buttons. "With Mason, it's as if we've been meant for each other our entire lives. I can't explain it, but being with him is like going home."

Home. What was home? Charlotte longed for that feeling of security. Between being uprooted from her childhood home in upstate New York, traveling across the country, losing her parents and moving into Charles's house, she'd never felt secure enough to call a place home.

"How wonderful that must be," she whispered, realizing at the same time that her plans had sent Holly's into a tumult. "Thank you for taking time away from Mason on your wedding day."

Holly chuckled. "That's all right. The house would have been busy anyway with Liam and his friends running in and out. It's going to be tight fitting three of us into the teacherage, but we'll get by."

Charlotte embraced her. "You'll be perfect parents."

"Maybe not perfect, but with God's help, we'll do our best." Holly surveyed her critically. "Time for the hat and gloves, but first you'll need to take off that wedding band."

Charlotte stared at her hand. She'd worn the ring Charles gave her for so long that she'd forgotten she had it on. She wrestled with it and finally managed to pull the band off, leaving behind a pale imprint around her finger.

"Do you feel different with it off?" Holly asked.

Charlotte shook her head. "I suppose I miss Charles in a way, but that's the past. Now I need to focus on the future."

"That's a good way to look at it."

Both of them knew Charlotte's marriage hadn't come close to the ideal. If anything, she was stepping into the same situation she'd known with Charles, with one exception. Wyatt stirred her emotions in ways Charles never had. His touch, the way his eyes changed intensity, the slight lifting of the corner of his mouth when he was pleased—all of those sent her reeling. But it was his kindness with Sasha that meant the most to her.

"All done." Holly clapped her hands as if she'd finished preparing the last of her students for a recital. "Are you ready to get married?"

Ready? Charlotte's heart nearly stopped. The word *married* hit her with a finality that she hadn't anticipated. Within the hour she'd be Mrs. Wyatt Reed. He would follow her back to this house. He would live with her.

Charlotte trembled. What had she been thinking? This would never work, not when his mere presence sent her into such a fit of nerves. She couldn't think straight around him. She couldn't stop blushing. If she was honest, part of her wanted him to touch her, to kiss her, to cherish her. But he was a loner. He'd insisted there be no emotional attachment. Could she do it? Could she cook for him and launder his clothes and wake up to him first thing in the morning without any emotion at all? She had to try, for as soon as Sasha was legally hers, he would leave.

She wrapped her arms around her queasy midsection. "I must be out of my mind."

Holly laughed. "Don't worry. You just have the jitters. Most brides do."

"Did you?"

"No, but that's different. I liked Mason for ages."

"Unlike me, who's marrying a man I barely know." The truth of how little Charlotte knew about Wyatt hit her hard. She didn't even know if his parents were alive or if he had any family. For that matter, she didn't know where he hailed from. Maybe ignorance was best since he was only going to leave, perhaps in a matter of days if the judge ruled the orphans could stay in Evans Grove and approved her adoption petition in a timely manner. The less she knew about Wyatt Reed, the less likely her heart would get broken.

Holly handed Charlotte her gloves. "Did you get the jitters with Charles?"

Jitters couldn't describe the terror that had seized her that day. She'd vomited until her stomach was empty and nearly fainted during the vows.

"Yes," she admitted, "but this is different."

"How?" Holly stood on a stool to tuck a few stray strands into Charlotte's upswept hair before pinning on the matching hat that blossomed with white satin roses and emerald-green ribbon.

How, indeed? To anyone else, the two marriages bore a striking resemblance, but Charles had never sent a single blush to her cheeks. Charles didn't inspire a fluttery feeling in her stomach every time he spoke. Charles's voice grated on her nerves whereas Wyatt's rich baritone made her… What? Swoon? Goodness, she was acting like a foolish girl.

"I guess I want Wyatt to like me a little."

"Oh, Charlotte." Holly hopped off the stool and engulfed her in a hug. "How could he not like you? You're beautiful."

That hadn't meant anything to Charles.

"I'm such a goose." She tried to smile through the tears. "Here I am fretting over a man when the only person that matters is Sasha. She adores him." Charlotte dabbed at her eyes. "She already calls him Papa. I can't imagine why. Maybe he looks like her father." She shook her head. "It doesn't matter why. Wyatt cares for her, and she trusts him."

Holly squeezed her arm. "That's important. Children have an uncanny ability to sense a person's true character."

Charlotte hoped her friend was right. Otherwise, Sasha's little heart would shatter when Wyatt Reed walked out of their lives. Hers would too.

Holly stepped back and surveyed her. "You look gorgeous. Wyatt Reed would have to be a fool not to fall in love with you."

Charlotte knew better than to think beauty could inspire love. She tugged on her gloves. "I'm ready."

As ready as a woman could be to marry a hired husband.

"Marriage is a solemn state, not to be entered lightly." Reverend Turner eyed Wyatt over his spectacles.

The meaning of the pause that followed wasn't lost on Charlotte, but thankfully Wyatt stood stoically by her side.

She couldn't calm her nerves. They buzzed like houseflies, reminding her of the terrible step she was taking. These were sacred vows, and she was not entering into them with the straightforward honesty that they demanded.

If truth be told, she'd hoped Wyatt would smile when she walked up the aisle, but his sober expression showed no joy or delight at her change of attire. The disappointment had led to doubt and the doubt to nerves. Only thoughts of Sasha kept her focused.

Reverend Turner didn't help. His downturned lips conveyed his opposition to this wedding. If Holly hadn't stood with her, she might have crumbled. Her friend smiled encouragingly and sent a spark of hope into Charlotte's heart, but Mason masked his feelings with the same taut expression as Wyatt. The men looked like they were headed into a battle they didn't expect to survive.

Reverend Turner's words echoed in the empty church. Only Mrs. Turner, Pauline and Mr. Brooks sat in the pews. True to their word, they'd kept the news of this ceremony quiet. The mayor had also suggested Sasha join the orphans and Miss Sterling at the schoolhouse until after the ceremony. Though Charlotte had initially protested, Pauline convinced her that the child would not understand what was going on.

Of course she wouldn't. Charlotte barely understood how she'd come to such a juncture. When Charles died, she'd vowed never again to tie herself to a man she didn't love, but she was about to do just that.

Her knees shook, so she straightened them. Her hands trembled, so she knotted them together. Her ears buzzed, but she didn't dare faint. Land sakes, she was hopping from the skillet into the fire. What was she thinking?

Then she reminded herself of Sasha's plight, and for a moment, her pulse slowed and all became clear again.

"Repeat after me," the reverend said. "I, Wyatt Earl Reed, take this woman to be my lawfully wedded wife…"

She held her breath. Would Wyatt say the vows?

When his voice rang out clear and firm, she looked up in surprise. How could he be so certain? He stretched out a hand, palm up, and she tentatively placed her small, pale hand in his large, rough one.

"Do you have a ring?" Reverend Turner asked.

Of course they didn't.

"No, sir," Wyatt answered.

"Very well, then," the minister said with undisguised distaste. "It's your turn, Charlotte. Repeat after me. I, Charlotte Rose Miller, take this man to be my lawfully wedded husband, to love, cherish and obey…"

The words buzzed in her ears, taunting her. *Liar, liar.* Was she lying before God? Or was she speaking the truth? She picked apart the vow. She was willingly and knowingly taking Wyatt for her lawful husband. She would cherish and obey him until death parted them. But love? Could she love him, knowing that he would break her heart?

Her lips quivered, and Holly squeezed her elbow.

Reverend Turner waited. Mason and Holly waited. It was time.

She ought to look at the man she was tying herself to for the rest of her life. Fighting doubt and fear, she lifted her gaze.

His steel-gray eyes bored through her, demanding to know why she hesitated.

Dear Lord, forgive me, she silently prayed. *I will do my best to fulfill this vow, even though it will hurt.*

The minister cleared his throat. "You may agree with the vow if you can't recite it."

Though her throat had squeezed to the size of a needle, she managed to squeak out her assent.

Then Reverend Turner pronounced them husband and wife. "You may now kiss the bride."

Excitement mixed with terror. Would he kiss her? What would it feel like? It had been years since she'd experienced anything other than a peck on the cheek.

Wyatt looked at her then at the minister and back to her. He was going to refuse to kiss her. Tears of humiliation threatened, but instantly vanished when Wyatt drew her near. This close, he was even more handsome. His eyes no longer appeared cold, and she could see hints of sun and sky in them. She caught her breath and shut her eyes, half-afraid, but that fear melted the instant his lips tenderly touched hers. Gentle as a whisper at first and then firm, yet tender. The room and everyone in it vanished in a swirl of emotion.

He cared for her. He must. Wyatt Reed spoke with his actions, and that kiss said he cared more than he would ever let on. Every buzzing doubt fled in that embrace. She threaded her arms around his shoulders and sank willingly into the bargain she'd just made.

Chapter Nine

Considering Wyatt had just hitched himself to a woman for the rest of his life, he ought to feel weighed down. Instead, he felt like kicking up his heels. At first, stepping into the church had scared him half to death. He'd waited for a lightning bolt to strike him dead or the minister to chase him off. Neither one happened.

Then Charlotte had walked down the aisle looking like a princess, and he'd been lost. It took every bit of steely nerves to stand there solemn, like a man was supposed to act in church. He'd had to tense his jaw and look at Miss Sanders, er Mrs. Wright, so he didn't betray how he felt about Charlotte. He could hardly believe a woman that beautiful would marry him.

If she knew what he'd done...

But she didn't, and it was going to stay that way. Once she legally adopted Sasha and no one could take the girl away, he'd slip off and head to San Francisco. Then she'd have everything she wanted and be rid of an unwelcome husband.

He could tell she regretted having to marry him. She wouldn't look at him almost the entire ceremony. When she finally did lift her eyes, he saw panic underneath those perfectly curved eyelashes.

Sweet stars, she couldn't even repeat the vows. He thought for a minute that the whole thing was done and over with, but she somehow managed to say enough to please that crotchety minister who'd glared at him the entire time.

Then he had to kiss her. He'd forgotten about that part, but it didn't hurt his feelings that he'd have to kiss such a pretty thing. She looked terrified at first, as if he would strike her. His dander rose at that first husband of hers. Though she'd insisted he didn't beat her, she could be hiding the truth. It wouldn't be the first time.

Her fear only made him want to help her more. He took it slow and gentle. It took every ounce of restraint he could muster, because deep down he wanted to claim those soft lips. He wanted to regain—even for a moment—all that he had lost. Yet, he held back.

Then the miracle happened. She responded. Her lips softened, and she wrapped her arms around him. So close to her, he lost his head and every ounce of resolve.

The embrace must've lasted longer than respectable, because the minister cleared his throat. That got enough of Wyatt's attention for him to break off the kiss.

Once he was separated from her, cold, hard reality returned. The marriage license had to be signed. The sheriff, mayor and banker wished him well. Mrs. Wright hugged Charlotte, and then it was over and they stood outside the church not sure what to do next.

"I suppose I should fetch Sasha from the schoolhouse." Charlotte stood just out of reach, wringing her gloved hands. "Y-y-you can bring your things to the house at any time."

Wyatt hadn't quite realized he'd have to live with her. "Maybe I should stay at the hotel."

"After we're married?" She lifted those glorious hazel eyes to him. "People will know."

Wyatt understood what she meant. People would know

their marriage was a sham. Still, living with her? That wasn't Wyatt's way. He preferred the open air and a campfire. He didn't get attached to anyone or anything.

"Are you sure?" he asked.

She nodded, her cheeks turning that pretty shade of pink, but she wouldn't look at him. Why not? He hated the way women thought he was supposed to understand what they wanted without them saying a word. That was one good reason not to get involved. One good reason to stand alone. He had to put a stop to those blushes and squash any idea she might be getting into her pretty head that they'd have a real marriage.

"You haven't paid me yet," he said flatly.

After a jerk of surprise, her shoulders sagged, and he regretted hurting her.

"You will get your money, *Mr.* Reed. I am not a person who goes back on a bargain."

He liked it when she showed a little feistiness. That was a Charlotte he could admire, one who spoke her mind, not one who cowered and fretted. It also kept her at a distance. "Neither do I."

Her lips pressed into a furious little pink knot. "Even if it means hurting children?"

They weren't back to arguing over the orphans, were they? He considered telling her he might change his mind, but women couldn't keep a secret to save their souls. If he told her, she'd tell Holly Wright, who'd tell the sheriff, and then he'd never discover why this town was so desperate to keep the children.

"Only four have been taken," he reminded her.

"Five now. Holly and Mason have taken Liam."

That explained the sheriff's personal interest in the case. It also meant trouble if the judge ruled for Greenville. Sheriff Wright wasn't going to give up the boy without a fight. He hoped the judge would at least let the five stay. "That still leaves three unclaimed children."

She braced her hands on her hips and elbowed past him. "Men."

"Mrs. Reed." He caught her arm.

She stiffened as if just that moment realizing she was no longer Widow Miller. Her voice caught when she asked what he wanted, and his conscience pricked. A good husband would show consideration. He'd share everything with his wife. That's why Wyatt could never be a good husband. Still, he owed her an apology.

"I'm sorry." He truly was. "But I don't know where you live."

"Oh." That pretty blush returned, chasing away the anger. "On Third Street, past Liberty. The second house on the right. There are the sad remains of a tulip garden in front."

Of course she'd have flowers. Beauty loved beauty.

She ducked her head as a wagon passed slowly, its occupants watching them with no attempt to hide their curiosity. Her fingers toyed with the ribbons on her hat. "I—I should be back from fetching Sasha by the time you get there." She rubbed her midsection, as if she had a stomachache. "Until later, then."

"Until then." He tipped his hat, not quite sure what a man was supposed to do at this point with his new wife.

Wife. That was going to take some getting used to.

Charlotte needed to explain Wyatt's presence to Sasha before he arrived, but she didn't know how. Even though they were legally married, she didn't want to get Sasha's hopes up that he would stay. The poor girl had lost two fathers already, and Wyatt had made it clear that he would leave after the adoption.

On the walk home, Sasha investigated every bug and flower until Charlotte's patience had worn thin. She couldn't broach the subject in public, and at this pace, Wyatt would be at the house before they arrived.

When they finally turned the corner onto Third Street, she was relieved that his horse wasn't in front of the house. She glanced back. Third Street ran all the way to the hotel, but it was so clogged with pedestrians, dogs, carts and the bustle of a normal late afternoon that she couldn't possibly spot him.

While she was looking backward, Sasha wandered into the neighbor's yard and plucked a handful of pansies. Charlotte gasped. Mrs. Ingersman would have a fit if she saw Sasha in her yard. Like Beatrice, she subscribed to the notion that the orphans were prone to criminal behavior.

"Stop that, Sasha." She bit her lip for sounding too harsh. The little girl didn't know any better. "Let's go in the house before..." Before what? Before Papa got home? The words stuck in her throat. What should she call Wyatt?

Sasha skipped to her and held out the flowers. "Pitty."

Charlotte's eyes misted as she took the bouquet. "Thank you, dear one." She hugged Sasha close. "They are pretty, but let's leave the rest in the garden so we can see them when we walk past, shall we?"

Sasha nodded slowly, though she probably didn't understand.

"Good girl." Charlotte thought up a reward. "Would Katya like a new dress?"

As she suspected, a new doll dress proved more enticing than Mrs. Ingersman's flowers. Sasha bounded to the house, climbed the single step and opened the door. Once inside, she climbed onto her chair at the trestle table and set Katya before her.

Charlotte tugged off her gloves and unpinned the fancy

hat while drinking in her daughter's eagerness. Oh, to embrace life with such excitement again. When Wyatt kissed her, she'd felt a stirring that had lain dormant for many years, but the next moment he'd stung her by reaffirming their marriage barter. Perhaps it was best he would soon be gone.

She glanced out the window. Still no Wyatt. Good. That gave her time.

The materials for the dress were in her trunk. While removing the fabric and thread, she began to broach the subject of Wyatt.

"You like Mr. Reed, don't you?"

As often happened, Sasha chose that moment to hold her tongue.

Charlotte smoothed a remnant of the royal-blue fabric that she'd used to make Sasha's dress, but then she spotted a bit of emerald-green taffeta at the very bottom of the trunk. Wouldn't that make a pretty dress for Sasha's doll? Then again, the blue gingham would be more practical. She'd let Sasha decide. Gathering both fabrics, she brought them to the trestle table and laid them out.

"Which would you like for Katya's dress?"

Sasha's eyes widened as she reached for the emerald-green taffeta. "Like Mama."

The words tugged at Charlotte's heart. "Yes, dear, just like Mama's dress."

"Pitty. Mama pitty."

Charlotte blinked back a tear. Sasha had accepted her as her mother in just a couple of weeks. She was everything Charlotte could have asked for in a daughter, yet the girl had nearly been taken from her.

If not for Wyatt, she would have lost Sasha forever. For that alone, he deserved a good and loving home. She would do her utmost to give it to him for as long as he stayed.

* * *

Wyatt Reed never walked into a situation without checking it out first. Experience had taught him that danger lurked in the unknown. Therefore, while Charlotte fetched Sasha, he surveyed her home.

The tiny house looked cozy enough with its fresh coat of white paint. A single chimney jutted from one side of the roof, and a narrow porch with no railing stretched along the front, just one step up from the ground. Two glazed windows faced the street.

For a wheelwright who must have worked with wood all day long, Charles Miller did nothing to ornament his house. That surprised Wyatt. He'd imagined a woman like Charlotte would favor a porch rail with fancy spindles and shutters on the windows.

The tulip garden along the porch burst with weeds. Only the yellowing stems marked where the tulips had once bloomed. He circled the block to view the house from the other side. The large backyard contained a small shed and the privy. No stable. She must not have a horse or wagon, unless she owned one of the teams housed at the livery. Dusty would have to stay where he was. Wyatt felt a little relieved. It gave him an excuse to get away. The whole notion of sharing a house with her did things to his insides that he didn't want to acknowledge.

He'd thrown his principles out with the bathwater when he let himself get involved with Charlotte Miller. Involved? He'd married her! What kind of fool notion was that?

He'd told himself that he'd done it for the money, and on the surface, that made sense. If he backed Evans Grove on Monday, he wouldn't get another cent from Baxter. The man would probably even demand he repay the partial fee he'd already received. If he was going to get to San Francisco, he needed Charlotte's money, but he wouldn't take a cent more than Baxter had planned to give him. And that's where his argument failed.

A man who didn't care would take everything she had.

His gut twisted. How on earth was he going to extricate himself from this mess?

Chapter Ten

The loud knock made Charlotte jump.

Wyatt had arrived, and she hadn't yet told Sasha that she'd married him.

Her pulse raced even faster than when he kissed her. She smoothed her skirt, buying precious time.

A second knock sounded, and Sasha lifted puzzled eyes before slipping off her chair.

"No, Sasha." Charlotte moved across the room. "It's just—" His name caught in her throat. What should she call him? "Mr. Reed."

Her hand trembled as she opened the door and it only got worse when she saw his dark, lean figure on her porch.

He surveyed her calmly. "Took so long I figured you were changing your dress."

"Oh." She looked down at the emerald-green taffeta. "No. Not yet."

Wyatt waited while she tried to gather her scattered thoughts. He wore the same trail-worn buckskin coat. The early evening light shadowed the stark planes of his face and the saddlebags he'd slung over his shoulder.

A distant rumble of thunder echoed the storm in her heart as memories and feelings bombarded her. His kiss. Her desperate wish that it would never end. In that moment, she'd seen the tenderness beneath his brittle exterior. She'd ached from emptiness when he stepped away. It all jumbled together with the gathering fear.

What would he expect?

"You did tell me to come here," he reminded her, and she realized she was blocking the doorway.

"Yes. Of course." She stepped back to give him room to enter.

He had to stoop slightly under the lintel. Once inside, he hung the saddlebags on the back of a chair and removed his hat.

"Papa," Sasha squealed. She stepped away from her chair and ran to him. Her thin arms wrapped around his legs.

Papa. Of course. Sasha had called him that since nearly the beginning. In some way that Charlotte might never know, Wyatt resembled her father. Sasha would think nothing of him living with them.

Wyatt lifted Sasha as if she weighed less than his saddlebags. "I'm glad to see you, too, pumpkin."

"Pumpkin?" Charlotte frowned. What an odd nickname for a dark-haired girl.

"That's what we called my kid sister, Ava. Sasha's the spitting image of her when she was that age."

So he had a sister. And Ava looked like Sasha. In one sentence, Charlotte had learned more about Wyatt than she'd known before she married him.

"You stay?" Sasha asked Wyatt.

He looked to Charlotte for guidance. At least he wouldn't break the girl's heart on the first day. No, he'd leave that painful task to Charlotte.

She found the words surprisingly easy to say. "Mr. Reed is going to stay with us for a while. Would you like that?"

Sasha nodded and threw her arms around Wyatt's neck.

A rare smile curved his lips, and he looked lost in a pleasant memory that Charlotte wished she could share.

"Is Ava your only sister?" she asked.

He stiffened, the moment lost. "Yes. I have three younger brothers and then Ava."

So he was the oldest. That explained why he clung so staunchly to his sense of responsibility. Could she make him see that Sasha was his family now?

"Do you ever see them?" she asked softly.

His darkening expression told her she'd pressed too far. "Not since the war."

Something had happened to split the family apart. What? The war? Had the brothers fought on different sides? Whatever it was, it had estranged him from his family. Though she longed to know more, the set of his jaw told her the subject was closed.

So she turned to the one thing Charles had appreciated in her. "Would bacon and potatoes be all right for supper? I don't have much else."

"You're not cooking tonight." Wyatt spoke decisively. "We're going to the hotel dining room to celebrate." His cheek ticked as if he resisted a smile. "After all, a woman shouldn't work on her...special day."

Charlotte wasn't sure she could bear being in public again, but it did postpone the decisions she dreaded.

Sasha walked her doll up Wyatt's arm. "Katya hungry."

"Then it's settled," Wyatt said. "We can't keep Katya waiting."

Charlotte allowed the corners of her mouth to curve. He was so good with Sasha, unlike Charles, whose size often frightened the little girl.

As Charlotte took his arm, she felt like they'd become a real family.

"By the way." Wyatt paused at the door. "I told Mrs. Allen."

Charlotte didn't have to ask what he'd told the hotel proprietress. Now one of the biggest gossips in Evans Grove knew she had married Wyatt. She squeezed her eyes shut at the thought of what people must think of her. By now, the whole town would know, and it wouldn't take long for comments to reach Sasha's ears. Charlotte had to explain the situation to her soon, but how could she tell a little girl that her papa would leave her in a few days?

Supper had passed more agreeably than Wyatt thought possible. Charlotte had chattered away with everyone who stopped by their table, accepting congratulations on her marriage as well as compliments on her dress. Even Beatrice Ward congratulated them, though Wyatt suspected that was because she counted Wyatt on her side against the orphans.

The spinster was going to be mighty displeased come Monday.

But Wyatt had no time to waste on Miss Ward when Charlotte sat before him, afire like a brilliant jewel. That reminded him of her empty ring finger. She deserved a wedding band. She deserved a loving husband. Even if he couldn't be the latter, he'd send her a ring once he set up shop in San Francisco.

Tonight he settled for feasting on her dazzling beauty and equally stunning gown. He was no tailor, but he could see that the precise stitching and perfect fit meant her late husband had hired an expert dressmaker. The man might not have improved his house, but he certainly spent money on her attire. Yet she'd claimed their marriage was loveless. Those two facts didn't fit. Either she'd gotten the gown from someone other than her husband, or she wasn't telling the whole truth about her marriage.

The idea that she was hiding something bothered Wyatt, but he had the sense not to ask questions on a woman's wedding day. Plus, he enjoyed having her on his arm. Imagine, a man like him married to a beauty like Charlotte. No one who'd known him since the war would believe it.

The skies opened before they reached her house, soaking them to the bone. He expected Charlotte to wail over her ruined gown, but she giggled like a girl as they ran through the pelting rain. He scooped up Sasha and followed her as she danced around the puddles. Her wet and muddy skirts tangled around her legs, but she only laughed more. This was a woman after his heart.

By the time they burst into the house and collapsed on the chairs around the table, Wyatt felt more at home than he had in years.

"You look like a soggy beetle," he joked.

"A beetle?" She feigned displeasure as she tugged the fussy hat off her head, releasing the pent-up curls that he'd longed to touch all day. The damp ringlets tumbled around her porcelain face, making her look even more like a doll. He ran a finger along her jaw, where the drips had gathered. To his surprise, she didn't pull away. Instead, she drew in her breath and gazed right into his eyes. He couldn't look away.

"You're beautiful when you're wet." Despite every effort, his voice came out ragged.

Her lips formed a perfect *O* as those eyes widened.

"And when you're dry," he added.

She ducked her head as the compliment flushed her cheeks. "I should get Sasha dried off and changed so she doesn't catch a fever."

The little girl played with her doll, oblivious to what had just happened between her new parents.

Charlotte darted a quick glance at him. "Will you light a fire?"

He knew she was being sensible, but he hated to let the moment pass. It couldn't last, of course. They both knew their marriage would never be real, no matter how tempting it was to pretend a little, just for now.

So he dripped across the plank floor and checked the stove's firebox. A good bit of stirring uncovered a few embers. He added coal from the scuttle, opened the dampers and poked at the coals until the fire took off.

Meanwhile, Charlotte changed Sasha into a nightgown and wrapped her in a blanket. Before long, the girl's lids drooped, and she slipped off to sleep.

To his surprise, Charlotte put her in the bed on the main floor. In most one-room houses, that bed belonged to the husband and wife. Then again, most houses these days had a separate bedroom, whereas Charlotte only had a curtain. He couldn't understand why her late husband hadn't built a wall for privacy.

The cabin—and that's really what it was—consisted of a single ground-floor room with the kitchen on one side, the table in the middle and the bed on the other side. A small desk and one of those newfangled home sewing machines framed the front door. Opposite, a ladder led up to a loft. That was usually where the children slept. Sasha was probably too small to sleep upstairs, especially by herself. The open trunk downstairs and Charlotte's mourning dress hanging on a hook by the bed meant she slept downstairs, too. But he saw no men's clothing. Either she'd packed her late husband's clothes away or the sleeping arrangements had changed prior to the man's death.

Once Charlotte pulled the curtain closed and tiptoed across the plank floor to join him, darkness shrouded all but the small area illuminated by the oil lamps he'd lit while she was singing to Sasha.

"She's asleep," she whispered. She bit her lip as she noticed he was still in his wet clothing. "I'm sorry. I should have told you that you could change in the loft."

So that's where she expected him to stay. "You go first." He motioned toward the ladder. "I'm used to being wet."

She blushed and looked away. "How do you stay dry on the trail?"

"Find cover when I can," he said flatly.

"And when you can't?"

Shiver. Endure. "I get by. I'm a lot tougher than you. Go on now. I promise not to look."

Her cheeks colored again, and she hesitated.

"I could go outside. In the rain."

"No." Her voice sounded strangled, just like it had in the church. "That's not it. I—I—I can't unbutton the back."

He laughed before he caught himself. That's what was bothering her? "I do know how to undo buttons."

Her face blazed red. "I hate to ask." Her voice quivered.

What did she fear? He wouldn't hurt her. "I *am* your husband."

After a flicker of uncertainty, she turned around.

Down the back of her dress ran a line of little round buttons inside a row of equally small fabric loops. Sweet stars, he'd never get his fingers around those delicate little things. They were so close together and so tiny.

"I knew it was hopeless," she wailed. "I should never have let Holly talk me into wearing this dress. Why didn't I think about how I'd get out of it?"

"It's not hopeless," he said through clenched teeth. "Hold still."

Again, she obeyed.

He gingerly fingered the first button. How in blazes did these things work? He tried to get his broad, calloused fingers between the buttons and under the fabric loop to no avail.

"Maybe try a button hook?" She whisked off to retrieve the metal hook.

Wyatt didn't see how that was going to make things easier. The hook was made for boots and shoes, not delicate wet silk dresses.

"Don't move," he instructed as he bent over her back. The lamp gave just enough light to pick out the fabric loop. With a little wiggling, he managed to get the button hook under the loop and pull it over the button. "Got it!"

"You did?" She sounded as amazed as he was.

That was just one button, but once he mastered the technique, he could unhook loops with relative ease—and speed. Standing this close to her, though, was wreaking havoc on his resolve to keep his emotional distance. Wyatt Reed did not feel anything for anyone. *Get in, do the job and get out.* He silently repeated the words, trying to convince himself.

She turned when he stopped, her brow creased. "Are you done?"

He could have nodded, should have just nodded, but in that moment he had to do something to stop the feelings raging through him. So he jabbed at her the only way he knew how.

"After you've changed, I want the money."

Her eyes shot wide as if he'd just leveled a gun at her.

But he couldn't stop the cruelty. If he did, she'd want a real husband and a father for Sasha. So he hit harder.

"I held up my end of the bargain. I expect you to honor yours."

Her color drained before anger took hold. Grabbing her shawl from the hook by the door, she wrapped it around her shoulders. "I always honor my word."

He hated himself for hurting her, but he couldn't let her close again. She might discover who he really was.

She strode to the small desk by the door and lifted its lid. "Please look away."

She didn't trust him? Annoyed, he pretended to close his eyes but kept them slitted enough to see her remove a drawer and rummage behind it before pulling out the wallet she'd shown him earlier. His irritation grew. She'd offered him all her money earlier and now she didn't want him to see where she hid it. As if he'd steal her money!

She handed him the wallet. "Take it. Take it all."

The leather burned against his palm. Blood money. The woman was a widow. She had no means to support herself and her child. He felt like Judas taking silver from the chief priests.

"Only what we agreed on." He opened the wallet and removed the same amount Baxter had offered him. "Keep the rest." He set the wallet on the desk.

She stared at it, her hand still clutched to her breast. "You'll stay until I adopt Sasha?"

"I always keep my word."

She slowly nodded. "Thank you." It came out in a whisper, as if the words hurt.

They stood in silence for long minutes, the lamp flickering. In the soft, yellow glow, she looked even more lovely, and he hated himself for hurting her.

"I'll sleep in the loft," he blurted out.

She didn't offer to follow him. Instead, her gaze slipped toward the curtained-off bed where Sasha slept. "That would be best."

He wanted to put his arms around her. He wanted to promise to be the husband she deserved, but he couldn't. His past carried too many mistakes that would eventually find their way here. For her sake he would complete this barter they'd made and be on his way.

"Good night." He crossed the room in four steps and hurried up the ladder.

Maybe alone in the loft he could forget the woman that slept below on this, their wedding night.

Chapter Eleven

"Time to get ready for church!" The clatter of pans and the bright command pulled Wyatt from deep sleep. A woman was calling him to church. Why? Where was he?

Wyatt rubbed his eyes and gradually took in his surroundings. A plank ceiling sloped above his bed. An open trunk stood at the head of the bed with men's trousers and shirts stuffed into it. At the foot of the bed, two shelves had been fixed to the wall. One contained half-burnt candles and a small, framed daguerreotype of a woman. The other held a few books. Beneath him, straw poked through the ticking of the mattress, which was damp from perspiration.

A girl's giggle came from below. Sasha. He was in Charlotte Miller's house. In the loft. And he'd married her.

Last night he'd lain awake for hours before falling into a fitful sleep, tormented with nightmares. This morning, every muscle ached. His head wouldn't clear.

He stretched his limbs before sitting up. Sometime during the night he'd pushed the quilt and sheets off the bed. It was hot here at the top of the house. He'd shed his shirt and trousers last night. They sat neatly folded on top of his saddlebags next to the trunk. His belt, coat and hat draped over a squat stool. He checked under the pillow for his gun.

Still there.

Sunlight peeked through the vents at the roof peak and the chinks in the siding. If he was staying, he'd fill those before winter, or Charlotte and Sasha would shiver from cold. But he wasn't. In a day or two he would wrap up the orphan business and legally adopt Sasha. Then he could leave.

He slipped into his trousers and buttoned them before taking advantage of the chance to look around the loft in daylight. From the looks of the clothes in the trunk, Charlotte's late husband slept up here. The man must have been large, broad across the shoulders and wide in girth. He riffled through the trunk. No women's clothing.

Odd. At least he kept a picture of her.

He put on his shirt and then crawled to the shelves. A small pewter spoon lay in front of the picture, which was ringed with the candles. It almost looked like a shrine.

As he reached for the spoon, he noticed the image in the picture was not Charlotte but another woman with a typically severe expression. Who was she? Charles Miller's first wife, the one Charlotte had mentioned to him before? Whoever she was, she'd meant more to him than Charlotte.

"Breakfast," Charlotte called out from below.

Her voice startled him, and he shoved the picture back onto the shelf. The aroma of bacon made his stomach rumble.

"Wyatt?" Her bright tone failed to mask fear and hesitation. "Are you awake?"

He hurried toward the ladder. "I'm almost finished dressing."

"Good. We'll have to eat quickly so we don't miss Sunday worship."

Wyatt swallowed his irritation. It'd been half a lifetime since he'd arranged his schedule to a woman's liking, and he wasn't about to start now. He buckled on his belt and holster.

With his gun on his hip, he felt himself again. Grabbing the buckskin coat and hat, he headed down the ladder.

"Good morning." She looked up from pouring milk into a tin cup for Sasha.

Three plates containing bacon, potatoes and eggs sat before three of the chairs. She'd placed him at the head of the table, doubtless where her late husband had presided. Charlotte wore a plain gray dress that did nothing for her sunset-kissed hair and porcelain complexion.

He set his coat and hat on the empty chair and noticed the open Bible at the empty table setting.

She offered a tentative smile. "I thought you might like to read the scripture this morning, but do pick a short passage. We're running a bit late."

His throat closed. Other than yesterday, Wyatt hadn't set foot in a church since Sherman's march. God might have spared him for the wedding, but He wouldn't want a man like Wyatt in His house on a regular basis.

He strode past the Bible. "You do it."

She looked startled, even a bit worried, but thankfully didn't harp on him. With the gentleness of the biblical Ruth, she lifted the Book and read the passage about loving your neighbor as yourself.

He frowned, annoyed that she'd picked that passage. He hoped she didn't expect him to love her, because that wasn't part of the bargain.

He dug into the potatoes.

She softly cleared her throat. "We need to say grace."

He gulped down the mouthful. It'd been so long since he'd eaten in a Christian home that he'd forgotten.

She had Sasha fold her hands and then turned to him. "Would you like to do the honors?"

The potatoes felt like lead in his gut. "No, ma'am." Best she know right away that he wasn't the praying type.

We'd like to send you two free books to introduce you to the Love Inspired® Historical series. These books are worth over $10, but are yours to keep absolutely FREE! We'll even send you two wonderful surprise gifts. You can't lose!

Each of your **FREE** books is filled with romance, adventure and faith set in various historical periods from biblical times to World War

GET 2 FREE BOOKS!

HURRY!
Return this card today to get 2 FREE Books and 2 FREE Bonus Gifts!

YES! Please send me the **2 FREE Love Inspired® Historical books** and **2 FREE gifts** for which I qualify. I understand that I am under no obligation to purchase anything further, as explained on the back of this card.

**PLACE
FREE GIFTS
SEAL HERE**

102/302 IDL FVU9

FIRST NAME

LAST NAME

ADDRESS

APT.#

CITY

STATE/PROV.

ZIP/POSTAL CODE

▼ DETACH AND MAIL CARD TODAY! ▼

® and ™ are trademarks owned and used by the trademark owner and/or its licensee. © 2012 HARLEQUIN ENTERPRISES LIMITED. Printed in the U.S.A.

LIH-IN-13

She stared at him, as if assessing why he'd refuse to say grace, before turning back to her plate. "Very well. I'll do it."

But she looked disappointed, and a small part of him wished he still believed in a good and generous God, full of love and mercy. As a boy, he'd believed what the Bible said, that all things turned out for good for those who loved the Lord. He'd celebrated God's creation. That had ended in the war. He'd seen no love or mercy there. Then came the fiery march… He fought the memories that still seared. That putrid smell of the dead and dying. That roar of flames not quite loud enough to drown the cries for mercy. That raging bloodlust of hatred that had turned him into a beast. No good and loving God would have created such a man.

She folded her hands and waited for him to do likewise.

He scowled, set down his fork and bowed his head. That was as much as he'd give her.

After a moment's hesitation, she softly prayed for blessing on the food. The lilt of her voice mesmerized him. He could get used to hearing that every day. He even appreciated her devotion to religion. Most women needed that. But he couldn't fit her idea of a good, God-fearing husband.

After she finished, he cleared his throat. "I have business to take care of while you're in church."

She stopped eating, fork in midair. "What possible business could you have on a Sunday morning? Nothing is open except the hotel, and that's only for guests."

He kept his focus on the plate, shoveling the food in as quickly as possible. The sooner he got out of this house, the better. "I need to ride to Greenville."

"Greenville?" A flicker of alarm tinged her voice.

He reached for the cup of steaming coffee. "That's right."

"What's in Greenville? You're not…" Her voice trailed off as it usually did when she got to something she was afraid to say.

No, he wasn't seeing Baxter, but he wasn't about to explain his investigation to her, not with Sasha sitting there.

"I'm going for business," he reiterated.

She frowned. "But everyone at church will ask where you are. They'll all know about the wedding by now, and those who haven't heard will learn about it the moment they arrive. They'll want to congratulate you."

"Accept their congratulations on my behalf."

"But they won't understand your absence. What do I tell them?"

"Whatever you want." He'd finished eating. "Better they don't expect me to be around." He pushed back his chair.

Sasha watched him with those big, blue eyes. His conscience pricked, but it was better this way. When he left for good, the townspeople would rally around her. The people of Evans Grove were warm and compassionate. They'd deem him the villain and do all they could for Charlotte and Sasha. He'd try to send money when he could, but he wasn't going to be tied to her or this town a minute longer than necessary.

"But we'd expected to spend time with you." Her shy smile vanished.

How could something as small as a missing smile hurt so badly?

"There'll be time enough," he said gruffly.

"Sasha wanted to see your horse."

"Hor-sey," the little girl echoed, beating her fork on the plate.

Wyatt felt the noose tighten around his neck, but he would not be trapped. He rose. "Maybe later." Like tomorrow.

Wyatt's departure ripped an unexplainable hole in Charlotte, as if the light had been sucked out of her life. Charles had never left such emptiness.

"Mama?"

Sasha's plaintive cry drew Charlotte's attention away from her own distress.

"It's all right," she murmured, though it wasn't. Wyatt didn't believe in God. His words had left her horribly unsettled.

She ran a hand over Sasha's silky, black hair. At least she could keep her daughter. He'd promised that much.

"Where Papa go?" Sasha's lips quivered.

Charlotte's heart wrenched. Poor girl. All the father figures in her life had left her. And now Wyatt had walked out, too. Didn't he see how much he meant to this little girl?

"He had some work to do, dear." Though she tried to sound cheerful, her voice cracked. She forced her smile wider. "You won't mind spending the day with Mama, will you? We have a busy day ahead of us, starting with church." Though part of her wanted to hide from the questions sure to come, she could not miss Sunday worship. "Would you like to wear your red or blue dress?"

The question diverted Sasha's worries, but it did nothing to ease the hurt in Charlotte's heart.

At church, she donned a smile to mask her feelings, but she heard the whispers. "Just married, and already he's wandering off." "Should have known better than to get mixed up with the likes of Wyatt Reed." "The man's no good. After all, he's trying to take away our orphans."

If not for Holly and Pauline, she could never have made it through the service. Holly's encouraging smiles and the mayor's bold congratulations stopped the flow of gossip—at least for the moment.

Reverend Turner spoke of tolerance and compassion, neither of which Charlotte felt from some in the congregation. She saw the uplifted eyebrows and heard the cruel comments. She prayed Sasha didn't.

When the service ended, Charlotte rushed out of the

church. She intended to hurry home, but Rebecca Sterling waited for her near the church steps. Charlotte's heart nearly stopped. Had the orphan society insisted Rebecca take Sasha away from Charlotte now?

The little girl slipped away to join Lynette and some of the orphans. Charlotte let her go. If this was bad news, best Sasha not hear it.

"Lovely morning, Charlotte." Yet Rebecca didn't look like she was enjoying it.

Charlotte hesitated. "Yes, I suppose it is."

The pretty blonde ducked her head a moment before drawing a shaky breath. "I wanted to offer my congratulations and to say I'm sorry that you had to go to such extremes. I didn't want it to come to that. I pleaded with Mr. Armstrong to grant an exception."

It took Charlotte a moment to recall that Mr. Armstrong was the head of the Orphan Salvation Society. If Rebecca had contacted him, then she'd done her best to help.

Charlotte's heart rate slowed. "Thank you. It means a lot to know you tried."

"Sometimes I get angry at the rules. I know they're there for a reason, but life doesn't always fall into place so neatly."

It certainly didn't. Charlotte forced herself not to think of Wyatt's departure.

"People shouldn't say such things," Rebecca whispered, nodding toward the gossips. "I'm glad Mayor Evans put them in their place. I'd have spoken up myself, but it didn't feel right, when I'm not really a resident of Evans Grove."

Rebecca's wistful gaze reminded Charlotte that the orphan agent was terribly young to have endured a train robbery at gunpoint, the murder of her fellow agent and handling the group of orphans all by herself. Her delicate shoulders bowed under the weight of responsibility that she must carry alone, and so far from home, too. While she rarely talked about her background, it was evident that Rebecca came from a much more glamorous lifestyle than anything Evans Grove had to offer.

Charlotte squeezed Rebecca's hand. "You did all you could."

The simple statement brought a hopeful smile to Rebecca's lips. "I wish I could have done more." She glanced toward Heidi, who was watching the other orphans. "I wish they'd all find homes here." She nibbled her lip. "It's a good town. The people here care, but today's Sunday. Tomorrow will be too late."

"No one has come forward?"

"The Monaghans have asked for Patrick."

Charlotte seized on this hopeful sign for the troublemaking boy. "They'd be perfect for him with their four boys. Mr. Monaghan is firm, yet caring. He'll have Patrick so busy there'll be no time for stirring up trouble."

Rebecca looked relieved. "I hope the selection committee agrees. They're going to meet this afternoon."

"Even Beatrice? I can't believe she'd agree to meet on the Sabbath."

Rebecca sighed. "I wouldn't put it past her to raise a fuss."

"But she's only one member of the committee," Charlotte reassured her. "Has there been any interest in Tom or Heidi?"

"Pauline said the Quintons asked who was still available. Maybe they'd take Tom." Rebecca's smile faltered. "I'd love to think they'd take Heidi as well, but I know that's not likely. They already have two girls, and with the farm… Tom is small and not terribly coordinated, but he's still a boy." She leaned close to whisper. "I'm so afraid that no one will take Heidi. What then? She would have to go to Greenville alone and could end up in the orphanage there. I just can't bear the thought of her growing up in an orphanage."

Charlotte felt a tug on her heart. "I could take her." But even as she said the words, she knew she couldn't.

"I know you would, and you'd be a wonderful mother, but—" Rebecca hesitated. "Three children would be a lot for your little house."

"Three?" Charlotte counted only Sasha and Heidi.

"Her brother Jakob. I made a mistake separating them, and now I fear he's trying to find her."

Somehow Charlotte had missed this news. "Heidi has a brother? Where is he?"

"He was placed in Glenwood, Iowa, our last stop before crossing into Nebraska. Until then, he and Heidi had been inseparable. Jakob is the oldest, and I gather that after they lost their parents, he felt his sister was his responsibility. The poor girl thought her brother would never find a home as long as they stuck together. The scars meant that no family showed interest in her, so Heidi tricked him into getting placed by himself."

Charlotte ached for the decision this girl had made. "But he didn't stay?"

Rebecca took a deep breath. "We learned he ran away and think he's heading this way, but he'll never know the children are in Evans Grove. He knew the stops we were planning to make, and this town was never on the itinerary." She fidgeted with the clasp on her bag. "So many terrible things could happen to him out there." She blinked back a tear. "If only we knew where he was."

Charlotte caught her breath as an idea came to mind. Wyatt was a tracker. He found lost and missing people. Maybe he could find Jakob. Moreover, it would give him a reason to stay in contact with Evans Grove. It was perfect.

"I wonder if—" she began but was cut off by Beatrice Ward.

"Miss Sterling!" The woman bustled toward them, shaking her finger at Rebecca. "If you won't look after those truants, that Society of yours should find someone who can."

Apparently, Beatrice had heard none of Reverend Turner's sermon.

The woman continued her tirade. "That boy of yours pulled all the blossoms off the peonies."

Charlotte's gaze followed her outstretched hand to see Tommy hand a single pink bloom to Lynette Gavin. "How sweet. Little Lynette loves flowers. Why, it's rather romantic."

"Romantic?" Beatrice kept her distance from Charlotte, as if getting too close would contaminate her. "What would you know about romance, Mrs. Reed?" She clucked her tongue. "You might think you've pulled one over on this town, but no sin can be hidden from God."

Sin? Charlotte's jaw dropped. Hadn't the woman congratulated her just last night? What had happened between then and now? Glancing over at the group of Beatrice's friends, Charlotte thought she knew why. Or, more precisely, *who*. Mrs. Ingersman gave her a scathing look. No doubt she'd seen Sasha pick her pansies yesterday and was exacting her revenge.

"As the Good Book says, the Lord sees all and judges accordingly."

Charlotte wondered why Beatrice didn't apply that scriptural teaching to herself.

Miss Ward returned her attention to Rebecca. "Keep those urchins under control, Miss Sterling. You'll only have to manage for one more day, since the judge arrives tomorrow." Her nasty business done, she returned to her cronies.

Rebecca sighed. "She won't approve any placements this afternoon."

"She's only one member of the committee." Yet Charlotte cringed as Sasha pulled a bloom off the peonies that Miss

Ward had planted at the church. "I'd better rescue Sasha before Beatrice gets to her."

Rebecca agreed. "And I'd better get the children back to the schoolhouse."

"I'll make dinner for everyone," Charlotte offered as they strode toward the children. It would distract her from Wyatt's absence.

"Thank you." Rebecca's weary smile touched Charlotte's heart. "It'll take the children's minds off the selection committee meeting."

"Would two o'clock be a good time, then?"

"Perfect." Rebecca then admonished Patrick, who was teasing Tom about giving Lynette the flower. After restoring order, she marched the restless group back to the schoolhouse. The children had to know this afternoon might be their last chance to stay in Evans Grove. Tomorrow, Wyatt would do his best to take them to Greenville.

Charlotte's stomach clenched.

"Pitty." Sasha held up the peony.

"For me?" Charlotte's heart warmed. A child's love could be so pure and unconditional, unlike the complicated way she felt about Wyatt.

"For Papa."

Charlotte's heart nearly broke. Wyatt had stormed out of the house this morning with no indication if or when he would return. Would Sasha wait all day in vain? For the little girl's sake, she prayed he would come back soon.

The church bells mocked Wyatt as he rode Dusty out of town. Cow-ard. Cow-ard. Each stroke accused him of running away from God. He had. Going to Greenville had been an excuse to not go to church. He did want to take another stab at discovering Baxter's motive, but that could have waited until after the morning service.

Instead he'd headed west along the stagecoach road to-ward the large-scale farmers out Greenville way. He couldn't cover the entire distance and back today, not if he wanted to talk to anyone, but he could get to the nearest farms. The Star Plains farm stretched for hundreds of acres more than halfway between Evans Grove and Greenville, and a handful more miles north. To get there, he'd have to cut across fallow lands and head up toward the curve of the Big Blue River.

Dusty snorted, enjoying the brisk pace after being cooped up in the livery all day yesterday. Wyatt could sympathize. He'd felt the walls close in on him this morning. Nothing beat fresh air and open country.

The morning had shimmered with the promise of a fine day, and, by the time he reached the point where he had to head north, the sun beat down hot. The road baked like a flapjack in a skillet.

After they left the road, the pace slowed to a crawl as Dusty picked his way through the fields. That gave Wyatt time to decide exactly what he'd ask once he reached the farm. The direct approach hadn't worked so far. Evans Grove farmers had eyed him warily or clammed up. Only Colton Hayes had said anything to raise a red flag, but the man wouldn't explain why he refused to deal with Baxter, prob-ably because he didn't know Wyatt. In these parts, relation-ships were built on trust earned over time. Wyatt had arrived in Greenville after March's storm, the one that had broken the dam and flooded Evans Grove. He hadn't had time to earn that trust.

Dusty whinnied and shook his head.

Wyatt automatically tensed and eased his left hand toward his gun. His horse had seen or heard someone.

He scanned the fields to the left. Low trees dotted the edge, but they were spaced too far apart and were too young to hide anything bigger than a squirrel. To the right, a small grove nestled by the road. Dense and heavily shaded. A perfect hiding place.

With a soft cluck of the tongue, he directed Dusty to stop. The well-trained horse responded at once.

Wyatt listened. Birds squawked and twittered. A light breeze rustled the leaves and grass. In the distance, wagon wheels cut a dusty path across the horizon. A horse whinnied, followed by a sharp command.

That wasn't a man's voice. Too high. It had to be a boy or a woman. By his calculation, the horse and rider were just beyond the grove. He eased off on the gun and with his knees, urged Dusty forward. A woman or boy wouldn't pose any danger. With luck, he'd find a boy. After a little friendly conversation, most lads would tell him anything.

He rode at an easy pace, hoping he looked like a man taking a Sunday ride. As soon as he rounded the grove, the plow horse and boy came into view. The lad's arms and legs looked thin as straw. The sun beat down on dark brown hair as he wrestled the horse and plow through the field. No hat. Ragged trousers.

That boy shouldn't have to work so hard on a Sunday. He should be in church.

Startled by the thought, Wyatt drew Dusty to a halt. Guilt washed over him again, but he brushed it aside. If he learned something bad about Baxter, those orphan kids could stay in Evans Grove, and that was more important than going to some stuffy church service.

He waited until the lad neared him. "Hello, there."

The lad's head jerked up. "'Lo," he muttered with a quick glance toward the grove.

The boy couldn't be more than thirteen or fourteen. Scrawny arms and bowed legs barely kept control of the plow. Moreover, the lad was barefoot. Most farmers worked their children from a young age, both from necessity and so they'd learn farming and could take over one day. But this boy looked half-starved despite the large size and apparent prosperity of the farm.

Wyatt set both hands on the saddle horn. "Mind telling me where I am?"

The boy halted the plow horse and wiped his brow. "Star Plains."

Wyatt looked around as if he hadn't a clue what that meant. "I'm looking for the road to Greenville."

The boy hesitated before pointing south.

"How far?"

The boy shrugged. "You'll run across it."

Wyatt pushed a little further. "Ever been to Greenville?"

Again the flinch. "Once."

"Big town?"

"Wouldn't know." The boy looked furtively over his shoulder again, as if afraid someone was watching him from that grove of trees.

Wyatt fought the urge to look. He'd check on his way back through, but he still hoped to get more from the boy while keeping up the ruse that he was out for a Sunday-morning ride.

"Much obliged." He clucked his tongue as if to instruct Dusty to head out, but he'd trained his horse to hold still on that command. "Worthless horse. It won't obey any orders." He clucked his tongue again. "If I'd gotten a better one at the livery, I wouldn't be in such a fix." He lifted his hat and mopped his brow. "Don't suppose I could go up to your pa's house and beg a drink of water for me and this worthless critter."

The boy wavered, his sympathies entirely with Dusty. After another glance at the grove, he lowered his voice and said, "I wouldn't go up there if I was you."

"Your ma and pa gone to church?"

The boy shook his head. "They ain't my ma and pa. I jess work here."

"That so? They hiring?"

"Didn't ya hear me?" His eyes darted toward the grove. "Head south, and you'll find the road." He called to the plow horse, slapped the reins and drove the plow toward the center of the field.

Wyatt would have to follow into the field to continue the conversation. Judging by the boy's constant glances toward the grove, any trespassing would not be welcomed by whoever was overseeing this operation.

A boy of thirteen hired out? It wasn't unheard of, but this lad hadn't an ounce of meat on his bones. His parents must be impoverished to resort to hiring him out to a farmer who worked his hands so hard, even on Sunday. It wasn't fair or just, but Wyatt had learned that fairness and justice often vanished before necessity and greed.

Turning Dusty around, Wyatt ambled toward the grove. As he neared, the shadows grew deeper. He'd have to plunge into the thick undergrowth to track whoever was hiding there. Though curiosity urged him forward, common sense told him he'd learn nothing. Moreover, the feared overseer would take out any trespassing on the boy's back.

No, he'd best head onward and leave Star Plains farm behind. He directed Dusty back to the road. With every step he grew more and more troubled.

Chapter Twelve

Despite occupying her hands with cooking Sunday dinner and occupying her mind by inventing games and stories to distract Sasha from Wyatt's absence, Charlotte had been unable to halt the mounting fear that he would not return. With every passing hour, her tension rose until she felt like she would burst.

Where was he? What was he doing? Her hands marked the fabric for Holly's dress with a piece of chalk, but her mind wouldn't settle on the task at hand. Surely Wyatt hadn't stayed in Greenville.

Yet part of her feared he had. She'd pushed too hard this morning. A man in love might change his ways in time, but she should never have insisted he go to church the first day of their wedded life. He wasn't ready for it, and she'd been too consumed by her hope of a future together to see that.

As a result, he'd left, and she had no idea if he would return. What would she tell Sasha? The little girl had asked for him all day, and Charlotte had been forced to make up excuses. How inconsiderate he was! How selfish. He should have thought of Sasha before running off to Greenville. No doubt he intended to consult with Mr. Baxter about tomorrow's court hearing. Nothing had changed Wyatt's mind.

She might be able to keep Sasha, but come tomorrow he would take away Liam and the rest of the unplaced orphans.

By the time she heard footsteps on the porch, she'd worked herself into a frazzle.

She clutched the chalk when Wyatt opened the door. "Where have you been?"

He paused, cold as stone, his hand still on the knob. "I told you I had business."

His resentment was palpable, but Charlotte couldn't stop the flow. He didn't know the taunts she'd endured. He didn't know how often Sasha had asked for him. He didn't understand how much his actions hurt others. Today of all days, Wyatt Reed should have stood at her side.

"They said terrible things about you this morning," she told him. "Mrs. Ingersman was worst of all, though Beatrice made it clear she did not approve of our marriage. And that after congratulating us the night before." Charlotte lined up two pieces of fabric that needed to be basted together. "I didn't know what to say."

"Don't say anything," he growled, closing the door. "Gossip doesn't deserve an answer."

"It's not only gossip. It's spiteful."

"They're just unhappy people." Only the hard planes of his cheeks were visible beneath the shadowed brim of his hat. He made no move to remove either his hat or his buckskin coat, and that worried her even more.

"Maybe *I'm* unhappy." She attempted to thread a needle, but her hands shook too much to get the thread through the tiny eye. Frustrated, she threw the harshest accusation at him that she could imagine. "Sasha asked for you all day."

"I told you I was going to Greenville."

Charlotte wouldn't let him make this her fault. She pointed at the peony propped in a mason jar. "She brought that home for you."

He gave the flower passing notice before looking toward the curtained bed. "She's asleep?"

Charlotte managed to get the thread through the needle's eye. "She was tired after our long day. I cooked Sunday dinner for Rebecca Sterling and the orphans. We were trying to distract them from the selection committee meeting. Did you know there was a meeting this afternoon?"

"I'm not surprised." He still stood near the door, ready to escape.

She set her jaw. "They approved sending Patrick to the Monaghans and Tom to the Quintons. Does *that* surprise you?"

"No."

"But it'll make your argument more difficult, won't it?"

His jaw tensed. "Listen, Charlotte—"

"Don't 'listen Charlotte' me. I didn't go running off when I was needed. I didn't show up hours later. Your dinner must be dry as jerky by now."

"That's fine." He finally took off his hat, and the sight of his steel-gray eyes shot uncomfortable needles of regret through her.

She stared at the fabric and reminded herself that he was at fault. She hadn't run off, leaving him to handle everything. She stabbed the needle into the fabric—and her thumb.

"Ouch." She shook her hand and sucked on the injured thumb, even more petulant. "We missed you. Sasha missed you. You promised to show her your horse."

"I said maybe."

"She wouldn't take her nap after dinner because she didn't want to miss it. I finally got her to fall asleep by assuring her you never forget a promise."

"I don't."

"I hoped that was true." But she was choking on that hope.

His dark, unyielding presence made her fear for their future. "I—I was so afraid you wouldn't come back."

"I told you I would." The words pelted her, hard as stones. "I always keep my word."

She bit her lip to stem the rush of tears. Careless emotion had gotten the best of her. She'd made up all sorts of terrible things that could happen when he had in fact done exactly what he said he would. She choked back a sob. "I—I'm sorry."

"No." He grasped her shoulders. "Don't be."

The jolt of his touch made her gasp, but he didn't seem to notice. Instead, he let go.

"I'm the one who should be sorry," he continued, oblivious to what had just happened. "I should have been more considerate. I should have told you how long I'd be gone." He drew in a deep breath. "I'm not used to considering anyone else in my plans."

His words swirled around her head, like puffs of cottonwood seed on the wind. She knew he was apologizing, and she did regret her words, but how could he not feel what she'd just felt? His hands had cupped her shoulders with both strength and tenderness. His touch sent shivers skittering all over her flesh, drawing up goose pimples.

Yet he didn't react.

How cruel to feel so drawn to a man who could never love her. This was worse than Charles, for she had never felt more than mild affection for him. This hurt. To the bone.

"Don't cry," he commanded stiffly, as if embarrassed by her tears. "I will keep every word of our agreement."

That only unleashed the flood. For the briefest moment she'd sensed the man beneath the cold exterior, a man starved of affection, but the unbreakable shell returned the next instant.

He thrust a handkerchief at her, and she buried her face

in the rough muslin, wishing she hadn't let down her guard. A chill whispered between them, unspoken, yet absolute. He had given his word, but he would not give his heart.

Why had he touched Charlotte? Even as Wyatt lay awake in the loft, he replayed the moment. Her thin shoulders beneath the plain cotton dress. The warmth of her. The way she'd tensed and then relaxed, leaning toward him.

None of it made sense. The moment he'd stepped in the door, she'd leveled accusation after accusation at him. Each word made him more furious. He'd wanted to turn right around and leave. What did she expect? They had a business agreement, not a real marriage. But then she'd laid out her fears, and he'd unthinkingly reached out to comfort her.

He ground his teeth. He should have known better than to touch her. From the beginning she'd gotten to him more than any other woman. She sent the same shivers up the back of his neck that he got from a crimson sunrise or drinking in the millions of stars overhead on a moonless night. And then he'd gone and made her his until-death wife.

He lay on the straw-stuffed mattress, perspiration beading on his skin, and listened to the wind whistle between the boards. It blew endlessly here, until it set a man's teeth on edge. Maybe San Francisco would be different.

He tried hard to imagine that city the way the old prospector had described it, with shining buildings perched on a slope around a clear blue bay. The island in the center. The fog that rolled in and out. It must be beautiful.

Just like Charlotte.

Now, why'd he gone and thought that? Must've been the tears. He couldn't stand to see women cry, and she'd wept over some promise he'd apparently made to Sasha. He blew the air from his lungs. That little girl was his weak spot. She deserved a good home after losing her parents at such a ten-

der age. Charlotte was a good guardian for a child, unlike
the Star Plains farmer. That encounter still angered him.
Wyatt couldn't forget the boy's furtive glances. He'd make
sure Sasha never had to endure that sort of life.

He flexed his aching knee. The army doc couldn't get
the bullet out, so it rattled around inside, grinding against
the bone. On nights like tonight, it throbbed, reminding him
of his guilt.

He closed his eyes and tried to think of Charlotte and
Sasha. In a perfect world, those vows he'd spoken in the
church would last more than a few days, and he could be a
true husband and father—but that wasn't possible. Even if
he could convince Charlotte to give him a real chance, eventually the truth of his past would come to Evans Grove, and
she'd learn to hate him. Better she never loved him, for like
the bullet in his knee, the truth would grind away against
something as gentle and kind as love.

The yells awoke Charlotte. At first she thought something
must have happened in town. She shot up, and then checked
Sasha to see if she'd awoken.

Thankfully, no.

She tucked the covers around her daughter and slipped
out of bed. The hard floor bit into her feet as she crept to the
window. The curtain filtered the waning crescent moon. As
she brushed it aside, she realized the yells hadn't come from
outdoors. They'd come from above.

Wyatt.

Her pulse quickened. What had happened?

She slipped past the curtain that separated the bed from
the rest of the room. The dim moonlight guided her across
the room to the ladder.

She shivered, but the house wasn't cold. No, this shiver
came from an intense feeling of vulnerability at the thought

of going to Wyatt, comforting him through what appeared to be a nightmare.

Perhaps she should return to her bed.

But then he yelled so loudly that she feared he'd wake Sasha. She darted across the room to check on her daughter. Still asleep, for now, but one of those yelps was bound to awaken the little girl. She'd have to shake Wyatt out of his nightmare.

When another volley of moans tumbled down from the loft, she hurried to the ladder.

Charlotte feared heights. When she was little, she'd lost her footing and fell from the loft in her father's barn. The resulting blow had knocked her unconscious. Her mama said they'd kept vigil at her bedside for two days until she finally awoke. Her limbs still froze when faced with heights.

Another moan followed by a thud unlocked them.

The poor man could roll clear out of the loft if he continued. That fear made her grip the sides of the ladder. That fear made her take the first halting step.

Foolish woman! How did she think she could pack up Charles's things if she couldn't climb into the loft? This had been her late husband's retreat. She hadn't entered it. He'd brought down the dirty linens and clothes. He'd made the bed with fresh linens. At first she'd considered it a kindness, but soon she'd suspected he wanted it that way.

She took another step.

Holly would have helped her, of course. Her friend wouldn't be afraid of heights. Holly was the bravest person she knew.

Charlotte pretended she was Holly and took another step and then another. She must be five feet above the floor now. If she fell… Her head grew woozy and her limbs shook. She couldn't fall.

"Burn," he mumbled, the urgency building. He sounded so utterly distraught.

Taking a deep breath, she scurried up the remaining steps and pulled her body onto the floor of the loft. The raw planks prickled against her palms and knees, but she'd made it.

"Mah-get," he muttered incoherently, followed by violent thrashing.

The light was poor up here. Strips of moonlight from the vent at the peak of the roof lined the floor and revealed the bed a few feet away. She crawled forward and halted.

He lay twisted in the bedsheet while he moaned and tossed his head so that his lean face fell into the moonlight. His usual calm confidence had been replaced with pain. Every feature was contorted.

She instinctively reached out to him. His forearm was damp with sweat. No wonder. The air up here was unbearably hot.

"Margare—" he shouted.

She shoved her hand over his mouth.

He twisted away.

"Hush!" She held his damp cheeks, rough with whiskers. "Please, you have to calm down. It's just a dream, Wyatt. Just a dream."

He wrenched from her grip. "Margaret."

Margaret? Who was Margaret? His wife?

"Margaret!"

Without another thought, she shook his hot shoulders. "Wake up, wake up." He flailed at her, but she persisted. She had to make him stop.

"Wake up," she said, ducking a hand.

With a start, he suddenly sat up, sending her sprawling. "Who's there?" he barked.

In the moonlight, she saw the flash of something metal. His pistol.

Heart in her throat, she whispered his name.

"Charlotte?" He said it shakily but lowered the gun. "What are you doing here?"

"You were shouting. I was worried—that you'd wake Sasha, that is."

He set the gun down beside him, still loaded she presumed, and scrubbed his face. "Must've been a dream."

"You were calling out for Margaret." When he said nothing, she asked, "Is she a cousin or aunt?"

"She's no one."

His tone implied he wanted no further questions, but Charlotte couldn't rest without knowing who this woman was. "Clearly she's someone who means a lot to you, or you wouldn't call for her."

"It's from the past," he growled.

This time Charlotte heeded the note of warning. He did not want to tell her about this woman. She fought a twinge of jealousy, but their marriage was only a business transaction. She had no right to demand more.

Wyatt rubbed his eyes, and his open-neck shirt shifted enough to reveal a jagged scar on his left shoulder.

Charlotte gaped at the old wound. "What happened?" She pointed to his shoulder, half fearing the answer.

His jaw tightened, and his shoulders tensed. "The war."

The war. Of course. Many men had joined the terrible struggle. She knew several in Evans Grove. All had fought to save the Union, but she knew so little of Wyatt. He could have been a Rebel.

"Which side?" she asked softly.

"Union."

She breathed out in relief. She wasn't sure how she would have felt had he fought for the Confederate states. "I'm sorry you were wounded, but at least your sacrifice brought justice."

"Justice?" He stared at her as if crazed, and her fear escalated. Would he harm her? Did the madness of the nightmare continue into the waking world?

"I—I didn't mean anything by it." She retreated until her back hit the edge of the shelves.

His tension eased. "I didn't mean to frighten you. Please don't run away."

She gulped at the emotion that rushed through her. Charles had never asked for her to stay with him. His presence had never stirred her this way. He'd been safe, predictable, uninterested. At first glance, Wyatt had seemed just as aloof, but beneath the surface boiled raw intensity. He was dangerous and unpredictable. She knew so little about him and wanted to know more. She wanted to drink in everything about him, to know him deeply, fully, as a wife should know her husband.

If they were truly married, they would start a family. Baby brothers and sisters for Sasha. She drew in her breath as she imagined what his child would look like. If a son, Wyatt would teach him to ride, to handle himself with confidence, to walk tall. If a daughter, he'd cherish her the way he cherished Sasha. Her eyes misted at the thought of the future that would be possible in the full, loving marriage she'd always wanted. The marriage she now could only imagine with him.

"Please don't be afraid," he said softly as he reached for her hand. She couldn't bring herself to take it. As much as she wanted more from their relationship, like Charles, Wyatt had never promised to love her. Taking his hand now would only make his imminent departure hurt more.

"What's wrong?" he asked.

She shook her head, unable to risk spilling her heart, and grasped on to the first thought that crossed her mind. "You look…different in the moonlight."

"More frightening?"

He was teasing, but she couldn't calm the pounding in her chest. "More handsome," she whispered.

He started at her words before the cold exterior returned. "The moonlight lies."

His stark denial extinguished the heat and revealed the truth. She'd remade him into the man she wanted, not the man he truly was, scarred and angry. Yet he didn't see clearly, either.

"God made you in His image."

His jaw tensed. "Then God is a fool."

She reeled at the blasphemy. "How can you say such a thing?"

He turned from her. "I've seen things that no loving God would allow."

"Evil does not come from God."

"But He allows it."

"To test and purify us, like in the forge."

He turned back to face her. "Is that what your husband did? Test and purify you?"

She gasped. "I already told you that Charles was a good man."

"But not to you."

The harsh words slashed deep into her soul. Charles had shown her the same kindness as everyone else in town, but she wasn't just another neighbor. She was his wife. She should have received more than gratitude for a meal well cooked before he retreated into this loft. She bowed her head and mumbled, "Married life is both trial and joy."

Wyatt snorted. "More trial than joy sometimes." But then his voice softened. "He never grew to love you, did he?"

She turned from him so he wouldn't see the truth on her face. The moonlight flooded the shelf above her head, illuminating a daguerreotype of Charles's first wife, Gloria, surrounded by candles. A shrine. That's why he'd retreated here each day. She could often hear him overhead as he mumbled and sobbed regrets.

Wyatt's hard gaze bored through her. "Tell me, and I'll never ask again."

Time stopped as she hesitated. Revealing her heartache wouldn't solve anything. It wouldn't erase the thirteen years of hoping Charles would change. It wouldn't bring back her youth or give her the family she'd always wanted. It wouldn't make Wyatt stay.

"Why do you care?" She summoned the courage to add, "Because your Margaret hurt you?"

The pause made her heart pound. Did he resent her prying? Or was he just like Charles, clinging to the past?

At last he answered. "Love can be cruel."

Though he didn't tell her exactly what had happened, she could imagine. A young man off to war. Wyatt would have been around twenty, perhaps younger, if he'd joined early in the conflict.

"The war?" she asked.

He nodded.

"She didn't wait."

His jaw tightened. "It wouldn't have mattered, anyway. War changes a man."

Enough to give him nightmares.

"I'm sorry." Her whisper belied the thudding of her heart against her ribs. Dare she tell him her heartache and dashed hopes?

"It doesn't matter." His voice was cold, devoid of the emotion that had been there moments before. "The past is done. I should never have asked you to tell me about your late husband. I won't ever again." He took a deep breath. "Tomorrow, everything will be settled. You'll have your daughter."

And he will leave us.

"You're a good mother," Wyatt added.

Mother. Not wife, though they were bound to each other for life. No man would sing to her like Solomon to his beloved. No man would hold her in his arms. No man would gaze into her eyes like Mason did to Holly. All she would ever have was her daughter. She lowered her head to hide her quivering lip.

Sasha should have been enough, but she wanted more. She wanted what she could not have. She wanted a real marriage.

Chapter Thirteen

After last night's encounter with Charlotte, Wyatt couldn't wait to get out of the house. She acted like everything was the same, even served him the same bacon, eggs and potatoes for breakfast; but they both knew something dangerous had happened in the moonlight.

He'd felt that spark when he touched her shoulder. He'd wanted to protect her, to comfort her, to be everything her late husband hadn't been, to make a family with Sasha. But it wouldn't work. Last night's nightmares proved he couldn't escape the past in Evans Grove.

"You should have seen Liam at Mason and Holly's wedding." Charlotte chattered away while she dished up breakfast. "The boy clearly adores Mason, but he had to act tough, like he didn't care. I think he's still trying to impress Mason, but I'm pretty sure Mason was impressed the moment Liam ran to town to tell him about the train robbery." She paused, deep in memories. "If it hadn't been for Liam, Evans Grove would have lost the money to rebuild, and the children might not have come here."

She smiled fondly at Sasha, but he could see the worry in her eyes. Today the judge would decide if any of the children had to go on to Greenville. He and Charlotte would also apply to adopt Sasha. That'd make any woman jittery. Probably why she didn't stop talking.

"Holly said she and Mason are going to officially adopt Liam. And then Patrick and Tom were taken. Isn't it wonderful?" She didn't pause long enough for him to answer. "That only leaves Heidi. Poor girl. That scarring frightens people. I'd take her, if…if I could manage." She bit her lip in that pretty way she had when she was troubled.

He wished he could assure her that all the orphans—even Heidi—could stay, but he didn't have the proof to ensure Baxter wouldn't press the matter. Nor could he predict how the judge would rule. He could only do his part.

"Surely someone will take her in." Charlotte dished the bacon-laden potatoes onto his plate. "She's a dear child, just a little shy, which is completely understandable, seeing what she's been through. I heard she was burned escaping her own home. Her parents died in that fire. It's too awful to imagine."

Her words seared Wyatt, bringing back horrific memories. The screams. The flames. He steeled himself and desperately tried to change the subject. "I won't ask the judge to send the children to Greenville."

Charlotte's jaw dropped. "You won't?"

"I won't." The nightmarish memories receded. "I changed my mind after seeing how the community took in those kids." He glanced at Sasha, well aware that she was one of *those kids,* but the little girl didn't seem to know what he was talking about.

Charlotte sank into her seat with a sigh of relief. "Then they'll stay."

"We don't know that," he cautioned. "Greenville has a written agreement with the Orphan Salvation Society. Even if I don't press the point, others might."

She wrinkled her brow. "Who?"

"The citizens of Greenville," he hedged, since he still wasn't sure of Baxter's role. "They want those children real bad."

"But why? These children were passed over stop after stop. Greenville didn't suffer from the storm that flooded our town. They didn't lose children like we did. Why would they insist?"

He gulped the scorching coffee, aware that she had come to the same conclusion he had. "I don't know, and that's what bothers me. It's also why I think the kids should stay here."

"All of them?"

He hated to admit just how far he'd come since he first arrived, but his gut told him this was where those children belonged. "At least the ones who have homes."

"But what will happen to Heidi and Jakob?"

"Jakob?" Wyatt hadn't heard that name before.

"Heidi's brother." Her eyes sparked in a way that he'd come to recognize meant trouble for him. "Rebecca—Miss Sterling—told me that he was taken by a family in Iowa, but word came that he ran away. She thinks he's trying to find Heidi, but he wouldn't know that the train stopped in Evans Grove." She waited expectantly.

"What are you getting at?"

"I've been thinking. You're a tracker. You know how to find missing people. Maybe you could find him."

She looked so hopeful that he hated to dash her expectations, but as soon as the adoption came through, he was headed for San Francisco. He sure wasn't going to look for some runaway.

"I work for hire." He didn't figure that orphan society would fork over money to find one runaway boy.

Charlotte jutted out her chin. "Then I'll pay you."

"You'll do no such thing. You need that money for Sasha."

The little girl's eyes widened, and he realized he'd raised his voice to her mother.

"Sorry," he muttered, "but I won't take another cent from you."

"Th-then maybe the town or the orphan society will hire you."

"I don't work on maybes." He scooped up a forkful of eggs.

Her lips pressed into a frown, and he thought for a moment that she would rebuke him further. Maybe she would have if Sasha hadn't sobbed.

"Mama?" The plaintive voice cut deeper than any blade.

Never argue in front of the children. His father had held strictly to that rule, though Wyatt had heard plenty through the walls of his parents' bedchamber.

He mustered a smile for little Sasha. "Would you like to visit Dusty later today?"

Her face lit up.

"If your mother agrees, maybe I can take you on a little ride."

Charlotte played along. "Isn't that nice of Mr. Reed?"

Mr. Reed. Despite their conversation last night, the formality remained. He should be pleased. That's what he'd wanted. But somehow it didn't sit right. Part of him wanted to be more than Mr. Reed.

Yet that's all he could ever be. He'd best remember it. A good woman didn't need a man like him. Sooner or later his past would catch up to him. He'd almost told her too much last night. Best he break free while he could.

He pushed away his plate and rose. "Got to be going."

"So soon?" A flicker of alarm crossed her face.

"The law doesn't wait."

Neither did Wyatt Reed. After grabbing his hat from the

hook by the door, he walked out of Charlotte Miller's house. If all went as planned, he'd be a free man by sunset.

Wyatt's departure put a lump in Charlotte's throat. The moment she asked for anything, he bolted. Just like last night. Tender one moment and then distant the next. She'd almost spilled her heart to him, and he would have crushed it the way he did every request that didn't benefit him. But that didn't explain why he wouldn't find Jakob. It made such perfect sense, but he'd looked like a cornered hare when she suggested it.

She soothed Sasha, who'd burst into tears at his sudden departure. Only the promise of a horseback ride could calm her. Charlotte hoped Wyatt would keep his word, or she'd have one disappointed little girl tonight.

If she still had Sasha at the end of the day.

Though Wyatt said he wouldn't oppose Evans Grove, he wouldn't go so far as to say the children were safe. No, he seemed to expect the judge could send the orphans to Greenville. That could include Sasha. If the judge ruled that the Orphan Salvation Society's agreement with Greenville excluded any placements in Evans Grove, then all the children would have to go.

She had to do something. Sasha, Liam and the rest of the children must stay. She paced the room, tidying up after breakfast, but kept her mind devoted to the problem. A solution for the whole mess came to mind, but it would take Rebecca's assistance. And that of Mason and Mr. Brooks.

Trembling, she put on Sasha's socks and shoes.

"We need to visit Miss Sterling. Won't that be nice? You can show her Katya's new dress." Charlotte felt for the orphan society agent, who was caught between her employer's rules and her desire to keep the children in Evans Grove.

Charlotte didn't allow Sasha to dawdle. If the judge had

arrived last night, then he'd open court this morning, perhaps as early as eight o'clock. Wyatt's hasty departure led her to believe he expected an early hearing.

They arrived at the schoolhouse, where Miss Sterling and Heidi were staying, while the dew still glistened on the grass.

She rapped lightly on the door. Hearing no answer, she cracked it open and called for Rebecca. "It's Charlotte Miller, uh, Reed." She would have to get used to her new name.

"Come in," rang out Rebecca's bell-like voice. "Is Sasha with you?"

Charlotte's stomach lurched. Today was the day that she was supposed to have given Sasha to Rebecca.

"Mama? Hurt."

Charlotte looked down at her daughter and saw she was squeezing the little girl's hand so tightly that Sasha's fingertips had turned red. She loosened her grip, but she had no intention of losing either her daughter or her husband. If she could get Rebecca Sterling to agree to her plan, neither one would leave Evans Grove.

"I have an idea," she said breathlessly as she stepped into the hot schoolhouse.

Rebecca sat in Holly's chair, combing Heidi's hair. The poor girl ducked her head away from Charlotte, self-conscious about the scars on her face. Sasha pulled free from Charlotte's hold and showed Heidi her doll's new dress. Bless little children. They didn't see disfigurement, only playmates.

"An idea about what?" Rebecca asked with a weak smile. The upcoming hearing must be wearing on her, too.

Charlotte glanced around the otherwise empty room. "Is there somewhere we can speak in private?"

Rebecca led her to the vestibule, where the students left their boots and coats in foul weather. Heidi and Sasha were far enough away that they wouldn't hear if she and Rebecca spoke softly.

Charlotte broached her worries first. "Mr. Brooks seems confident that Evans Grove will be able to keep the children. Has he told you exactly why? Is it something in the agreement?"

Rebecca nodded. "The agreement with Greenville doesn't name the prior stops. It only states that any available children may be selected. He believes that since the agreement doesn't say exactly which cities were going to hold distributions, the addition of Evans Grove isn't a breach of contract."

Charlotte breathed out a sigh of relief. "Then we have nothing to worry about."

"I wish I had your confidence." Rebecca worried her lip.

Perhaps Charlotte could ease her mind on that. "I think Wyatt is wavering."

Rebecca gasped, and a hand fluttered to her throat. "Then he won't press Greenville's position to the judge?"

"That's what he told me. But he also said that Greenville might challenge his position."

"Then nothing has changed."

"Yes, it has." Charlotte's idea took hold. It was the perfect solution. "We don't have to give up. Does the agreement say anything about who can take in the children?"

Rebecca's brow creased. "That decision is made by the selection committee."

"Which is made up of community members, correct?"

Rebecca nodded hesitantly. "I don't understand what you're trying to say."

"If the worst happens, and the judge rules against us, what's to stop those of us who took in the children from going to Greenville and applying again?"

"Yes, I suppose you could, but the committee might prefer Greenville citizens."

"Not if half the committee is made up of those who favor our position."

Rebecca frowned. "How do you propose to accomplish that?"

"How big does a committee have to be?"

"Three to five, usually, though some have larger committees."

"Suppose it's just three people. The Prairie Trust Bank of Nebraska has an office in Greenville, too. That means Mr. Brooks could be on that committee. Since Greenville is in the county, it falls under Sheriff Wright's jurisdiction."

Rebecca's brow furrowed. "It does? But isn't Greenville larger than Evans Grove?"

"Evans Grove is centrally located between Greenville and Newfield. The sheriff's office has always been here, I suppose to make it easier for the sheriff to get around the county. So that means Mason could be the second committee member. We might even be able to convince Wyatt to serve."

At that, Rebecca's eyebrows rose. "A tracker?"

It was a bit of a stretch. Committee members were supposed to be upstanding citizens of the community. Wyatt didn't quite fit into that category. She searched her brain for the rest of her argument. "You could urge them to apply for the committee. You could also tell everyone in Greenville what a fine job they did here. And then the children will have a say. When they see us, their parents, in Greenville, they'll insist on going home."

Rebecca smiled softly. "It's an interesting idea, and I hope you're right, but it would be better for everyone if it never comes to that." She sighed so wistfully as she looked at Heidi that Charlotte recalled the rest of her mission.

"Remember when you told me about Jakob?"

Rebecca brightened. "Have you heard news?"

"I haven't, but I got to thinking that finding him is something Wyatt could do. I asked him today at breakfast."

"He'll do it?" Rebecca's hope exploded into a smile.

Charlotte bit her lip. "For a fee. Would your agency pay him to find Jakob?"

Rebecca's doubt returned. "I can wire New York. It'll take time for a response. Do you think your husband would wait?"

Husband. So he was. The good along with the bad. If Charlotte convinced him to take this job, she'd keep Wyatt here a little longer, perhaps long enough to discover what was paining him so, maybe even change his heart toward God and family. That had seemed impossible yesterday, but Charlotte couldn't give up hope. Hadn't he reversed his position on the orphans?

"Leave that part to me. But if the Society won't agree to hire him, we need an alternative. I think Mayor Evans could be convinced." Her mind whirled with plans. She had to get this in place before the judge gave his ruling and Wyatt left. "Wyatt's headed for the town hall. I'll go talk to him. You can cable New York, but who will speak with the mayor?"

"I will," said Holly, who stood in the front doorway.

"But doesn't class start soon?"

"I can think of no better way to teach children about local government than to introduce them to the mayor and the judge." Holly grinned. "A little visual support at the hearing won't hurt our cause, either."

Charlotte's hope doubled. "It will work. It has to work."

No one was at the town hall. Wyatt frowned at the locked door. No notice. No explanation.

Where was the judge? He looked up and down the street. Business as usual. Wagons kicked up dust. Horses waited at hitching posts. Women strolled toward the butcher or the general store, basket in hand.

Seeing as he didn't know where to find Mayor Evans, Wyatt headed to the one man who would know what was going on—the sheriff.

Sheriff Mason Wright's office was only half a block away, but the mass of wagons, horses and commerce slowed Wyatt's progress. Most of the women and some of the men he passed stopped to offer congratulations. Wyatt nodded without replying. It kept conversations to a minimum.

By the time he reached Sheriff Wright's office, Wyatt had endured more claps on the back and tittering ladies than a man should have to face in a lifetime.

He bounded inside and found Mason sitting behind his desk with the feisty redheaded Liam at his side. The lad looked up when Wyatt entered, bristling with defiance. Wyatt had been just as cocky and sure of himself once, before life bit him in the backside.

"Reed." The sheriff nodded his acknowledgment of Wyatt before turning his attention back to the boy. "Best head on up to school now. Wouldn't want to be late on your first day as the sheriff's son." The man shot an equally defiant glance Wyatt's way.

"And after the judge says so, I'll be Interim Assistant Junior Sheriff Liam *Wright*," the boy pointed out.

So Charlotte was right. The sheriff and his new bride were also planning to adopt an orphan today.

The sheriff grinned and tousled the boy's hair before sending him off. Liam gave Wyatt another scowl before heading out the door.

With both the sheriff and his new bride sitting on the selection committee, no wonder the town refused to hand over the unclaimed orphans. No doubt the boy knew Wyatt had opposed their staying in Evans Grove. Wright certainly did.

Still, Wyatt ached for the kind of relationship the sheriff

had with his new son. In those two minutes of interaction, the bond was evident.

Sheriff Wright settled back in his chair. "What brings you here so early?"

Wyatt took off his hat. "I was just down to the town hall and noticed it's locked up tight."

The sheriff nodded. "Judge Broadside was delayed in Newfield."

Wyatt battled impatience. "Delayed?"

"That's right." Wright toyed with a bosun's whistle sitting on his desk.

Though Wyatt recognized the whistle from his time in Savannah during the war, he wouldn't expect to see one on the prairie. "Were you in the navy?"

Wright looked perplexed until Wyatt pointed to the whistle. "Naw, my uncle sailed." He tucked the whistle into his vest pocket.

They didn't have the war in common, then. Near as Wyatt could see, they shared nothing. Best get down to business. "Do you know when the judge'll get here?"

Wright shook his head. "No telling. He's usually delayed a bit. Sometimes as much as a month."

"A month? I can't wait a month."

"You could always go back to Greenville."

Wyatt gritted his teeth and leaned both hands on the man's desktop. He could tell the sheriff that he'd changed his stance, but the man had threatened him the last time they talked. "It would be better to finish this business sooner rather than later."

"That's your opinion." Sheriff Wright leaned back in his chair and braced his hands behind his head as if he hadn't a care in the world. "I hear you've been busy."

Wyatt stared. Wright knew he'd been asking questions?

"Concerned about Baxter?" the sheriff asked, leaning

forward to prop his elbows on the desk. "I would be, if I were you."

Wyatt sucked in his breath. "What do you know?"

"That you're new to the area. That Baxter's got his fingers pulling more than a few politicians' strings."

"Are you saying he's a crook?"

The sheriff's easy grin vanished. "I can't find anything on the man, and that's what worries me. He has no history, no family, no past. A bit like you."

Wyatt clenched his teeth. "I'm not from these parts."

"Maybe Baxter isn't, either."

"It would explain his lack of history."

Wright's blue eyes pierced through him. "You don't trust him, either."

Wyatt hated that the man assumed he knew Wyatt's mind, especially since he was right. "I can't put a finger on it. It's more a gut feeling."

The sheriff nodded. "What have you found out so far?"

Wyatt had pegged the sheriff as a square shooter from the start. He also preferred to work with law enforcement, not against them. The deputy sheriff in Greenville was a fool, more interested in his wages than dealing with crime. Wright, however, was clearly cut from a different cloth.

"Not much more than you." He eased into the chair across the desk from Wright. "That rancher a few miles north of town, Hayes, doesn't trust him. That much is clear, but he wouldn't say why. I'm guessing that's because he thinks I'm the enemy."

"Are you?"

Wyatt could appreciate the man's directness. "I plan to tell the judge the children should stay in Evans Grove."

If Wright was surprised, he didn't show it. "Fair enough. I'll pay Colton Hayes a visit. Anything else?"

Wyatt paused, considering whether to say anything about

the boy at Star Plains farm. That had been nothing more than a feeling, too. No evidence. Nothing to suggest it wasn't just an ornery man working his kid seven days a week.

"Nothing solid." He looked the sheriff in the eye. "I don't have your clout around here."

Wright's eyebrows rose. "The badge can slow a man down, too." He leaned forward, earnest. "I can only investigate crimes. You can look into matters that I can't touch, and get into places I can't. If we work as a team, we just might be able to find out what's really going on."

Wyatt knew the sheriff had a point, but he wasn't sure he wanted to get that involved. "Maybe the judge will rule in Evans Grove's favor."

"Do you want to take a chance that your Sasha ends up in Baxter's hands?"

Wyatt gagged on the thought. "No, but if this man's as crooked as I think, he'll get real nervous once I'm onto him."

"You saying what I think you're saying?"

Wyatt nodded. "I wouldn't put anything past the man. Even murder."

"That's a mighty bold accusation."

"A cornered man either fights or gives up. Baxter cares too much about his reputation to give up. Anyone going up against him needs the law on his side in case it comes to a fight." Or gunfire.

The sheriff rubbed his jaw. His gaze drifted down to Wyatt's hip, where the buckskin coat covered his holster. He must know Wyatt carried a gun. No tracker went without one.

"I wouldn't want anyone shot unlawfully," the sheriff drawled, "but self-defense is another matter."

"I hate killing. Did too much of it in the war."

"War takes the fight out of most men." Wright tapped his

fingertips on the desktop. "I've seen 'em come back shaken, but I've also seen 'em come back angry. Which one are you?"

Wyatt steeled his jaw. "Neither." He had no intention of explaining the nightmares. "I just want justice."

"We agree on that." The sheriff's gaze narrowed as he assessed him. "Well, then, I think I can help you. It just so happens I could use a deputy."

"It sounds to me like you have one in your boy."

The sheriff chuckled. "I need one who knows his way around a gun. Bucky Wyler would step in when needed, but with his wife expecting, she's not keen on him getting in the path of any bullets."

Wyatt could hardly believe what he was hearing. Was the sheriff offering him a job? "I don't have that problem."

"Charlotte wouldn't mind? You do have a young daughter to consider."

Wyatt brushed off the sheriff's concerns. He didn't intend to pass this by her or anyone. Wyatt Reed made his own decisions, and the best thing he could do for Charlotte was to ensure she kept Sasha. That meant taking down Baxter, and the badge just might give him the authority to do it.

"I don't see why she would." After all, she only wanted him around long enough to adopt Sasha.

A smile teased the corners of Sheriff Wright's mouth. "Maybe you'd better ask."

Ask? Wyatt didn't ask a woman what he could and couldn't do. Still, he could tell Wright expected him to get her approval.

"She's not a fearful young bride," he argued, hoping that was true. "Besides, she wants me to find a way to keep the orphans in Evans Grove. This will do just that."

"Then it's settled." Sheriff Wright rose and extended his hand. "Welcome to the job, Deputy Reed."

Wyatt shook his hand. "Thank you, Sheriff."

"Best be calling me Mason," he said as he pulled a tin star from his desk.

Wyatt took the symbol of his new position and ran a thumb over the engraved word that made him a deputy of the law. "Call me Wyatt, then, but if it's the same to you, I'm going to keep this badge under wraps for now. At least until we get the truth on Felix Baxter."

Mason nodded. "Makes sense to me, but keep it handy."

Wyatt pinned the badge to the inside of his coat. He was now a lawman. It felt good. Real good. For the first time in years he was doing something that helped people. This was his chance to erase the sins of the past.

He wouldn't tell Charlotte just yet. She'd only worry and try to talk him out of it, the way Bucky Wyler's wife had. He wasn't about to blow this chance for redemption.

Chapter Fourteen

All of Charlotte's worry had been for nothing. Judge Broadside was delayed indefinitely. So, too, was Wyatt. She'd expected him to return to the house once he learned the judge wasn't arriving that day, but hour after hour passed with no word.

What could he be doing? No doubt he rode off on his horse, like yesterday. No explanation. Not even the courtesy to tell her he'd be gone. Moreover, he'd promised to give Sasha a horseback ride, which the little girl did not forget. She fussed and whined, unhappy with everything Charlotte attempted to do with her. Even Katya went flying across the room during a tantrum.

Charlotte's head pounded. Her nerves frayed. How on earth had Rebecca managed eight children in the schoolhouse when the orphans first arrived in town? Charlotte could barely endure one ill-tempered child.

She tried to work on Holly's dress, but every time she approached her sewing machine, Sasha clung to her and cried that she wanted to play.

By the time Wyatt returned, she'd lost the last shreds of patience.

"Sit," she commanded Sasha as Wyatt opened the door.

His eyebrows rose. "That's a fine welcome home."

Home. His use of the word would have pleased her if she hadn't been so overwrought. "I was speaking to Sasha. Though I might ask where you spent the day, considering the judge never came to town."

"Papa! Papa!" Sasha's shrieks of joy gave him the chance to avoid answering.

Wyatt scooped up the little girl and whirled her around until she laughed and giggled.

Frustrated and exhausted, Charlotte sank into a chair. "You promised her a horseback ride."

"So I did." Wyatt cradled the little girl so easily in his arms. "Do you want to meet Dusty, my horse?"

"Hor-see," Sasha squealed, the tantrums and whining completely gone.

Charlotte resented that she'd had to struggle all day while Wyatt got to enjoy the perfect little girl. No doubt he thought caring for Sasha was easy. He didn't teach her proper behavior. He didn't wash her and feed her and clothe her. He didn't have to scold her when she misbehaved.

Her irritation grew as she followed them outside. As promised, his horse awaited. The chestnut gelding munched her overgrown flowerbed. At Wyatt's approach, the horse lifted its head and snarled out a whinny.

Charlotte drew in her breath. The horse was huge, nearly as big as Charles's team. She would never consider putting such a little girl on one of Charles's horses, yet Wyatt intended to carry her on top of that enormous animal. Her head spun just thinking about the distance to the ground. Adults broke necks falling off horses. What would happen to a four-year-old?

"Are you sure?" she choked out.

Wyatt must not have heard her. He held Sasha near Dusty's head, and she reached out to pet the animal.

"Horsee," she squealed.

Dusty nipped at the air, away from Sasha but still too close for Charlotte's liking.

"I don't think this is a good idea."

"Now don't go getting yourself out of sorts." Wyatt placed Sasha on the saddle. "I've got a good hold of her, and we're only going a few steps."

Sasha's eyes were round as teacup saucers as she grabbed on to the pommel. "Horsee." She banged her shoes against the horse's flanks.

"Don't do that, Sasha!" Charlotte cried.

"Just a few steps, nice and easy," Wyatt said, one hand on the bridle and the other holding Sasha by the back of her dress.

Without a verbal command from Wyatt, the horse began to walk. Sasha swayed, and Charlotte hugged her arms, terrified. She wanted to beg Wyatt to stop, but he had hold of Sasha, didn't he?

Then Sasha squealed, the horse's ears pricked, and he shot out of Wyatt's grasp.

"Dusty!" Wyatt clucked his tongue.

Why was he encouraging the horse to run? Charlotte screamed as Sasha slid sideways. Not her daughter! Not her only child. Sasha was all she had left.

She raced toward them. "Stop, stop!"

In those moments, she relived the frightful moment in her past when she fell in the barn. Her foot slipped. Her hand grazed the ladder. The barn floor came closer and closer until…

All went black.

She dropped to her knees.

"Charlotte? Charlotte." The voice called her out of the darkness. "It's all right. Everything is all right."

Only she wasn't a child, and her father wasn't calling to

her. Wyatt was. A strong arm held her close. She caught the scent of him, the scent of the outdoors, rich with wood smoke and prairie grass.

"Mama?" A little hand pressed against her cheek. "No cry."

Charlotte hadn't even realized the tears had fallen, but she'd never heard such a wonderful sound before.

"Oh, Sasha." She pulled her daughter close, reveling in the squirming bundle of energy. "You scared me."

Wyatt brushed the hair from her forehead. "I had hold of her the whole time."

Still, Charlotte couldn't stop trembling.

"I'm sorry," he said, his eyes softened to mist. "I didn't realize it would upset you."

Charlotte struggled to find her voice. "Your horse. He took off, and you urged him to go faster."

"Faster? I did no such thing." He looked so puzzled that he must be speaking the truth.

"But you clucked your tongue."

"Oh. That." He cupped her jaw in his worn, yet comforting hand. "I taught Dusty to stop on that signal."

"But usually…" Charlotte felt a little foolish.

He brushed his thumb against her cheek, sending an entirely different sort of trembling through her limbs. "It's my fault. I should have realized you didn't know. Forgive me?" His eyes had darkened, but not like an approaching storm. No, they took her in, like a snug night before the fire.

Charlotte drew a ragged breath. They were on the step of her porch, in full public view. And Sasha was sitting beside them while Dusty leveled her garden. But that look promised a future, the kind of future she desperately wanted, the kind that promised he'd stay.

"Forgiven." She sank deeper into his arms. How warm

and welcoming. How perfect. How… What just poked into her ribs?

She looked down to see a tin star—a lawman's badge—attached to the inside of his buckskin coat. Too late, he pulled his coat shut. She'd seen it. But trackers didn't wear badges, did they?

"Who are you?" she breathed.

What had happened? That morning Wyatt had been determined to complete his part of the bargain before nightfall. He'd gone so far as to pack his saddlebags. But then the sheriff offered him a job, Sasha ran to him as her papa and Charlotte sank into his arms. By the end of the afternoon, he'd fallen into the domestic life he'd craved for years.

"Sheriff Wright offered me the deputy position."

Charlotte's hazel eyes widened. "And you took it?" She said it with such wonder that his heart did a double take.

"For now." He couldn't tell her what he was investigating. If his gut instinct was right, Baxter moved in rough circles, the kind filled with men who wouldn't hesitate to threaten a woman or child.

"Oh." Her disappointment hit him hard. She looked down at her hands, which plucked at her skirt nervously. "It's just temporary?"

He couldn't lead her to believe otherwise. Once the past caught up to him, once the nightmares worsened, he'd have to go.

"It is."

Her shoulders squared as she accepted his decision. Disappointment gnawed at the pit of his stomach, but he had no choice. No one could know the truth, or Charlotte and Sasha would be in danger.

She started to rise, but he caught her arm to keep her on the stoop beside him. "Please don't tell anyone. It's important so…" He paused trying to figure out how to say it without giving away his mission. "Kids could be affected if we don't keep this secret."

Her eyes widened in alarm, and for a moment he feared she'd ask too many questions.

Instead, she placed her hand over his. "I promise."

Relief flooded through him. "Thank you."

Her eyes dropped. Before they did, he realized she hoped for something more, but he couldn't give it to her. He couldn't promise her a future together. Her delicate hands knotted in her lap, knuckles white.

"I understand," she whispered.

Then Sasha offered her a beetle. Charlotte calmly suggested they let the beetle go home to his family. The frazzled, frantic woman had disappeared. Calm, gentle Charlotte returned. Such a woman deserved a child. He wouldn't let her down.

"I'll stay no matter how long the judge takes," he promised. "Even if we have to wait for him to come back a second time."

Her head bobbed very slightly before she turned to the little girl. "Come inside, Sasha. We need to make supper."

She withdrew from his side, and her absence tore a bigger hole out of him than any cannonball could.

Days, then a week and more passed without news of the judge's arrival. Charlotte hoped she and Wyatt would grow closer during that time, but he withdrew even more than before he'd hired on as deputy sheriff. He did get a good price for Charles's team of horses and wagon, but he didn't even smile when he handed her the money.

She'd offered it back to him. "It's yours now, too."

He'd shaken his head. "Keep it."

The wall still stood between them. He would not share,

would not commit, would not become a real husband. He rose at dawn, downed breakfast before Sasha was completely awake, and didn't return until nightfall. After supper, he retired to the loft.

Just like Charles had.

With a sinking feeling, Charlotte realized she'd committed herself to exactly the same kind of marriage. The only difference was the spark between them. Surely he noticed, for she'd felt him tremble when he held her that day on the porch step, but as quickly as a connection formed, he severed it.

Her hope that he'd stay after the adoption dwindled and died. To compensate, she did what she'd always done—kept busy. It helped pass the time.

Charlotte hated waiting, but it seemed that was all women could do. Rebecca waited for permission from Mr. Armstrong to hire Wyatt to find Jakob. Pauline waited for the rebuilding projects to be completed so Mr. Brooks would return to his bank. Holly joined Charlotte waiting for the judge and the chance to permanently claim their children.

Each day Charlotte asked Rebecca if she'd gotten word. Each day she shook her head.

"Mr. Armstrong's not in the office. I fear he took his family on holiday."

Judging by Rebecca's resignation, she held out little hope for a positive reply. What could one lost boy mean to a man of industry? To Armstrong, the trouble that had befallen this group of orphans must seem insignificant compared to decisions that affected scores of workers in his factories and children in his orphanage.

Rebecca's shoulders sagged. The seemingly endless obstacles must be taking their toll.

Charlotte wanted to reassure her, but Mayor Evans hadn't given her better news. Sure, Pauline had been supportive when Charlotte outlined her request to pay Wyatt to find Jakob, but she couldn't promise any funds.

"We're using every cent of the bank loan to rebuild the town. Even though having the orphans help on the chore teams has saved on the cost of labor, the materials are so expensive that we haven't anything to spare. I will ask Mr. Brooks, however, when he returns." She said the last with obvious irritation. "That man is testing my patience. First, he insists on approving every expenditure, then he disappears with no reason just when I need that approval."

Charlotte could sympathize. Wyatt was acting exactly the same way. If she didn't know better, she'd think the two of them were sneaking off together.

To occupy her hands while waiting, Charlotte worked on the dress for Holly. If her friend would let her take measurements, it would have been done days ago, but Holly always had an excuse for not coming by the house.

Charlotte supposed her friend was too busy, so she tracked her down after school let out on Thursday. Once the children finished pouring out of the schoolhouse, Charlotte entered to find Heidi and Rebecca with Holly.

Rebecca averted her gaze, while Holly greeted her a little too cheerfully. "Charlotte. What brings you here?"

Something had happened.

Charlotte let Sasha join Heidi at the back of the room. "I came to get measurements." She held up the dressmaker's tape. "You've been too busy to stop by my house, so I thought I'd come to you."

"That can wait." Holly stacked each primer in perfect alignment.

Rebecca still hadn't looked at Charlotte.

"Did I interrupt something?" Charlotte tentatively asked.

Holly mustered a tense smile. "No, no. We were just discussing tomorrow's proceedings."

Charlotte's stomach clenched. "The judge arrived?"

"Probably," Holly stated. "He was due to arrive on the midday train."

Rebecca finally looked up, and no one could mistake her distress. "He will hold court in the morning."

Tomorrow? After all the waiting, it suddenly seemed too soon. "But…" She let her voice trail off. With Heidi near, she couldn't bring up the fact that no one had heard a word about Jakob. Nor dare she mention that Heidi hadn't been placed. No wonder Rebecca was worried. Even if Evans Grove won the right to keep the placed children, Heidi would probably have to go on to Greenville. Charlotte sank onto one of the low chairs and leaned onto the desk. The black ironwork creaked under the unfamiliar weight.

Tomorrow they would know if the other children could stay. If so, she and Wyatt would adopt Sasha, and then Wyatt would leave. Hope battled dread. Even if she kept her daughter, she'd lose her husband.

"I'd hoped by now we could at least have a reunion." Rebecca glanced toward Heidi, her meaning unmistakable.

Jakob.

"No word?" Charlotte asked.

Rebecca shook her head.

"Did you hear from your office yet?"

Rebecca's shoulders slumped. "Mr. Armstrong refused."

"We can't give up." Holly, who'd once hung back in public, now glowed with purpose and determination. "We'll find a way to reunite the siblings. And tomorrow," she said, looking at Rebecca and then Charlotte, "we stand our ground. We will state our case and make the judge understand that the best interests of all the children have to come before any document."

Rebecca looked skeptical. "Will he listen?"

Charlotte caught Holly's optimism. "We'll make sure he does."

"Above all, we'll put it in God's hands," Holly added.

Rebecca grasped on to that slender thread. "We can use all the help we can get."

"Don't worry," Holly said, her confidence unshakable. "Everything works out for good for those who love the Lord."

"I hope so." Rebecca glanced at Heidi, who was admiring Sasha's new doll. "For the children's sake."

Chapter Fifteen

Court was packed the following morning as Charlotte made her way to one of the scattered empty seats in the town hall meeting room. She'd wanted to leave Sasha with the Gavins, but the entire town had turned out for the hearing.

To her left sat the Regans. They nodded at her with the sympathy borne of shared hope and fear. Their Lina sat between them, and Mrs. Regan clutched her new daughter's hand fearfully.

Wyatt should have sat to Charlotte's right, but as plaintiff, he took one of the reserved chairs at the front. Instead, Mrs. Gavin nestled beside her.

The woman leaned close to whisper in a voice loud enough for all to hear, "I hope you've straightened out that husband of yours."

Charlotte's cheeks flamed when she saw Wyatt stiffen ever so slightly. She wanted to blurt out that he'd changed his mind, but that news belonged to Wyatt. Her heart swelled with anticipation.

"All rise." Sheriff Wright acted as bailiff.

Everyone shuffled to their feet as Judge Nelson Broadside entered the room. Gray-haired with bushy, white eyebrows, the man cut an impressive figure as he gazed out at the assembly. Only the twinkling blue eyes betrayed that he was a kindly man.

After he settled behind the table at the front of the room, everyone returned to their seats.

Mason directed the order of business. "First up is the claim by Greenville for the orphans."

Considering the short introduction and the way Judge Broadside nodded, Mason must have briefed the judge on the subject last night.

The judge looked from one side of the room to the other. "If there is no objection, an informal hearing should settle the matter. Will the two parties involved come forward?"

Mayor Evans, along with Mr. Brooks and Wyatt, took their places in the front of the room. No one from Greenville joined Wyatt, nor did Charlotte see a strange face in the crowd. That must mean Greenville hadn't sent anyone else to contest the placements in Evans Grove in person. Hope soared.

First Mayor Evans explained the town's case, outlining in detail each step they'd taken to get approval and follow the Orphan Salvation Society rules.

"As you can see, your honor," she wrapped up, "with all but one of the children placed in good homes, there is no need to break up families in order to place these children in jeopardy again. The stated purpose of the Orphan Salvation Society is to find good homes for the orphans. Miss Sterling can testify to that."

With a clear, resolute voice, Rebecca affirmed Pauline's testimony.

"Moreover," Pauline continued, "Mr. Brooks has examined in detail the agreement between the Orphan Salvation Society and Greenville and can find no promise that any children would be available to them by the time the train reached their town."

"Do you have the paperwork?" Judge Broadside asked Mr. Brooks.

The banker handed over a sheaf of papers.

The judge frowned as he read through them. Then he turned to Wyatt. "Mr. Reed, I understand you represent the interests of Greenville?"

"I did, your honor."

Did. The crowd didn't catch the little three-letter word, but it shot so much pride and joy through Charlotte that she longed to applaud.

The judge didn't miss the change in verb tense. "Do you no longer represent the town, Mr. Reed? Should I be speaking to someone else?"

"No, your honor. I'm still Greenville's chosen representative. But after thinking on it and seeing how good the people are here, I agree with them. The children should stay."

Wild cheering erupted in the room, and no amount of banging of the gavel would quiet them. Finally, the judge shouted that since no one opposed the placements and the paperwork confirmed Mr. Brooks's assertion, he was dismissing the case and calling a recess.

Mrs. Gavin hugged Charlotte from one side, and Mrs. Regan wept on her shoulder on the other. Men clapped Wyatt on the back, and Charlotte saw the sheriff shake Wyatt's hand. Not only had Wyatt backed the town, he'd gained their respect.

Charlotte burst with pride. The children could stay. Sasha was hers. Wyatt had stood by her and the town.

Then she saw Beatrice Ward weave through the crowd until she reached the judge. The din was too loud for Charlotte to hear what she said to him, but his response couldn't have pleased her, because Beatrice stormed out of the hall, fire in her eyes.

Charlotte didn't have time to think on it, though, because

Wyatt directed a rare smile her way. She picked up Sasha and pushed through the crowd until she reached his side.

"Thank you." She couldn't find words enough to tell him how she felt, so she settled for kissing him on the cheek.

His expression softened as he took their daughter into his arms.

"It's over," she gushed. "Praise God."

He shook his head. "Baxter could still appeal."

Charlotte recalled Beatrice's displeasure. "Could anyone else?"

"Anyone with cause."

"Do you mean…?" She clutched her daughter's arm. "We couldn't lose her, could we?"

"Not after the adoption."

At that instant Charlotte wished the judge hadn't taken a break. "How soon can we do it?"

"Mason said the judge will handle the adoptions this afternoon. Miss Sterling had the paperwork for both Sasha and Liam sent from New York. It shouldn't take long."

Her stomach unclenched. Beatrice couldn't do anything to stop them that quickly, could she?

Judge Broadside handled the adoption petitions quickly, and by the end of the day, Sasha and Liam had been officially adopted by their new parents.

While Holly and Charlotte exchanged hugs, Wyatt settled for shaking Mason's hand. Liam paraded around testing out his new name and title after Mason assured him he was still Interim Assistant Junior Sheriff. Sasha probably didn't understand what had happened, but she squealed with joy when Wyatt swung her around and gave her a big hug.

After Sasha joined her friends and the women bunched together to relive every moment of the proceedings, Wyatt stood outside the town hall marveling at the changes that had happened in a couple of weeks. He was now a married man, a father and a deputy sheriff. Two weeks ago, he wouldn't have thought any of it possible. The best he'd thought he could hope for was a fresh start in San Francisco.

Since the women showed no sign of wrapping up their conversation, Wyatt strolled down the street toward the hotel, where everything had first started. On that very street he'd heard Sasha crying. Little had he known that finding one lost girl would change his life.

He could see staying here. He could imagine raising a family. He sure wouldn't mind loving a woman like Charlotte. She was kind, sweet and so very beautiful, even when she pestered him about where he was going and when he'd be back. That had been an ongoing bone of contention between them because he couldn't tell her. But now that the children could stay in Evans Grove, the secrecy could end.

"Reed!"

The familiar male voice stopped Wyatt cold. He whirled around, hand instinctively reaching for his gun. "Baxter."

The man scampered down the steps of the hotel. He looked furious. "We need to talk. Now." He pointed in the direction of the creek, where the forge lay silent and the grain mill had yet to be completely repaired.

"We have nothing to discuss."

Baxter glared. "You're still in my employ." He headed toward the mill.

Wyatt considered walking away, but he had to end things with Baxter before he could get a clean start. He wasn't about to go in the mill, though. The battered building stood alongside the fast-flowing creek, its wheel turning nothing until the new gearing could be put in place.

"The building's not safe. We can talk down here." Wyatt loped past Baxter and headed for the creek.

Baxter scowled but followed, though he veered toward the back of the mill.

Not perfect, but better than inside. While Wyatt sauntered to Baxter's chosen meeting place, he tried to piece together what had brought the man to Evans Grove at this hour. Judging by the angle of the sun, the eastbound stage had just deposited Baxter at the hotel. If he'd been concerned about the outcome of the hearing, he should have arrived earlier. The fact he was standing here now meant someone in Evans Grove had wired him *after* the judge ruled against Greenville. Someone was keeping Baxter informed. Wyatt intended to find out who. This little chat promised to give him the answers he hadn't unearthed in ten days of investigation.

"I paid you good money," Baxter sputtered the moment they stepped behind the mill.

Wyatt pulled out his wallet. "You can have it back." He hated giving Baxter one cent of Charlotte's money, but once Mason paid him his wages as deputy, he'd pay her back.

"I don't want your money. I want your loyalty. You have a reputation for finishing the job. So what happened today?"

Wyatt didn't have to explain his actions to anyone. "The judge ruled against you."

"You were supposed to make sure he didn't. You were supposed to get those children to Greenville at once. Instead, it's been nothing but delay after delay. I even heard you got married."

Now, who had told him that? It had to be the same good citizen of Evans Grove that had relayed the outcome of this morning's hearing. Baxter had a contact, a spy, nestled deep in this town. Brooks? The man vanished regularly. He'd ride off one day and return the next. Wyatt had tracked him a couple times, but each time he'd headed toward Newfield, and Wyatt had figured the man was going to his bank to handle business. Besides, Brooks had supported the town's position and had been the one to suggest they could fight Greenville in court. No, definitely not Brooks. It had to be someone else, someone determined to send the orphans to Greenville—someone like Beatrice Ward. The thought that a woman could be involved in something so underhanded sickened him, but he'd seen it before. Women could go bad as easily as men, especially under duress. He wondered if Baxter had some leverage on the spinster.

"A widow," Baxter sneered. "One who took in an orphan. Your failure makes sense now. You're protecting her and the runt."

Wyatt fisted his hands. "Leave Charlotte and Sasha out of this."

"Hit home, did I?" Baxter stabbed his finger into Wyatt's chest. "Well, how do you suppose she's going to feel about her new husband when she learns the truth about you?"

Hot anger pounded in Wyatt's head, but he kept outwardly calm. Baxter knew nothing. "What truth?"

Baxter grinned. "Does Atlanta mean anything to you? Part of Sherman's forces, weren't you?"

How did Baxter find out? Wyatt hoped he'd gotten far enough west this time. Clearly he hadn't.

Baxter's sneer set Wyatt on edge. "I'm sure the little woman would love to hear about your exploits there."

How dare Baxter tell Charlotte about his past? Wyatt gripped his gun, feeling its smooth, cold handle against his palm. In one second, he could end it all. A single shot. Fury pulsed white-hot. To protect Charlotte, he would kill. He'd done that in the war. When his boyhood friend was shot in the back, he'd run after those yellow-bellied Rebels and shot every one he could. Then, during the march through Georgia, he'd polished off his revenge.

But that was war—and even then, the memory of what

he'd done sickened him. There'd be no excuse this time. If he killed Baxter, it would be murder. Wyatt took a deep breath and eased his finger off the trigger. "What do you want?"

Baxter's smug look almost made him replace that trigger finger. "Finish the job."

"It's too late. The judge has already made his ruling."

"A resourceful man like you can find a way, especially when there's so much at stake." Baxter drew a purse from his pocket and pulled out a handful of gold coins.

That was enough to take care of Charlotte and Sasha for years, but it was blood money. Wyatt would never betray Charlotte or Sasha or a single one of those children.

"Some of the children have been adopted. Pretty near all the rest are in homes. They're beyond your reach now."

"Nothing is beyond reach," Baxter snarled. "Find a way."

"I won't give up Sasha. She's legally mine."

"I don't want your toddler," Baxter spat. "I need the older ones."

The man's words chilled Wyatt. "Why just the older children?"

Baxter started as if he realized he'd just blundered. "The families in Greenville are mostly farmers. They want children who can help on the farm."

Baxter was lying. He couldn't hold Wyatt's gaze. His normally florid face flushed even darker. He swiped at his mouth repeatedly. Something else was afoot. Something evil. Baxter wasn't representing Greenville at all. Wyatt suspected Greenville's mayor was in Baxter's pocket. The deputy sheriff might be, too. That made this doubly dangerous.

Baxter jingled the gold, seeming to regain his confidence from the sound of the rattling metal. "Well? What will it be? Life as a rich man or getting run out of town?" His grin tempted and lured. "I'm sure the wife would like to live in luxury, and you could give your little girl everything her heart desires." He pocketed the bag. "Well, Reed, what's your answer?"

Chapter Sixteen

Charlotte should be happy. She had Sasha. She had a home. She had everything she'd thought she wanted, but when Wyatt walked away from her after the proceedings, she'd acknowledged to herself that she longed for more.

She wanted the family that they'd become in that moment when Wyatt stood up for Evans Grove. Sasha needed a father, and none could be better than Wyatt. The little girl sparkled whenever she was with him. He'd become her hero, and, if Charlotte was honest with herself, he'd become hers, too. Not only had he married her and helped her adopt Sasha like he'd promised, but he'd stood on the side of justice and supported Evans Grove's petition.

So many people congratulated her and remarked on what a fine man she'd married. Not Beatrice Ward, of course. Thankfully, the formidable spinster hadn't returned after storming out of the town hall at the end of the morning session.

"Congratulations, Charlotte and Holly." Mayor Pauline Evans embraced each of them warmly, almost chasing away Charlotte's blues.

Maybe all the acknowledgment would help Wyatt see how much he was wanted and needed here. He had looked pleased when man after man came forward to clap him on the back. But then, after adopting Sasha, he'd slipped away. The terms of their marriage agreement settled like lead in her stomach. Once they adopted Sasha, he was free to leave. He'd insisted upon it, and she'd agreed.

She closed her eyes against the storm of regret.

"I'm so happy for you both," Pauline continued. "We fought and won. All the children can stay."

"Except Heidi," Holly reminded her.

In all the excitement, Charlotte had forgotten about Heidi. Poor girl. That explained Rebecca's subdued reaction and her retreat from the afternoon session as soon as her part was over.

"Isn't there any way that Heidi can stay?" Charlotte asked.

Pauline blew out a sigh of frustration. "A family needs to step forward. I would consider it if Robert was still alive."

In the pause that followed, Charlotte felt the depth of the woman's loss. Pauline and Robert Evans had been close, still acting like newlyweds after years of marriage. Her heart must ache. Charlotte hurt at the thought of losing Wyatt, and she barely knew him.

But Pauline was strong. With determination, she snapped out of her sorrow and back to business. "Speaking of men, have either of you seen Mr. Brooks?"

Charlotte searched her memory. "I saw him with you this morning, but I don't remember seeing him this afternoon."

Holly agreed. "When did you last see him?"

"Curtis joined me for lunch but then said he had to send a wire and never returned."

Holly nudged Charlotte. Pauline had used Mr. Brooks's Christian name.

"I'm sure something came up with the bank," Holly said.

Pauline frowned. "At the end of the day? What could be so important that it needs to be taken care of at once? Why, that man buzzes around like a housefly. I just wonder what he's got himself into now."

Holly and Charlotte had to chuckle. Pauline complained that Mr. Brooks nitpicked her every move, when everyone could see that he wanted to win her favor. Pauline was the one who wouldn't budge an inch.

"Maybe he went to check the post with Rebecca," Holly suggested.

Since the mail was distributed at the telegraph office, there was a chance Mr. Brooks would still be there.

"The post. That's what I forgot to do," Pauline said a little too brightly. "I should check for mail before they close down for the day. I'll see you both later. Congratulations again."

The mayor bustled off, leaving Charlotte alone with Holly and the worry that Wyatt was preparing to leave. He'd headed toward the livery. He must figure his job was done, so he'd saddle up Dusty and go back to Greenville. Would he really leave without saying goodbye?

Her chest constricted so she could hardly draw a breath. His name floated on her lips, but even if she didn't have Sasha to watch, she hadn't the strength to chase after him.

Holly squeezed her arm. "What's wrong? You look pale."

"It's nothing."

"It's most certainly something. What happened?"

Charlotte hesitated. She hated to reveal anything personal. It's what had kept her silent all those years of marriage to Charles, but look what that had brought her. The town adored Charles and believed their marriage perfect. She'd lived a lie. Never again. She needed to talk to someone. If she couldn't confide in her dearest friend, who could she tell?

She took a deep breath. "Wyatt's not going to stay. He, that is, *we*—" This was difficult to say. "We agreed to stay together only as long as it took to adopt Sasha."

To her surprise, Holly didn't seem shocked. "Does he know you love him?"

"Love him?" Charlotte pulled out her handkerchief and wiped away a tear. "Do I?"

"It's obvious to everyone," Holly said. "You look at him the way I used to look at Mason, like you're afraid to let him know how much you care about him."

Charlotte bowed her head. "It's true."

"But you have to tell him how you feel. Trust me on this. It's frightening and risky, but there's no other way."

"Just like that?" She fussed with her skirts and checked on Sasha, who was playing with Lynette and the other children.

"Just like that. For too long Mason and I made the mistake of not saying how we felt toward each other."

"It's not the same." Charlotte shook her head. "Everyone could see you and Mason were meant for each other. I knew that in time he'd see it, too."

"So will Wyatt."

"I'm not so sure." Charlotte bit her quivering lip. "He's been so set on leaving, and once Wyatt sets his mind on something, he won't change course."

"He changed his mind about the orphans," Holly pointed out.

"That's different. He loves children." She lowered her gaze. "But me? No."

"What a fool notion. I don't believe it for a minute. I've seen the way he watches you when you're not looking."

Charlotte's cheeks heated. "You must be mistaken."

"That's what I said when people told me Mason looked at me that way, but they were right."

Charlotte held her breath. Did she dare to believe that Wyatt felt something for her? "But..." She choked on the reality of the bargain she'd made with him. "He made me agree to let him go once Sasha was adopted." She shook her head. "He hasn't said he changed his mind."

"Maybe he hasn't said he wants to stay, but he does. I saw that from the start. If I hadn't, I would never have agreed to witness your marriage. Just tell him how you feel and hand the rest over to the Almighty."

Holly made it sound simple, but Charlotte knew from experience that whenever she pushed, Wyatt retreated. "But what if Wyatt doesn't feel the same way? What if he leaves?"

Holly smiled knowingly. "What if he doesn't?"

"Well?" Baxter glared at Wyatt. "What's your decision?"

Wyatt knew better than to answer from this secluded spot behind the mill. Though Baxter didn't strike Wyatt as the type to do his own dirty work, he did have a temper, and Wyatt doubted he'd respond politely to someone telling him no.

"I'm thinking it through." Wyatt ambled toward the front of the mill.

"Where are you going? We're not done yet."

But, as Wyatt anticipated, Baxter followed. Wyatt continued walking until he stepped onto Liberty Street in full view of the sheriff's office. People still clustered outside town hall. Charlotte stood there, as pretty as a summer rose. Sasha played with a couple of girls her age. His chest swelled. They were his family. His responsibility.

"You walk away, and I take my business elsewhere," Baxter threatened as he trotted along on Wyatt's heels.

"Fine by me." Years of duress had taught Wyatt to keep his voice low and calm when threatened. It generally rattled the other person into thinking he was holding something back. He usually wasn't, but this time he wanted out of this job, plain and simple. Everything about it was wrong. "I'm done with this job."

"No, you're not. I'm not letting you out of it. We made an agreement, shook hands on it. I expect you to make good on your word, or—"

Before Baxter could add to his threats, Wyatt spun to face him, spread his feet, and exposed his pistol.

Baxter flinched when he saw Wyatt close his hand on the weapon. "No need to get riled. I'm just asking you to enforce the agreement Greenville made with that orphan society. It'll be to your advantage."

"Not mine." Wyatt hated the man's wheedling. "Take your business elsewhere. I don't want it."

Baxter feigned shock. "I'll triple the rate."

The man definitely had something suspicious going on, something that Wyatt was going to discover if it took the rest of his life. He itched to reveal his deputy sheriff badge, but that would only send Baxter running.

He set his jaw. "I won't do it at any rate."

Baxter's face darkened. "Then you'll pay the price. No one takes a job from me and doesn't finish." He glanced down the street to where Charlotte stood. "Don't get too comfortable here. So many tragedies have happened in this town. Funny how they tend to come in bunches."

"That had better not be a threat."

"Just an observation." Baxter glanced back at the mill. "You never know what will happen."

For a second, Wyatt wondered if Baxter had something to do with the dam break, but that was nonsense. It'd washed out in a storm. Besides, Baxter had nothing to gain from it. Or did he? The man operated a supply store. The town needed supplies to rebuild. He'd have to ask Brooks if the town was buying from Baxter.

"I'm not changing my mind," Wyatt said.

The weasel's black eyes glittered like the gold in his bag. "If you do see reason, I'll be eating dinner at the hotel before heading back to Greenville." He made a show of looking at his gold pocket watch, engraved with the swirling letters *F. B.* "That gives you two hours to come to your senses."

"My senses are just fine." At that moment, they screamed *danger.*

"Are they?" Baxter paused before leaving. "If they are, then I'll see you later."

Baxter's smugness unsettled Wyatt as he watched the man return to the hotel. Baxter didn't make idle threats. He intended harm if Wyatt didn't do as instructed. And he wouldn't—couldn't—do what Baxter wanted. But that meant that he'd made a powerful enemy, who wouldn't hesitate to lash out. Wyatt had no choice. His presence here endangered Charlotte and Sasha.

For their sakes, he had to leave.

Charlotte stayed at the town hall until only she and Holly remained. Sasha, minus her playmates, whined and tugged at Charlotte's skirt, but she couldn't face an empty house. If she returned to find Wyatt's saddlebags gone, she'd know he left.

"I need to fix supper," Holly finally said. "Will you be all right?"

Charlotte nodded. She couldn't put it off much longer. "I'll walk with you to your house."

Holly raised an eyebrow. "It's out of your way."

How could she explain the terror building inside her? If Wyatt was gone, she didn't know how she'd carry on.

Her friend seemed to understand. "Better to find out sooner than later."

Charlotte supposed she was right, but she dreaded learning the truth. She had made the bargain. Now she must accept the consequences.

"Come along, Sasha."

But before she got ten steps, Rebecca hurried toward them

waving a piece of paper. From the look on her face, something horrible had happened.

Holly retraced her steps and met Rebecca at the same time Charlotte did.

"What's wrong?" the two women said simultaneously.

"I-i-it's Heidi." Rebecca's pretty face crumpled, and the tears flowed.

Charlotte located her handkerchief while Holly comforted the younger woman. "It's all right. Tell us what happened."

Rebecca dabbed at her eyes with Charlotte's handkerchief and then handed the paper to Holly. "Read for yourself."

It must be a telegram. Charlotte's heart started to pound. Heidi was at the general store. She'd seen her leave with the Gavins and Lynette. What urgent matter could affect her? She gasped as realization dawned. "Something happened to Jakob."

Rebecca shook her head violently, and the tears welled again.

Holly handed the telegram back to Rebecca. "They've given up placing Heidi. Rebecca's supposed to take her back to New York."

"H-h-how will she ever get a home?" Rebecca stammered.

Charlotte ached for the girl. "I wish I could take her." But she didn't dare with Wyatt leaving.

Rebecca drew a quavering breath. "And how will her brother find her? He's out there all alone, enduring who knows what hardship all to find his sister, and now they want me to take her back to New York. He'll never find her. Oh, what am I going to do?"

"Delay," Holly said emphatically.

Rebecca blinked, her tears stemmed for the moment. "Delay?"

"Yes." As always, the ever-sensible Holly seized on the solution. "The telegram doesn't say *when* you need to return, so take your time. Wait until Jakob shows up in Evans Grove."

"But what if he doesn't?" Rebecca whispered. "What if he never does? I wish Mr. Armstrong had hired Mr. Reed."

Charlotte did too. It would have kept Wyatt here longer. "I could try again to persuade him to look for Jakob." But only if he was still in Evans Grove.

Holly started. "That's it! It's the perfect solution. The way I see things, Jakob is a missing person who has probably reached the county by now. That makes this police business."

Charlotte understood what she was getting at. This could solve both Rebecca's problem and hers. This could keep Wyatt in Evans Grove. Give him another job, one sanctioned by the sheriff.

"Would Mason agree?" she asked Holly.

The schoolteacher grinned. "If he doesn't, he'll discover just how persuasive I can be."

Chapter Seventeen

By the time Wyatt finished his business with Brooks and hurried down the hotel staircase, he hoped Baxter would be gone. Unfortunately, the weasel was still in the dining room, engrossed in conversation with someone. Thanks to the wall, Wyatt couldn't see who it was, and he couldn't risk going into the dining room where Baxter would see him. He tried to catch a glimpse from the porch, but the sun reflected off the windows and obscured his view.

His next stop should be the sheriff's office, but Mason was probably home with his new bride and son. Wyatt's resignation would have to wait until morning. After that, he'd head out. Once Sasha fell asleep tonight, he'd tell Charlotte that he was leaving. He owed her that much. Hopefully the provision he'd just made for their daughter would soften the blow.

The stagecoach rolled to a stop in front of the hotel. Baxter could come out at any moment, so Wyatt hurried toward the telegraph office. From there he could spot who left the hotel with Baxter while staying out of the man's sight.

He stepped onto the office's low porch and pretended to examine the rates posted on the window, while keeping an eye on the hotel. An elderly couple got off the stagecoach.

The bustle of removing their luggage blocked his view for a time. Then a wagon pulled in front of the coach, making it impossible to see who'd boarded. Wyatt growled in frustration and hurried toward the livery to get a better angle of the front of the hotel.

"Mr. Reed!"

The sharp command made Wyatt jump to the side before he crashed into Beatrice Ward.

"Ma'am." He touched a finger to his hat.

"Humph." She shot him a withering glare. "I would think a man would be home with his wife and child at this hour."

An ordinary husband would, but Baxter had just taken that away from him.

Charlotte held supper as long as she could. Thankfully, it was only salt pork and cabbage. When Sasha complained that her tummy hurt, Charlotte fed her, but she waited and waited to eat herself.

Surely Wyatt wouldn't have left town without his saddlebags. The moment she'd arrived home, she'd climbed the ladder to the loft and found them still there. But if he hadn't left town, what was he doing? Had Mason cornered him already? Had Wyatt gone to look for Jakob Strauss?

Sasha sighed, and her eyelids drifted shut. The little girl had curled up in her chair with Katya. The day's excitement had prevented a nap, and despite a valiant effort to stay awake, she finally succumbed. Charlotte carried her to the bed and laid a quilt over her. Rising, she couldn't help but see the ladder to the loft.

What if Wyatt's saddlebags were empty? She hadn't looked inside. Maybe he'd taken what he needed and left the bags behind. No, that was ridiculous. Either journey he might take—to find Jakob or to leave her—required saddlebags. Unless he was trying to mislead her. He wouldn't do that, would he?

After wringing her hands and pacing back and forth until twilight fell, she decided to check. She climbed the first two rungs of the ladder, but the shifting shadows made her less surefooted. She saw herself falling from the ladder again, felt again the impact of hitting the barn floor. She clung to the ladder, frozen in place as the front door opened.

"Charlotte? What are you doing up there?" Wyatt strode across the room.

She felt a little foolish. "I—I wondered if you left town."

"So you were climbing to the loft."

"To see if you'd taken your things," she admitted, unable to look at him.

"Well, I'm right here." To her surprise, she felt his hands on her waist. "Let go, darlin'. I'll catch you."

Darling? Her heart fluttered precipitously. Had he just called her darling?

"Let go," he urged again.

She forced her fingers to relax, and he lifted her as easily as he'd lifted Sasha. A thrill ran through her. His arms felt so secure, so perfect. The warmth of his chest, the beating of his heart, the way his touch sent tingles all over her. She could stay there forever. She ran a hand across his cheek and down to the little dimple in his chin.

"Thank—" The expression of gratitude stuck in her mouth when his frown didn't ease. "What's wrong?"

"Don't you go climbing that ladder again." He deposited her in the center of the room. "Promise?"

She didn't understand. One moment he was calling her darling and the next he scolded her and set her down like a sack of flour.

"I want your promise," he insisted. "You can't go getting hurt when you have a little girl to take care of."

Charlotte wanted to say that he could take care of Sasha if something happened to her. That's why God gave children two parents. But the hardness in his eyes frightened her.

He'd made up his mind.

"When do you leave?" The words stuck in her throat.

He drew in his breath and glanced at Sasha. "Tomorrow at dawn."

She wrapped her arms around her midsection, unable to stop the shivering. Against all reason, she hoped he was going to look for Jakob. "How long do you think it will take to find him?"

"Find who?"

"Jakob." She swallowed hard. "Didn't Mason talk to you?"

Wyatt's eyes narrowed. "No."

The trembling got worse. She shut her eyes, unable to look upon the man she'd come to love. He was leaving, just as they agreed, but didn't he see that everything had changed? Didn't he feel a thing? The steely eyes told her he didn't.

She drew in a shuddering breath. Holly had told her to tell Wyatt she loved him, but what would it change now? He'd made up his mind.

"Please don't," she whispered. Those two little words were all she could get out without breaking down.

"I have to."

She heard the creak of wood and opened her eyes to see him climbing into the loft. Moments later, he returned with the saddlebags slung over his shoulder.

"Maybe it's better if I go now." His voice betrayed no emotion. It was cold, hard as the day they met.

Charlotte shook her head, unable to speak. Her throat constricted and burned. Tears threatened. How could he? After all they'd been through? After all they'd shared? After the way he'd stood up for the town and been welcomed as a hero?

He paused at the door, and for a moment his gaze softened. "I'm sorry."

It wasn't enough. Nothing could be enough to mend the jagged tear in her soul. Yet another person was leaving her. She wasn't supposed to care for him in such a short space of time. This was supposed to be only a business transaction. That's all she'd asked of him. Help her keep Sasha.

She looked over at the little girl. "She'll miss you."

The silence lasted so long that she feared he'd gone, but when she looked back at the door, he was still there. The hat cast a dark shadow over his eyes.

"Tell her I'll miss her, too," he said softly.

A dose of uncharacteristic boldness struck Charlotte. *Tell him you love him,* Holly had said. Charlotte couldn't admit that. She wasn't entirely sure herself. But Sasha loved him. This she knew. "Tell her yourself."

His head snapped back as if she'd struck him.

Once her tongue had loosed, she could not stop it. "Tell her in the morning. It's only right." This time Wyatt Reed had to face the repercussions of his actions. This time she would not make excuses to Sasha or anyone else.

He stood at the door, unmoving. Behind him, night crept over Evans Grove with the hum of crickets and the pale light of a waxing moon. "It will only hurt her to see me leave."

"Better than to wonder why you don't come back. Tell her. She deserves that much, at least."

For a long time he hesitated. "All right. But in the morning, I go."

Thank You, God. She had one night to figure out a way to change his mind.

Wyatt should have resisted Charlotte's plea. He could more easily face a gun leveled at his head than that woman's tears. Now he'd gone and promised to stay until morning, which would only double the pain tomorrow. Sweet stars, he'd have to walk out on Sasha. What would he tell her?

As the evening progressed, he began to realize that Charlotte seemed to think she could change his mind about leaving. Why? Other than a few brief moments when emotion got the best of her, she kept her distance. From the start she'd known he had to leave, but now she was acting like she wanted him to stay. It made his head spin. It also didn't change the fact that he was putting both Charlotte and Sasha in danger every moment that he stayed in Evans Grove.

The woman gave him no chance to talk. She picked at her plate of cabbage and salt pork while he ate. The entire time, she prattled on and on about the missing Strauss boy and how his sister was doomed to return to New York. Better New York than Greenville, Wyatt was beginning to think.

What he couldn't get through his head was why she thought he'd take the job.

"Let me make this clear. No one's hiring me."

Charlotte smiled broadly. "You'd be working in your capacity as deputy sheriff."

The pieces fell into place. "And you think Mason will ask me to go after the lad."

She jutted out her chin. "Of course. We figure by now Jakob must have reached the county."

"And how exactly did you figure that?"

She looked at him as if he was plumb out of his mind. "It's been more than a month since he ran away, and it's only seventy miles or so from Glenwood to here. Even though he's on foot, he'd have made it this far by now."

The lad would have made it here a whole pile sooner barring disaster. Wyatt didn't bother to mention all the calamities that could befall a boy on his own. Hunger, coyotes, Indians, outlaws. None of them were fit for a woman's ears.

"When will you start looking for him?" Charlotte asked as she cleared the empty plates from the table.

He hesitated as a new idea took hold. While he was working on bringing Baxter down, he could look around for that boy at the same time, ask a few questions. If the boy could be found, then once he took care of Baxter, Wyatt could send Jakob to Evans Grove for that brother/sister reunion that had Charlotte so excited. Then she might not even mind that Wyatt wouldn't be returning. At least it would take the sting out of it.

No matter how much he wanted to stay in Evans Grove, he couldn't. He wouldn't shirk his responsibilities, mind you. He'd do his best to take care of the wife and child he'd taken as his own...but he'd do it from a distance. Charlotte deserved better than a man with such horrors in his past. He'd give her this one last gift—the boy Jakob Strauss, if he was anywhere to be found—and then he'd head out to San Francisco like he'd always planned. San Francisco. Funny how that place didn't hold near as much appeal as it had just a week ago.

He cleared his throat. "I'll talk to Sheriff Wright in the morning."

Just like he figured, the announcement made her clasp her hands together with joy.

"Oh, thank you, thank you."

Her infernal tears started again, but he didn't much mind the happy kind. Her cheeks flushed that pretty shade of rose, like Sasha's day-old wild geraniums stuffed into a mason jar in the center of the table.

Charlotte fairly glowed in the lamplight, her eyes bright. "A fourteen-year-old boy shouldn't be too hard to find."

Fourteen? Wyatt's skin crawled. Baxter wanted only the older kids—fourteen-year-olds like Jakob. He wondered about the boy at Star Plains farm. He'd been older. The farm owners weren't his ma and pa. Was Baxter sending those kids into what amounted to indenture? If so, and if Jakob Strauss had already reached Greenville, Baxter might have sent him off already.

"Promise me you'll look until you find him." Charlotte placed her delicate hand on his large, rough one.

No need to tell her about the danger he feared the boy might be in. Not until he had more information. Information that he would gather while he uncovered Baxter's plans. "I'll talk to Mason in the morning."

Only it wouldn't be to discuss taking on this job she'd concocted. He'd be handing in his badge.

Chapter Eighteen

Wyatt's nightmares returned that night. Charlotte awoke sometime in the early hours and heard him thrashing and groaning in the loft. Though he did not cry loudly enough to wake Sasha, his torment pulled at Charlotte. What had he gone through to lead to these horrible dreams? How could she help him get past this?

She hesitated at the foot of the ladder. Wyatt had made her promise not to climb it, but so had Charles, and that ladder had separated them for thirteen years. This time she could not let something so insignificant stand between her and a chance at the future she wanted. Though Wyatt had told her he'd talk to the sheriff about looking for Jakob, she sensed he was holding something back, something he would not tell her. Maybe that's what had brought on the nightmares again. Maybe she could provide the comfort and assurance he needed.

Please, Lord, help me find the words.

She crawled up the ladder, and with each step her certainty grew. What Wyatt needed most was the peace that only God could give. That resolve propelled her up the steps and into the loft, where the moonlight revealed Wyatt's torture. He still tossed and moaned, the bedsheet wrapped around him like a shroud. Up here near the roof, the heat was so oppressive that she could barely draw a breath. No wonder the poor man was feverish.

He groaned and rolled away from her, wrapping the sheet even tighter around his body. She tugged at the sheet. It was soaked with perspiration. Poor man! Charles must have suffered the heat, too, yet he'd never said a word. Charlotte bit back regret for all the times she'd scolded him. She should have done more to soften his grief. All that time she'd thought only of her needs, not his. Maybe if she'd gone to him with patience and understanding, he could in time have overcome the loss of his wife.

She'd failed Charles.

She would not fail Wyatt.

"Wyatt," she said softly into his ear. "Wake up."

He groaned and rolled back toward her. "Sarlot," he mumbled.

Had he just spoken her name? It had come out so garbled, that she wasn't sure, but at least he hadn't called for Margaret.

She placed a hand on his damp forehead. "It's me. I'm here."

His face contorted. "Charlotte! Run!"

His arms flailed, and she ducked below a punch that would have knocked her senseless. The move made her lose her balance, and she fell backward to the edge of the loft.

Her backside landed on the boards. The momentum carried her toward the edge. Her hand grasped air.

She shrieked.

He bolted upright. "Charlotte!"

In the moonlight, his eyes were wide as they searched for her. She didn't dare reach for him lest she lose her precarious balance.

"Wyatt!"

But he didn't see her. Her vision began to blur and fade, and she slipped back, back, until something jerked her forward.

"Charlotte, come back to me." Wyatt held her so tightly that she could feel the pounding of his heart against her cheek. "Why did you come up here? I told you not to climb that ladder."

Only it wasn't an accusation. Fear trembled his voice, and his arms held her tightly, as if he'd never let go.

She threaded her arms around his broad chest and looked up to that perfectly chiseled face. In the moonlight he looked as fine as a marble statue, utterly perfect in every way, and she knew she was falling in love with him. Yes, she was. Old hurts warned her to be cautious, but if Wyatt offered up just one more sign of commitment on his part—to the town, to God, to her and Sasha—she'd be willing to give him her heart completely.

"I'm not afraid of the ladder anymore. God was with me." She held her breath, half-afraid of his reaction.

Instead of stiffening, he held her closer. "I'm glad."

She wasn't sure if he meant her burst of courage or God's protective presence. At least he didn't close his heart like he'd done in the past. She laid her head on his shoulder. "You were having nightmares again."

He kissed the top of her head and ran his fingers through her hair. "I remember. I didn't want you to…" He never finished the sentence, instead dropping his lips to her forehead.

Then he gently tilted her head, and Charlotte's breath caught in her throat. Was he going to truly kiss her this time? Would this be the moment when he made that commitment, and told her that he wanted this marriage to be more than a business deal? Would she finally get the love and family she'd always wanted?

* * *

Sasha's cries startled them both, making Wyatt pull away. He couldn't believe how close he'd come to revealing the depth of his feelings to Charlotte. He should thank Sasha for interrupting them before he made a fool out of himself. He was leaving in the morning. He couldn't let himself forget that again.

What had he been thinking?

But she'd been there, the vision of his dreams only lovelier. Her profound faith had touched something deep inside, that part of him that still wanted to believe in a loving God, and for a moment he'd longed to seize that life with all his heart. Her very real presence had erased the nightmare that she'd died in Atlanta's flames. Charlotte wasn't in Georgia. She'd never been to Georgia. No, she lived a perfectly safe life in Evans Grove, Nebraska.

Safe only if Baxter didn't come after her.

That reality hit him hard the next morning. He had to leave. At once. If he stayed much longer, he'd put her in jeopardy. And it wasn't enough to just leave—he had to make it clear to Evans Grove that he wasn't coming back. Baxter had to believe Wyatt didn't care one ounce for Charlotte. Only then would she and Sasha be safe.

So he packed his saddlebags and descended for breakfast. She was so happy to believe he was heading out to find Jakob that he couldn't bring himself to tell her the rest—that whether he found the boy or not, he wouldn't be returning.

"I hope you find him quickly," she said with a shy smile. "I can't wait for you to get back." Her eyes said what her lips would not. She cared for him. Maybe even enough to want to make their marriage real.

The thought nearly made him lose his head. How easy it would be to stay. He could stake out the place, use his sharp-shooting skills to keep Baxter and his cronies at bay. Maybe Mason would help.

But Baxter knew about his past. Once he told Mason, Wyatt's stint as deputy sheriff would be over, anyway. *Killers don't become lawmen. They're hanged.* And a dead man was no good to Charlotte. Better he live and send her everything he could earn than die and leave her destitute.

Sasha banged her spoon on the table and refused to eat her oatmeal. He couldn't blame her. Oatmeal had never been his favorite.

"You'll need to eat up for our Saturday-morning play-time," Charlotte said brightly. "We'll see Aunt Holly and Miss Sterling and all your friends."

"Aunt Holly?" Wyatt was surprised by this new title Charlotte was using. Were they related?

"It's easier than explaining the change of last names," Charlotte said before turning back to Sasha. "Won't it be fun to see everyone again?"

The week before, the women had decided to make Saturday mornings a time for the orphans to play together and share what was happening in their lives.

"Some of them see each other at school," Charlotte had explained, "but the little ones only see each other at church. Rebecca and Holly think this time together will be good for them."

Wyatt didn't see much harm in it, unlike what he was about to do.

"Rebecca will be so excited to hear you're going to find Jakob," Charlotte said, oblivious to what was about to happen.

He felt terrible about it. He felt worse than terrible. The poor woman had just lost a husband. Now she'd be publicly abandoned. But he didn't see any way around the hurt. Like a festering blister, best to lance it to get the infection out.

She didn't know it yet, but he was the germ inside that boil. Best he get out before his presence killed her.

He shoveled down his oatmeal and made a show of heading out to see Mason. After handing in his badge and waiting for her and Sasha to head to the schoolhouse, he'd double back to get his saddlebags and leave her the note explaining the provision he'd made for her and Sasha. Telling her in a note was the coward's way out, but he couldn't say it to her face. He cared too much for her. He wanted a life with her. If he looked in her eyes, he would stay, and that would bring death to her doorstep.

Charlotte would be hurt when she read the note, but she had lots of friends here. She'd get over it.

He wasn't so sure he would.

Charlotte had never been happier. She had a daughter, a home and a husband who might be starting to love her, just as she was starting to love him. Once he found Jakob and came back to town, they'd finally talk—and then they could take the first steps toward making their marriage real.

When Wyatt gets back. She savored the life they'd have together. Shared meals, evenings strolling by the creek, Sunday picnics. She might even let him take Sasha on a horseback ride when she got older.

She hoped it wouldn't take him long to find Jakob. All he had to do was backtrack to Glenwood. Jakob would stay on the train route. The task was so simple that she wondered why no one had attempted it yet. She supposed everyone had been too caught up in the train robbery, rebuilding the town and the fate of the orphans. She certainly had.

She sang as she combed and braided Sasha's hair. Maybe if Rebecca couldn't find someone to take Heidi, she'd talk to Wyatt when he returned with Jakob. The house was small, but the yard was big. They could add another room. Why not? Charlotte wanted a big family, and Wyatt loved children. If Jakob made a good impression on him, then maybe he'd agree. Oh, she knew it was silly to make all these plans when things were still tentative and unsettled between them…but it felt so wonderful to be silly, and happy and hopeful for the first time in years.

She pressed a hand to her lips, hardly able to bear the excitement. Soon.

Soon.

Chapter Nineteen

"Can't say I understand," Mason said as he stared at the deputy badge Wyatt had set on his desk. "Does this have anything to do with what Miss Ward told me?"

Wyatt narrowed his gaze. "What did she tell you?"

"About your service for the Union in the war."

The raw taste of blood stained Wyatt's tongue. It didn't matter how the old woman had found out. Now everyone would know what he'd done. Everyone. "I'd take it kindly if you don't tell Charlotte right off."

"I figure that's your responsibility."

It was, but Wyatt couldn't go back to her or he'd be tempted to stay. He set his jaw. "My responsibilities are met. I'm leaving."

Mason's gaze pierced through him. "Running away won't solve anything."

The sheriff had come too close to the truth. Wyatt was running, had been running since the war. Only in these past couple of weeks had that changed, and he'd liked it. He'd liked everything about this life, but now the past, and Baxter, were catching up to him.

He hated disappointing Mason. The man had given him his first real chance to come clean and start over. But to protect Charlotte, he had to convince everyone, including Mason, that his marriage was a sham. That meant portraying himself as the worst sort of man on the face of the earth—a man who cared for no one and nothing but money.

"You can't say anything to change my mind."

Mason rose to his feet. "I can't accept that. You have the makings of a fine lawman."

Wyatt reveled for the briefest moment in the sheriff's vote of confidence, but for Charlotte's sake, he had to break all ties. He took a deep breath and put his plan into motion. "Believing that would be your first mistake. The second was hiring me. I work for the highest bidder, and that's not some lowly deputy job."

Mason looked rightfully angry. It was working.

Wyatt moved to the next stage. "That's why I married Widow Miller—for her money. That's right. She paid me. Now she has the kid she wanted, and I've got the cash. My end of the bargain is done, and I'm leaving."

Before Wyatt knew what was happening, the sheriff's fist slammed into his jaw. Wyatt staggered but didn't fall.

"Get out of here," Mason growled.

Wyatt hated the feeling in his gut, like he'd betrayed the best man he'd ever known, but he had to do this to save Charlotte and Sasha.

"My pleasure," he spat out, each word taking a chunk out of what was left of his soul.

He yanked open the door, strode out and plunked his Stetson back on his head. His jaw was going to swell and turn purple. Good. It would both disguise his appearance and make his sudden exit all the more believable.

"Everything will turn out perfectly," Charlotte said to Holly as she watched the children sort themselves into groups of boys and girls.

After meeting at the schoolhouse, they'd walked to the wide-open land north of the last house on First Street. The empty fields gave the boys plenty of room to hit a baseball while the girls gathered wildflowers to press.

"Of course it will," Holly replied. "Especially if Wyatt finds Jakob."

"He will, but that's not what I meant. Stop trying to change the subject. You need to let me take measurements."

The schoolmistress frowned. "I don't need a new dress. Besides, Mason loves me just the way I am. I don't need a fancy dress to attract his attention. Why don't you keep it for yourself?"

"You know I can't wear that color with my peculiar red hair."

Holly laughed. "Your hair is neither peculiar nor red. It's strawberry-blond and the envy of every woman in Evans Grove. Trust me, you'd look good in any color." She leaned close to whisper, "And Wyatt will certainly notice."

Charlotte's cheeks heated. She'd been bursting to tell someone that her relationship with Wyatt was moving closer to a real marriage, but she hadn't wanted to explain what that meant in front of Rebecca. The orphan agent might not take kindly to knowing that they'd circumvented Society rules in order to keep Sasha.

After Rebecca left them to ask Heidi why she hadn't joined the play, Charlotte had her chance. "I think he already notices."

Holly laughed. "Of course he notices. He's been noticing you since the day he got here."

Before last night, Charlotte would have doubted it, but today she felt new life blossoming. Like the world around her, she'd awoken from a long winter and looked forward to a new day. By this time next year, perhaps her family would grow.

Holly stared at her. "What happened?"

Charlotte giggled like a girl. "It's just, well, I think things will work out." Against all reason, tears rose to her eyes, and Holly squeezed her hands.

"Of course they will. God's in charge, after all, and all things work for good for those who love the Lord."

Charlotte smiled at her friend's solid faith. Charlotte did love the Lord, truly she did, but she had for as long as she could remember, and nothing had worked out. Charles wouldn't or couldn't love her. Then he'd suddenly died. Was God at work in that? Surely not. And yet, Wyatt's arrival in town certainly hadn't seemed like a blessing at first. Even the arrival of the orphans had started with a tragedy—one that the Lord had turned into a gift for the town, and especially for Charlotte.

"Holly! Charlotte!" Rebecca interrupted their conversation. "Do you smell smoke?"

Charlotte hadn't noticed, but now that Rebecca mentioned it, she did. She scanned the horizon to see where it might be coming from, but Holly found it first.

"The schoolhouse!"

"Impossible," Charlotte said. "Nothing seemed amiss when we left the school, and there hasn't been any lightning. Did you light the stove this morning?"

She and Holly looked to Rebecca, who shook her head. "I haven't lit it in days."

Holly's expression wound tighter than a watch spring. "It's either the schoolhouse or my house."

The sickening feeling hit them all at once.

"Go," Charlotte urged. "We'll watch the children and keep them busy." She could see the boys had already noticed the dark column of smoke.

Rebecca agreed, though she looked just as anxious to discover if the fire was at the school. "Bring us word as soon as you know."

"I will," Holly shouted as she bolted toward town.

"I hope it's an empty building." Rebecca gnawed her lip. "Not the schoolhouse. And I hope it's not Holly's house. Where would she and Mason and Liam live?"

"His old place, I assume." But Charlotte knew that a roof overhead wasn't all Holly would lose. Her house held her beloved books, her grandmother's teapot and her cat, Dickens.

"But what if it *is* the school? Everything Heidi and I brought with us is inside. What would we do? Where would we go?" Rebecca blinked back tears.

"I can manage the children if you want to go." Though in truth, the smoke had so captivated the boys that she was beginning to doubt the two of them could keep control of the group.

Rebecca looked at the children before shaking her head. "It won't matter if I'm there or not. Better we keep the children preoccupied."

What a brave woman! Charlotte hugged her. "Don't worry. Whatever happens, we'll take care of you and Heidi." She offered a hopeful smile. "As Holly would say, everything will turn out for good for those who love the Lord."

Wyatt finished the note to Charlotte and set it in the middle of the table where she would find it. The letter detailed the arrangements he'd made with Curtis Brooks. The money Charlotte had given him would be held in a special account for Sasha. The banker assured him it would earn a good rate of interest. Wyatt had also set up another account where he'd deposit money whenever he could to help support Charlotte and Sasha. Brooks had assured him Charlotte would have full access to that account.

Then he'd ended the note by telling her he'd fulfilled the terms of their agreement and was leaving for San Francisco. Better he jab the knife in deep and cut through her heart in one stroke. That way only her emotions would suffer. In time, she'd recover, for she had Sasha. That little girl meant everything to her.

His hand shook as he set Sasha's jar of drooping geraniums on top of the note. Pinkish pollen sifted onto the paper.

"Goodbye, Charlotte. Goodbye, Sasha."

He pressed a kiss to the paper and then gathered his saddlebags. Next he'd get Dusty from the livery and head west. By the end of the day, he'd reach Greenville, where he could start trailing Baxter.

Hope flickered for an instant as he ran his fingers one last time over Charlotte's chair. If he discovered the truth about Baxter soon enough, he could tell Mason and have the man arrested. Maybe then, he could return.

He shook his head. Foolish hope.

She'd still know innocent women and children had died in the fires he'd set. The worst woman on earth didn't deserve such a man.

He rubbed his sore jaw. The best thing he could do for Charlotte was stay away—and ensure that Baxter wasn't in a position to harm her or anyone else ever again. That man was doing something terrible with the orphans that came into his care, and Wyatt would put an end to it and Baxter in one final blaze of retribution.

His gaze slipped over the bed, neatly made, the sunburst quilt vibrant in the morning light. Charlotte must have made it. He walked to it, drawn like a moth to flame. A fine, curling hair shimmered in the sunlight. He wound it into a coil and put it in his breast pocket, closest to his heart. If matters got out of hand and Baxter shot him, he'd take a part of her with him.

Then, before the pain got too much, he walked out of their lives forever.

Chapter Twenty

The fastest route to Greenville was to cross Evans Creek at the mill and then head west across open country. The train dipped to the south, and the stagecoach road meandered through the northern villages between Evans Grove and Greenville.

Wyatt rode toward the mill at a brisk pace. The livery boy had asked too many questions already, and Wyatt didn't want anyone else to stop him. Misleading Mason had been tough enough.

Coward. The word rang in his head as he headed up Fourth Street. He should have told Mason the truth. The man deserved that much. So did Charlotte. Leaving a note was the coward's way out, but the less she knew, the better off she'd be.

He stiffened his resolve, but he couldn't help looking down Liberty toward his former job. To his surprise, men raced away from him. Wagons stormed in the same direction. Men shouted. Women stood on their porches, staring toward the other end of town. Something big was happening.

Wyatt halted Dusty.

"We need a bucket brigade," someone yelled.

Then Wyatt spotted the column of smoke. Fire. A big one.

He squinted into the bright morning sun. The building was located past the town hall, but on the same side of the street.

Wyatt's heart stopped.

The school!

Charlotte and Sasha had gone to the schoolhouse to talk to Holly and Rebecca. They might be trapped inside. Visions of Atlanta flashed through his mind. The buildings a ball of flame. All civilians had been ordered out of town. Wyatt had seen the columns of people carting their life's belongings with them. But he'd felt only anger toward them for all the death they'd caused. Sherman ordered the troops to burn anything that could aid the military, but Wyatt laid his torch to houses. That's when he heard the screams, saw the shadows flitting across the blaze. Women, old men, children... he didn't know. All he knew was that they'd died horribly, and he had lit the blaze.

Not again.

Wyatt spurred Dusty into a gallop and raced toward the fire. Charlotte. Sasha. He imagined them trapped inside the burning school, pounding on the window as the flames consumed them.

No, not Charlotte. Not Sasha.

No, God. If You exist, please don't make them pay for my sins. Take me. Take me. Take me instead.

He wove Dusty around the scurrying people, but a mass of carts and wagons blocked the street near the fire. Wyatt spurred Dusty over a water trough and down a porch. Emerging on the other side, he saw what he'd feared.

The school was ablaze. Flames shot high in the air. All four walls were on fire, and the front door was still shut.

Wyatt leaped off Dusty and ran for that door.

Charlotte. Sasha. He had to save them.

Strong hands grabbed his shoulders and yanked him back. "Hold on there, Reed. You're not going in there."

Wyatt spun away, frantic. "Charlotte. Sasha." Nothing would keep him away.

He raced for the door. Flames had blackened it. They licked through the hole where the knob had once been.

Men shouted, but Wyatt blocked out their words. He knew only one thing. He had to save his family.

Three more steps before he reached the door. Three little steps.

Then something hit him from behind. The impact sent him sprawling and knocked the wind from his lungs. He gasped and dug his fingers into the earth, determined to crawl into the building if he had to, but a heavy weight came down on him.

"Stop fightin' me," grunted a man. Mason.

"Ain't gonna do you no good." Bucky Wyler.

The two men tried to pin him down, but Wyatt writhed and fought.

"Now don't make me bring you in," the sheriff drawled. "We got more important things to do than keep your sorry behind from roasting."

"Let me go," Wyatt seethed. "I have to save Charlotte. I have to get Sasha." He thought he could hear them screaming, wailing, begging for mercy. "I can't let them die."

"Thought you didn't care about your wife and daughter." Mason forced Wyatt's face into the dirt. "Thought you only married her for the money."

Wyatt did not want to get into a debate while the two people he loved most were dying. Summoning all his strength, he jerked to his right and kicked Bucky Wyler aside while elbowing Mason.

He scrambled to his knees but got no farther because Mason walloped him in the gut. The blow bent him over double.

"It's too late," Mason shouted, shaking Wyatt. "Anyone inside is already dead. You can't save them."

"I have to," Wyatt choked out. Not again. It couldn't be happening again. Charlotte dead. Sasha dead. Just like those people in Atlanta.

With a roar, something inside caught fire and flames shot into the sky. The window panes shattered.

Wyatt buried his head in his hands. Mason was right. Anyone inside was already dead. The fire was too hot. It broiled his face.

"It should have been me," he yelled into the heavens. "Do you hear me, God? It should have been me."

Not the innocent. Charlotte and Sasha shouldn't have had to pay for his sins. His gut twisted into a knot, and his jaw ached. None of that mattered. He'd cast away the woman and daughter he loved. Nothing he could do could bring them back. There was only One with that power.

Closing his eyes, he bent into the dirt like the penitents of old. "Take me, God. Do anything to me that You want, but bring Charlotte and Sasha back. I'll do anything, pay any price if they can live."

The fire still blazed. The shouts and cries of those fighting the flames still continued, but Wyatt felt different. The despair had gone out of him, and a semblance of strength took its place. Maybe there really was a God. Maybe He actually answered desperate prayer. Maybe Charlotte and Sasha lived.

Wyatt opened his eyes, hoping to see his wife and daughter.

They weren't there.

People ran every which way, but no Charlotte and no Sasha.

"Why, God? Why take them?" He dropped to the ground, crushed, and his hand landed on something hard. He pulled back to see the glint of gold. Was this all the answer he'd get? Wyatt brushed aside the dirt to reveal a pocket watch. A watch? What kind of answer was that?

Furious, he grabbed the watch and stumbled to his feet. While cocking his arm back to hurl the worthless thing into the fire, he saw the impossible.

Charlotte, with Sasha clinging to her skirts, stood next to Miss Sterling and the rest of the orphans a block away.

"Charlotte." He gasped for air.

She was safe. And Sasha too. They'd never been in the fire at all.

Stunned by the turn of events, he absently pocketed the watch and staggered toward his wife and daughter.

Mason caught his arm. "I just saw Holly. Charlotte's not in the school. Neither is Sasha. No one is. They're all safe."

Wyatt nodded, still overcome that his prayer had been answered.

"We could use your help." Mason steered him toward the bucket brigade. "Don't want it to take down the teacherage and half this town."

Wyatt took halting steps toward the two lines of citizens. One threw water on the fire. The other soaked the teacherage, which hadn't suffered any damage yet. Everyone had pitched in. Mr. Brooks took buckets from Mayor Evans who got them from Theodore Regan. Wyatt joined the line after Brooks, who took advantage of a pause to roll up his sleeves, revealing a jagged scar.

"You can take the next one from me," Brooks said to Wyatt before reaching for the bucket that the mayor held.

Instead of handing off the bucket, Pauline Evans stared at Brooks's arm. "Where did you get that scar?"

Brooks took the bucket from her hands. "Old injury. Nothing to worry about." Though after Wyatt took the bucket from him, he rolled his sleeve back down. "Why don't you take a break, Mayor, now that Mr. Reed is here?"

Mayor Evans jerked from his attempt to steer her out of the line. "I'm not about to rest when Evans Grove needs me." She grabbed the next bucket from Mr. Regan.

"Sheriff, we found the culprit," shouted Bucky Wyler. "Got him 'round back."

"That so?" Mason stepped out of the brigade. "Coming, Deputy?"

At first Wyatt thought Mason was talking to someone else, but the sheriff was looking straight at him.

"I could use your help, Deputy."

That title sure sounded sweet. Wyatt could hardly believe Mason still trusted him. First Charlotte and Sasha were safe, and now his job was intact. That was some answer to prayer. He mopped his brow. He'd just promised God to do whatever He asked, but Wyatt had no idea how to figure out what that might be. So he'd start by helping Mason.

He followed the sheriff to where Bucky Wyler stood guard over an unconscious man lying on the ground near the privy.

"Is he hurt?" Wyatt asked.

Mason shook his head in disgust. "Drunk. I wouldn't have figured Vern Hicks as someone who'd light buildings on fire."

"You think he did it on purpose?" Wyatt's skin crawled.

"Might've been an accident," said Bucky. "You know he smokes them cigars. Might've flicked a lit one too close to the school afore he dropped off."

Mason rubbed his chin and surveyed the distance to the smoldering schoolhouse. "That would have had to be one long flick."

Wyatt estimated it at twenty feet or more.

Bucky tucked his hands in his trouser pockets. "Well, he might've dropped it down there and then toddled over here ta relieve himself."

Mason sighed, but he didn't look convinced. "Guess he's the only suspect we have."

"But why would anyone want to burn down a school?" Bucky asked.

Wyatt knew one person who might. One man had leveled threats yesterday. Would Baxter have hired Hicks to do the job?

"For mischief, Mr. Wyler."

The three men started at the sound of Miss Ward's voice.

"What do you mean, ma'am?" asked Mason.

All prim and proper, Beatrice held her bag before her like a shield. "Those street-urchin orphans, is what I mean. First the thefts and now this. Who else was here this morning except those children?"

Wyatt clenched his fists. If Beatrice Ward weren't a woman, he would knock some sense into her. Sasha could have died. All the children could have died. And she blamed them?

Mason's jaw tightened. "My wife was here. You're not accusing her, are you?"

Miss Ward flinched. "I'm sure she had nothing to do with it. The orphans probably waited until she wasn't looking."

"They're innocent children," Wyatt growled.

"Unlike some men who frequent saloons." Miss Ward glared at him before returning her attention to Mason. "Now, I'm not saying they set the fire deliberately. Ill-mannered children will get into mischief."

"They're not ill-mannered!" Wyatt yelled. "They're just like any other children."

Mason cut off the rest of Wyatt's rant. "Now, Miss Ward, there's no reason to think the children had anything to do with it."

The spinster wouldn't back down. "Your wife does keep

matches on hand to light the stove, does she not? From what I recall, they are within reach of any child inside the school."

Mason looked like he'd punch Miss Ward the way he'd clocked Wyatt, but the sheriff managed to maintain control. "A good lawman never jumps to conclusions, Miss Ward. All possibilities will be investigated."

"Well." She sniffed. "That's the most a *law-abiding* citizen can ask."

No doubt she was referring to Wyatt's tarnished past.

Miss Ward drilled Mason with a pointed look. "I can count on you to keep me informed?"

Mason managed a curt nod.

"Very well. Good day, gentlemen." Satisfied that she'd accomplished what she'd come to do, Miss Ward picked her way past the weary citizens dumping buckets of water on the remaining fire.

"That old biddy didn't lift a finger ta help," observed Bucky. "Jess picked fault."

Wyatt couldn't have summed it up better.

Mason sighed. "Suppose we'd better get Vern to the jail. Wyatt, why don't you and me cart him there so Bucky can continue fighting the fire? He's part of our fire department."

"Thanks, Sheriff." Bucky headed back to the blaze.

At this point, they had the fire under control and men were taking axes to the remnants of the walls. Wyatt shuddered. The building had gone up so quickly. If anyone had been inside, they would never have been able to get out. Just like Atlanta. Yet the memory no longer carried the pain it once had. Maybe because this time, he'd been one of the people fighting the fire, doing the right thing—and possibly even with God on his side.

Wyatt looked toward the spot where Charlotte had stood, but she was gone. With the fire almost out, she'd probably taken Sasha home.

"If you take one side, and I take the other, we should be able to drag the lout to the jail," Mason said.

"That's a couple blocks." Wyatt eyed the distance. "We could lay him on my horse and take him that way."

Mason agreed to that plan, and Wyatt hurried off to fetch Dusty from where he'd left him unhitched in front of someone's house. The crotchety horse had discovered the owner's pansies and was making a feast of them.

The elderly woman slapped at the horse with her bonnet. "Stop that. Shoo! I said get out of here!"

Wyatt stoppered a chuckle. "Ma'am? My apologies. Let me compensate you for your loss."

"Oooh." The woman drew up, her eyes round as he handed her a few coins, more than covering the cost of her half-eaten flowers. "Thank ye."

In the process of retrieving the coins, Wyatt felt the gold watch in his pocket. Maybe it belonged to Hicks. If so, then he'd gone very close to the front door and probably was at fault, putting to rest Miss Ward's accusation against the orphans.

He'd have to show the watch to Mason.

Charlotte simply wasn't tall enough to see over the crowds of people surrounding the fire. All that mattered was that everyone was safe. She'd wondered if Wyatt might be there. If he saw the fire before leaving town, he might have stayed. But the ladies she talked to hadn't seen him, so he must have left to track Jakob.

Since Sasha got antsy standing around, she brought her home. As soon as she opened the door, she knew something was wrong.

The house felt empty and lifeless, like after Charles died, only worse. But Wyatt hadn't kept much here, and the few things he did bring fit into his saddlebags, which he would have taken with him, anyway. She rubbed the goose pimples on her arms.

"Pitty!" Sasha stood on her chair and reached across the table for her jar of geraniums, which wasn't in the center of the table anymore.

Charlotte darted over to stop Sasha from climbing onto the table, and her heart sank. A folded piece of paper with her name scrawled on it sat underneath the jar.

With trembling hands, she slipped the note from beneath the jar and handed the flowers to Sasha. A smudge marred the paper beneath her name. His fingerprint? She touched it, wanting to believe it was a love letter, that he'd said in writing what he couldn't express aloud, but deep down she knew it wasn't. Part of her wanted to throw the note into the stove unread, but the larger part had to know what he'd written. So she unfolded the paper.

His handwriting scrawled across the page, as if he'd hurried to get it all down. The opening sentence drove a knife through her heart.

Dear Charlotte, I've provided for you and Sasha.

She didn't need to read the rest to know what it would say. He was leaving—truly leaving, with no intention of coming back. He'd already gone. But he'd eased his conscience by setting aside some money for her. Every cruel word confirmed that supposition.

When she reached the bitter end, her knees gave way. She sank to the floor. The sobs came next. She could stifle them at first, but then they came with greater urgency until she could hold them back no longer. Had the way he held her been nothing more than pretense? Did he never care?

Sob after wrenching sob tore from her, washing away thirteen years of loveless marriage, Charles's death and the cruelty of loving another man who couldn't love her in return.

"Mama?"

Sasha's slender arms wrapped around her neck, and Charlotte held her close, held her tight, held her forever.

"Sasha, dearest. I will never stop loving you. Ever. Ever." That's all she had now.

After locking Vern Hicks in the jail cell, Wyatt showed Mason the pocket watch. "Found this near the door of the schoolhouse. Thought it might belong to Mr. Hicks." He rubbed the watchcase against his trouser leg to remove the dirt and grime.

"Looks like gold," Mason said. "Can't see Vern having anything that expensive unless he won it gambling. They're always scrabbling to get by, thanks to Vern's drinking. Do you think it could be brass?"

Wyatt took a closer look. "Looks like gold to me. No tarnish anywhere." He flipped the watchcase over and stared. The scrolling monogram gave its owner away. He'd seen this watch before. "Felix Baxter."

"Baxter?" Mason stepped forward. "Are you telling me this watch belongs to Baxter?"

"I saw him take it out yesterday when we talked. It's engraved with his initials." Wyatt showed him the watchcase.

"Hold the cavalry. You saw Baxter yesterday?"

"He cornered me by the hotel. Acted like he'd just arrived and said he was leaving that evening."

"Hmm." Mason examined the watch. "Now why would he come to town for only a few hours?"

"Somehow he'd learned the outcome of the hearing, and he wasn't happy."

Mason narrowed his gaze. "Is that why you came up with that cockamamie story about marrying Charlotte for her money? Did Baxter threaten you?"

Wyatt supposed if he was ever going to get the life he

wanted with Charlotte, he'd better start telling the whole truth. "He threatened to harm Charlotte if I didn't finish the job and find a way to get the orphans to Greenville. Since there's no way I'd take those kids away from here, I figured I had to get away from Charlotte and make sure people thought I didn't care about her to protect her from retaliation."

Mason drew in a sharp breath. "I can't blame you for doing what you did, then. I'd have done the same. Sorry I clocked you in the jaw."

Wyatt rubbed the tender spot. "I deserved it."

Mason set the watch on his desk. "You said you found this at the schoolhouse. Could Baxter have been on the scene sometime yesterday afternoon?"

"I don't think so. I saw the watch late in the afternoon. Four-thirty or later, I'd say. After we finished talking, Baxter went to the hotel dining room to eat supper. I took care of some business upstairs with Brooks, and when I came down, Baxter was still in the dining room, talking to someone."

"Who?"

"That's the trouble. I couldn't see who it was. The wall blocked my view from inside the hotel, and the sun was reflecting off the outside windows so I couldn't see in."

Mason drummed his fingers on the desktop. "Doesn't matter. The hotel staff will know. They'll also know if he checked out."

"You don't think he took the evening stage?"

"Considering that watch, I highly doubt it."

"Then that means we've locked up the wrong man."

At that moment, the office door opened and a pale, nervous woman entered. She twisted and kneaded the bag in her hands. She looked familiar, but Wyatt couldn't place her.

"I understand you have Vern?" She looked at the floor as she spoke.

A grumble echoed from the jail cell as Vern Hicks came out of his stupor. "Dat you, Meelie?" he slurred.

The plump woman cringed, and Wyatt felt sorry for her.

Mason shook his head. "I oughta keep you here, Vern, until you sober up."

The woman looked up hopefully, but Vern shouted obscenities from within the cell, and she shrank again, like a wilted flower. She was no match for that bully in the cell.

"Sorry, Mrs. Hicks," Mason said with genuine concern. "We can't keep him here without charges."

She nodded in resignation and fiddled with the clasp on her bag. "Do I owe bail?"

Mason stilled her hands. "Not a cent." He tossed Wyatt the keys. "Why don't you let him out?"

Wyatt hated to subject the woman to the tirade her husband would unleash on her. "Are you sure we can't keep him until he's sobered up?"

Mason shook his head. "It's tempting, but he didn't cause a ruckus." Mason turned to the drunk. "You going to behave yourself, Vern?"

"Course." Hicks quieted down a lot. "Come on, Meelie, and get me outta here."

Wyatt gritted his teeth. That man did not deserve a wife.

"Best let Vern out," Mason said to Wyatt. "From what you told me, we've got a dangerous man to find. The sooner we get going, the better chance we have of catching him."

We? Wyatt reveled in the undeserved confidence. It'd been a long time since a good man like Mason placed his trust in Wyatt. Two men stood a better chance than one of taking Baxter down, especially when one of them was the sheriff. The risk was still high. Baxter could have gunmen protecting him. The man could be lying in wait, but Wyatt had never stepped away from danger. He'd also had nothing to lose then. Now he had a wife and daughter.

"Charlotte!" he exclaimed, remembering the terrible note he'd left for her. She would have found it and read it by now. She'd think he'd abandoned her. He couldn't head for Greenville and let her think he'd left for good. He had to get a message to her.

"Meelie!" Hicks banged on the bars.

Wyatt would leave the man to rot if he could. He gave Amelia Hicks a look of apology. She hung her head, and he realized where he'd seen her. She'd sat with Charlotte at that first town meeting.

"Do you know my wife?" he asked her.

She nodded. "She's kind."

"I need you to tell her—" He stopped, unsure how to formulate a simple message that this skittish woman could remember and convey. "Just tell her I'm coming back."

"Yes, sir. I will. Just as soon as I get Vern home."

Home. Nothing had ever sounded so good. He couldn't wait to get back home to Charlotte.

Assuming he survived.

Chapter Twenty-One

After Charlotte cried herself dry and Sasha fell asleep for her nap, she climbed the ladder into the loft. Maybe Wyatt had left something behind, some trace that she could cling to, some hope he might one day return.

Despite nearly falling the last time she went up there, she managed the ascent. Daylight revealed a hideous room. Spiders strung their webs across the vents at either end. Dark and dreary, the room offered no hope or cheer.

She focused on the bed, neatly made. The pillow still bore the indentation of his head. She ran her fingers across the cotton case.

Wyatt, Wyatt. Why did you leave me?

Though she'd thought herself wrung dry, tears flowed again. Her salty offering mingled with the last trace of him. This wasn't how it was supposed to be. He cared for her, didn't he? Then why leave her? Why disappear with only a note?

She hugged the pillow to her chest and surveyed the tiny room for anything he might have left behind. If he'd forgotten something important, he'd have to return. She ran her hands along the floorboards on every side of the mattress. She stripped the sheets. Nothing.

Charles's trunk contained nothing of Wyatt's. Did the shelves? She bit her lip. Wyatt wouldn't have set anything on the shelves, would he? Yet she had to look. She had to face Charles's shrine.

Though she knew Charles had clung to Gloria's memory, she'd hoped he would eventually pack the mementos in his trunk. But no. Her image in the daguerreotype still stared out at Charlotte. Cold, harsh, judgmental. No, not judgmental—fearful. What she'd once seen as harshness looked more like fear. Pauline had once told her that Gloria barely said a word to anyone, that she was timid. And Charles had protected her.

Charlotte touched the daguerreotype, surrounded by all those candles. "You won. He was always yours and never mine."

For the first time, that didn't hurt.

Now that the sting was gone, she could dismantle Charles's shrine. But what to do with it? He would have wanted Gloria's photograph buried with him, but it was too late for that. She stretched out her hand to pick it up, but the frame tipped over. Something fell off the back of the shelf and clunked onto the floor.

What on earth? She lay on her side and reached her arm under the shelves. Her fingers found balls of dust and plenty of dirt until they finally rested on a small metal object. She pulled it out. A baby spoon. But Charles and Gloria had no children. She brushed off the dust to reveal an inscription. By moving the spoon until the light hit it just right, she was able to make out the words: Baby Boy, June 12, 1861.

Charlotte's head spun. That was the same day Gloria died. Her hands shook as she stared at the spoon. Charles's wife had died in birthing a boy, who also died. Why had no one told her this? Why hadn't Charles said anything?

Charlotte clutched the spoon to her chest. No wonder he'd feared giving Charlotte children. No wonder he'd agreed to take in Sasha. He could give her the child she craved without endangering her life.

The sob bubbled to the surface.

Dear Lord, he blamed himself for Gloria's death. He never forgave himself.

The years of anger and resentment came crashing down. Poor man. Poor, poor man. He hadn't despised her. He'd been afraid to love her.

And all she'd done was beg and throw fits and criticize because he wouldn't give her what she wanted. She'd never asked why. She'd never tried to listen to him. She'd never given him what he needed most. Instead, she'd withheld her affection and denied him the compassion he so desperately needed.

She ached from the knowledge of what she'd done. And what she'd continued to do, for she had acted the same way with Wyatt.

Charity suffereth long, and is kind; charity envieth not; charity vaunteth not itself.

The Bible verse rang in her head. She hadn't shown charity or patience or consolation. She'd thought only of herself. Bitter tears ripped out from deep inside her.

And now it was too late.

While Mason saddled his horse, Wyatt sorted out events. "If Baxter didn't take the stagecoach to Greenville last night, he'd still be in town. He's not the type to walk twelve miles."

"He could've hired a mount."

"Baxter hates to part with a dime."

Mason grunted as he cinched the saddle. "He's probably not tightfisted when his neck is on the line."

"True. He paid for the stagecoach to get here."

Mason frowned. "When exactly did he say he arrived?"

"He didn't. I assumed he came on the afternoon stage."

Mason looked up sharply. "Yesterday's stage from Greenville was delayed. I think it got here around seven or eight."

That meant the evening stagecoach Wyatt had seen had been the eastbound one, not the westbound. "Then he definitely didn't leave last night."

"Probably rode here already knowing what he planned to do so he could head out the minute he finished setting that fire."

Wyatt calculated quickly. "He has at least two hours on us."

Mason frowned. "But where would he go?"

"Back to Greenville."

"You sure? Wouldn't he want to throw off any pursuers?"

Wyatt knew in his gut that he was right. "Baxter's overconfident. Trust me. He'd head straight back to where he has the officials in his pocket." And the henchmen to "convince" people of his point of view. "Besides, he doesn't think anyone would suspect him, and no one would if he hadn't lost that pocket watch. He probably saw Hicks passed out in the yard and figured we'd blame him."

"We did at first." Mason patted his horse's flank. "Do you think Baxter would've put Hicks up to it?"

The idea had crossed Wyatt's mind. "You know Hicks better than I do. Would he set a fire if Baxter paid him enough? Baxter had a purse full of gold coin."

"Might have." Mason considered Wyatt's question while he finished saddling up. "Except Hicks didn't have any gold on him when we found him, and even Vern couldn't drink away that much that fast. More'n likely this falls squarely on Baxter. At least I hope so. I'd hate to think we released an accomplice."

"I think you're right. Baxter had to be at the schoolhouse to drop the watch. He wouldn't have given it to a drunkard."

Mason looked relieved as he mounted. "We'll check at

the hotel to make sure Baxter stayed the night and then ride hard for Greenville, try to make up some time. The railroad grade'll get us there faster than the road."

Wyatt pointed toward the mill. "The quickest route is through open country. It'd give us a chance of cutting him off."

"You know the way?"

"In my sleep." Wyatt itched to loose Dusty. "We'll get him."

Mason nodded his approval. "But if you don't mind, I'll bring in a little higher help."

"Higher?"

Mason pointed upward. "God."

Charlotte couldn't dwell in emptiness. Somehow she had to find Wyatt and beg his forgiveness. Holly had been right. Charlotte should have told him how she felt. She should have shown it each and every day.

Well, God willing, she was going to start right now. If anyone knew where to find Wyatt, Mason would. So she woke Sasha from her nap, got her shoes on and headed for the sheriff's office.

The air still reeked of acrid smoke, though only wisps rose into the clear blue sky.

"Where, Mama?" Sasha trotted along obediently, probably hoping they were going to get candy at the general store.

"We're going to see Sheriff Wright."

"Why?"

The poor girl didn't understand, and Charlotte didn't see how she could explain without frightening her, so she kept her reply to the bare minimum. "I hope to catch your papa before he rides off on his horse."

"Hor-sey." Sasha skipped beside her, picking up on the one thing that excited her most.

Charlotte sighed. Before long, Sasha would beg to get back on a horse. It was natural she would, but it would still frighten Charlotte.

They soon reached the sheriff's office, but the door was locked.

In the middle of the day? Charlotte looked around. Maybe Mason was investigating the fire. Or he might have gone home. Even though the teacherage had survived the fire unscathed, Holly had wept over the loss of the school. Mason was the kind of man who'd stay close to his wife when she was hurting.

Though Charlotte hated to intrude, her mission was urgent. Wyatt could be across the county by now. Holly would understand.

While keeping a tight hold of Sasha's hand, Charlotte turned and headed for her friend's house.

God? Wyatt stumbled over the concept of praying for every little thing, but after the fire, he knew prayer could be answered.

"You always pray for help in your investigations?" Wyatt asked as they rode side by side through town after Ned Minor confirmed that Baxter left late this morning.

"You bet. God's the best help a man can get. He sees everything and knows just what to do."

Wyatt was skeptical. "And He answers you? Every time?"

"I didn't used to think so. In fact, I'd pretty much run from Him since my first wife died. Blamed myself because I was gone when the homestead was attacked. I lost her and—" His voice cracked. "Phoebe was with child."

Wyatt caught the quiver in the man's voice, and he looked away. Mason had lost even more than Wyatt had. While Charlotte and Sasha had never been in danger in the fire,

Mason had lost his wife and baby. If anyone could understand the hurt Wyatt was going through, Mason could.

"But that's the past." Mason cleared his throat. "And God blessed me with a second chance. Can't believe it sometimes—" he chuckled "—but I sure am mighty grateful. I know God's behind it all, and I'm doing my best to trust Him with things."

Wyatt mulled Mason's words as they neared the mill. The man had a real, practical faith and didn't claim he was perfect. In fact, he made it sound like God would answer even though he wasn't always centered on the straight and narrow. The idea was a breath of fresh air, and considering Wyatt had promised to do whatever God asked if He would spare Charlotte and Sasha from the fire, he warmed to this new way of thinking about God, as if an ordinary man could partner with the Creator of the universe.

It gave him strength. "We'll cross here and then head west."

The new footbridge easily handled their weight. Once they crossed, Mason brought his horse up alongside.

"Before we head out, I gotta know if you found something on Baxter that you haven't told me."

Wyatt had no reason to hold anything back now. "From what I can tell, the orphans that end up in his orphanage disappear in quick order."

"Disappear?"

"He says they're sent to families, but I've scoured the countryside and can't find a single one of those families except maybe Star Plains farm. Found a scrawny boy there. Scared half to death and struggling to do a man-size job on a Sunday. That doesn't sound like it'd fit that orphan society's rules."

"What'd the owner say?"

"Didn't hunt him out. I was afraid the boy would get

in trouble, so I left well enough alone. The man probably wouldn't have talked to me anyway."

Mason pondered his words, and Wyatt could see that steely determination set in. "You think Baxter's selling the kids?"

"Selling. Slavery. Call it what you want. Baxter takes in pretty near every orphan that comes to Greenville and near as I can tell, none of them are ever seen again."

Mason spurred his horse to a trot. "Then let's get to business."

While they rode across the open country, Wyatt pondered Mason's words of faith. The man was honest and trustworthy, the kind of friend Wyatt had missed since the war. Moreover, Mason trusted Wyatt—after clocking him, that is.

Wyatt grinned. He deserved to get some sense knocked into him, and there was no better man to do it than Mason.

He eyed the sheriff. He was tough as nails yet could melt at one look from his new bride, all while handling a rambunctious boy. Mason had everything Wyatt wanted. And faith, to boot.

Wyatt gnawed on that as he slowed Dusty to a walk.

Mason came up alongside. "Where now?"

"We'll drive hard until we reach the creek and then let the horses have a swallow before driving hard again."

Mason nodded, and they took off, side by side when possible, Wyatt leading the way when necessary. With every hoofbeat, Mason's words pounded into Wyatt's head. *God knows what to do.* Could He straighten out the mess Wyatt had made? Could He show Wyatt how to stay in Evans Grove? When Wyatt thought Charlotte was trapped in the fire, he'd known he loved her. The thought of his wife and child dying tore him up worse than anything he'd ever experienced. Yet he'd pushed Charlotte away when she wanted more. He'd given her no hope. He'd left that letter.

The words he'd scrawled burned into his head. *Now that the job's done, I'm leaving, just like we agreed.* They were cruel, heartless and a lie. Something had changed in him, and he no longer wanted to run. San Francisco no longer beckoned. He didn't care if he ever saw it. What could a city offer compared to the love of a wife and daughter? Nothing. Not one thing.

With all his heart he wanted to stay in Evans Grove, but how could she ever take him back after his cruel words? And anyway, once she learned he'd burned women and children, she would run from him. He couldn't keep that a secret now that Miss Ward knew.

It was too much to hope Charlotte could love him. She was a good, kind woman who'd known the loss of parents and a husband, yet hoped for the future. What kept her walking forward? Was it the same faith that Mason had expressed?

By the time they reached the creek and rested the horses, Wyatt wondered if faith was what he was missing. He'd had it once, years ago, but the war had taken it away. He glanced at Mason. Would the man understand?

"Sorry again that I had to get rough with you back at the fire," Mason said after a long draw on his canteen. He wiped his mouth on his sleeve and offered a drink to Wyatt.

"No, thanks." Here was the perfect opportunity. Wyatt rubbed his sore jaw. "You got a solid swing. Reminds me of a friend in the war." A friend who'd died in his arms.

"Must have been awful." Mason didn't look at Wyatt, but the set of his jaw said he understood.

"That's one way to describe it. Did some things I'm not proud of."

"We all have."

But this wasn't the same. Killers didn't become deputies. Miss Ward might have told Mason some of it, but surely she hadn't told him all. Once Mason knew everything, he'd ask for the badge back. But it was time to come clean. Wyatt had carried this burden for too long. Before he faced Baxter and risked his life, he had to get this off his chest.

"I was with Sherman." Wyatt paused, but Mason didn't react. "Marched with him through Georgia. Fought to capture Atlanta, and then moved south to Savannah. We stole what we wanted, slaughtered the livestock and set fire to everything that would burn."

Still Mason stayed silent.

Though every word hurt, Wyatt had to continue. Confession wasn't supposed to be easy. "I lit my share."

Mason finally faced him, his eyes expressionless. "You didn't light the one today."

"You don't understand." Wyatt gritted his teeth. "Everyone was supposed to be gone, but I saw them. Women and children. Old men. Innocent people. I don't know exactly who, but I saw their shadows in the flames. I watched them die. I'm responsible. I killed them." The words brought a cold sweat even on a hot day.

Mason kept his silence. He could have said what the pastors tried to tell Wyatt, that he'd been seeing things, that the flames played tricks on his eyes, but Wyatt knew what he'd seen and heard. He knew the price he had to pay.

"I thought…" Wyatt choked on the words. "I thought Charlotte and Sasha would have to pay for my sins, that they would die because I'd killed the innocent."

Wyatt couldn't look at Mason, couldn't see the man's disappointment and revulsion. He waited for Mason's recriminations, but only the wind and the babble of the creek pierced the air. Long minutes passed, but the sheriff said nothing.

"You see why I had to leave," Wyatt said flatly. "Charlotte and Sasha deserve better."

He heard Mason set down his canteen and draw a breath, but the sheriff didn't speak right away.

"Did you know that Jesus forgave murderers?" Mason's voice was rock-solid.

The unexpected words shot through Wyatt's head. He thought back but couldn't remember that in the Bible stories of his childhood. "He did?"

"Yep. He forgave the men who killed him."

The pounding of Wyatt's heart couldn't blot out the truth of Mason's words. Jesus forgave the men who'd killed him. He'd hung on the cross and asked Father God to forgive them. Who else could do such a thing? Surely not the people Wyatt had killed.

He shuddered. "The people I killed wouldn't forgive me, even if they had a chance. I can't forgive myself."

Mason spoke slowly, each word hitting with force. "That's hardest of all to get past. I hung on to a pile of guilt. Thought I didn't protect my wife. Blamed myself. See, it was easier to hang on to all that guilt than to let it go."

Wyatt understood what Mason went through. He'd experienced it, too. "That's how I felt when I thought Charlotte and Sasha were in the schoolhouse. That's how I still feel about what happened in Atlanta."

Mason acknowledged his words. "Thing is, I couldn't move on until I made things right with God. It's the only way. He'll forgive any mess we've made as long as we're sick about doing it and don't want to do it again."

"But it won't bring back the people who died."

"Nothing will. But if they had Jesus as their Lord, then they're in heaven with Him now. I know my Phoebe and our baby are there."

Wyatt grappled with what Mason was saying. The man had lost his wife and child. Wyatt would have given up living if Charlotte and Sasha had died. Yet Mason persevered, became stronger and even found a new family.

"How? How did you do it?"

"By getting God's forgiveness and letting Jesus lead the way." Mason clapped him on the shoulder. "Trust me. There's not a thing you've done that God can't forgive. Jesus already paid the price for our sins. All you have to do is let Him be your commander. Put all your faith and trust in Him, and He'll lead you to the right path."

With shocking clarity, Wyatt knew Mason was right. He wanted what Mason had. He wanted to move past his terrible sins. But… "Will Charlotte forgive me when she knows the truth?"

"I don't know, but women have a right uncanny way of setting aside our faults. Amazes me every time."

Wyatt had to cling to that hope. He knew he couldn't go on the way he had since the war, slowly dying inside. He needed the new life that Mason had.

"What do I do?"

Mason swallowed. "I'm no preacher, but it seems to me you just gotta get on your knees and speak man-to-man with God. Tell Him what you did wrong and surrender to Him." He stepped away, leaving Wyatt in private.

Wyatt didn't hesitate. After removing his hat, he dropped to his knees and spilled out everything to God.

"I'm sick about it," he said after choking out the terrible deeds he'd done in the war. "I wanted to be a good man. I wanted to do what was right, but then my friends got killed, and hatred got hold of me. I stopped feeling anything, and when they ordered us to burn, I lit everything on fire. I thought revenge would take away the pain of losing the people I loved. When I got Margaret's letter, saying she'd married someone else, I got angry. Then the Rebels killed my friends. We'd grown up together. I convinced them to join the army. They had wives and girls back home and whole lives ahead of them. I blamed the enemy. I wanted them to suffer, but I didn't expect women and children to die. Can You forgive such cruelty?"

Wyatt hadn't wept since his best friend died in his arms, but tears flowed now as he choked out each word.

"Mason says You can. That You already have. I don't understand it. I don't deserve it. But if You can find a way…I'm begging You. I'll do whatever You want. You're in charge from now on. Take what's left of me, and do what You want."

Exhausted, he sank onto his heels. The wind smoothed across his face, ruffling his hair and drying the sweat from his brow. The creek still rushed past. Dusty nickered and stomped impatiently. Everything was still the same outside, but not inside. The darkness in Wyatt's heart had been scoured out, the slate wiped clean. It still hurt, but in a good way.

He lifted his gaze and saw Mason readying the horses. Time to finish this job. As Wyatt slapped his hat on his head and stood to meet the task at hand, he knew that the outcome was no longer in his hands.

Strangely enough, that felt right.

Chapter Twenty-Two

"Wyatt is with Mason." Holly poured tea into her dainty porcelain teacups. "He figured they'd be heading for Greenville. I'm sure they'll be back as soon as they can."

Charlotte couldn't sit still for tea. She paced back and forth across the teacherage's tiny parlor, which, despite Mason and Liam moving in, still reflected Holly's tastes.

"Mason will come back, but not Wyatt. He wrote that he's leaving." Charlotte had already explained Wyatt's letter to Holly, but her friend didn't seem to grasp what Charlotte was saying. Maybe she was still reeling from the loss of the schoolhouse.

"Yes, he left with Mason." Holly motioned to the empty chair across from her, inviting Charlotte to sit.

"That's not what I mean." Charlotte withdrew the note from her pocket. At first she'd wanted to burn it, but then she realized it might be all she'd ever have from Wyatt. Even though the words hurt, they were his. "He said he's leaving forever."

Holly eyed the folded paper. "Are you sure you want me to read it?"

Charlotte's eyes misted. "There's nothing intimate in it." That thought made her throat constrict again.

"Perhaps you misunderstood him."

"I hope I did. Tell me what you think." Charlotte handed Holly the note and nervously rubbed her arms as she watched Sasha scribble on one of the slates from the school. A pile of them sat beside the table.

"The slates survived the fire?" Charlotte asked.

Holly looked up from the note. "They weren't at the school. I decided to bring them home last night for a good scrubbing."

Charlotte felt a twinge of guilt. Here she'd been so concerned about her own troubles that she'd ignored her friend's distress. "Oh, Holly, what can I do to help? You'll need somewhere to hold classes. My house isn't large enough, but you can use my yard in fair weather."

Holly shook her head. "Pauline already insisted we use the town hall to finish out the school year. Fortunately, school is almost done. Most of the older children are already busy on their farms. So, in a way, it's a blessing that if this had to happen, at least it happened when it did."

In comparison to her friends, Charlotte's troubles appeared small. Holly had lost her school and Rebecca her home. "Where will Rebecca and Heidi stay? I have a bed in the loft."

Holly's lips curved into a smile. "An anonymous benefactor paid for them to stay at the hotel. Isn't it marvelous how people step up when the need arises?"

Charlotte had to agree. In her hour of need, Wyatt had stepped up to help her keep Sasha. That's all she'd asked of him, and he'd fulfilled his end of the bargain and more, for he hadn't kept her money. Instead, like that anonymous donor who paid for Rebecca's stay at the hotel, Wyatt had given that money back to her by putting it into a trust for Sasha in Mr. Brooks's bank. He even promised to send her money. Yes, Wyatt had stepped up. He'd done his part. She was the one who wanted to change the terms of their bargain.

Holly finished reading and folded the paper. "Oh, Charlotte." She didn't condemn, but Charlotte felt the sting anyhow.

"I did wrong by marrying the way I did. I see that now. It wasn't fair to anyone." She bit her lip and glanced at her daughter, who was transfixed by what she was drawing. "How will I tell her?"

"You'll have to find a way."

Charlotte knew Holly was right, but she wasn't willing to accept that she'd done all she could. "I won't have to if I can convince him to stay. I *have* to convince him."

Holly sighed deeply. "Do you love him?"

That most direct of questions reminded Charlotte of Holly's earlier advice to tell Wyatt how she felt. She perched on the edge of the chair. "I can't imagine living without him. It's like a whole part of me has been torn away. It hurts so bad I can't bear it. Is that love?"

Holly smiled. "I felt the same way about Mason. Every time he backed off or turned away, I thought I would die."

"But he came around and realized he loved you."

Holly reached across the table and grasped her hands. "Wyatt will too. Give him time."

Charlotte shot to her feet. "I don't have time. He's gone, and he's not coming back." The bleakness of that realization sank in. "You read his letter."

"I read the words," Holly acknowledged, "but I also read the man."

"What do you mean?" If anyone knew Wyatt, it should be her. She'd spent the most time with him. She'd felt his arms around her, the gentle heart beneath the fierce exterior.

"Mason looks at me exactly the way Wyatt looks at you."

Charlotte caught her breath. She'd heard Holly say this over and over but never quite believed it. "You mean…?"

Holly nodded. "He loves you. Hopelessly and madly."

Still the fist squeezed her stomach tight. "Then why would he leave?"

Holly didn't say anything for a long time. Maybe she couldn't answer that, either. Charlotte knit her fingers together and watched Sasha. She'd always wanted a child. She'd prayed for a child. She just hadn't expected to get only a child. The most important part was missing. She and Sasha needed a family. They needed Wyatt.

"I used to think I had everything figured out." Holly spoke softly, her gaze faraway. "I even had the audacity to believe I could mold Mason's heart. What false pride. None of us can truly change another person. Only God can do that. We can only accept each other as we are and love the best we can."

Holly's words stung Charlotte. She'd failed Charles and then Wyatt in just that way.

"Mason was still struggling with his wife's death," Holly continued. "He blamed himself."

Charlotte flushed in shame. Charles had too. And Wyatt struggled with nightmares. From the little he'd said, something from the war tormented him. He was hurting. He needed to talk about what had happened, but she hadn't pressed hard enough. She'd let him turn away and keep it bottled up inside, just like she had with Charles. If she'd urged her first husband to confide in her, they might have had a real marriage. And now she'd gone and done the same thing with Wyatt.

"Love Wyatt for who he is now," Holly said. "Pray for him. If Wyatt is meant for you, God will bring you together."

Charlotte hoped she was right.

"It might take time and patience," Holly cautioned.

Time, patience and faith. All were impossible, perhaps the last most of all. Charlotte dropped to her chair again. "He doesn't believe in God."

Holly didn't look shocked. "Maybe God is working with him right now."

"I doubt it." Charlotte hung her head. "He won't even say grace before a meal. He turns away when I mention God." She choked down the clot in her throat. "How can God reach him if he won't listen?" And how could they ever have a real marriage without faith at its core? She bounded up again in frustration. "Maybe I'm reaching for something that just isn't there. Maybe our marriage *is* nothing more than a business transaction."

"I don't believe that, and you don't, either."

"Maybe I should." Charlotte coiled a lock of hair around her finger and yanked. Physical pain was easier than this emotional torment.

"You've just hit a rough patch." Holly smiled softly. "You know, Wyatt's a lot like Mason. It's going to take time and prayer on your part."

Charlotte knew her friend spoke the truth, but she couldn't just sit and wait. In a split second, she made her decision. "I'm going to Greenville."

"No, you're not." Holly sprang to her feet and halted Charlotte's pacing. "You can't."

"But don't you see? I have to. It's the only way to save our marriage." The pieces all clicked into place. "I'll take the evening stage."

"No, you won't." Holly spoke firmly, and Charlotte knew she meant business.

Still, she couldn't let Wyatt leave without knowing how she felt. She'd made up her mind. "I must. Will you watch Sasha until I return? I'll bring over clean clothes and everything she needs."

Without waiting for an answer, Charlotte headed for the door, but Holly got there first.

"Listen to what you just said. You're leaving your daughter? You can't. It's crazy."

Deep down, Charlotte knew Holly was right, but she hated to admit she'd lost control. Her entire world was caving in, and she felt certain that if she didn't do something, she'd lose the man she'd come to love. "I can't let him go."

Holly shook her head and pushed her back into the room. For such a tiny thing, she had surprising strength. "Now, sit down and listen to me." She was using her schoolmarm voice now. "You are not going to shirk your responsibilities here to go to Greenville."

"But—"

Holly cut her off. "Mason and Wyatt are pursuing a criminal, a dangerous criminal who was willing to kill children by lighting the schoolhouse on fire. Do you think they want you in the middle of their investigation? If they have to worry about your safety, Felix Baxter could get away."

"Felix Baxter?" Her eyes widened at the name of the man who'd hired Wyatt to bring the orphans to Greenville. "He's the one who lit the fire?"

"They think so."

"He's the one who hired Wyatt." Charlotte's heart sank into the pit of her stomach. "And Wyatt refused to finish the job. Oh, no. Mr. Baxter must be furious with him." Fear sucked all the strength from her legs and she collapsed onto the chair again. "If Mr. Baxter set the fire and was willing to harm children…" She couldn't bring herself to say the rest, but they both knew.

Baxter wouldn't hesitate to kill lawmen.

Baxter's orphanage was located in a three-story brick building off the main street in Greenville. Baxter had money.

Wyatt would give him that. It cost a pretty penny to build a building like this. Even in this last of the larger towns before the frontier, it looked too big. The forbidding facade with its curtained windows betrayed nothing suspicious. A passerby would assume the prosperous owner kept a neat and tidy orphan house.

"Think he's here?" Mason asked.

"Best find out now." Wyatt ran up the five steps, his boots barely touching the concrete.

The solid oak front door was shut. Wyatt pressed the latch and was surprised when it opened. He started to step inside, but Mason halted him.

"You know where his office is located?"

Wyatt nodded. "Straight ahead. Last door on the left. We'll go there first."

Mason took his gun out of his holster, and Wyatt followed suit. Wyatt had pegged Baxter as a coward, but yellowbellies were even more dangerous with a gun because they fired at anyone and anything.

Since they couldn't move silently, they moved fast. Wyatt's pulse pounded, and his senses heightened as the two men rushed down the hallway like a stampede of wild horses. He felt every loose board, heard every wagon rolling down the street, smelled the sharp mix of varnish, coal dust and bleach.

Farther inside he heard drawers open and shut, muttered oaths and the frantic bangs of a panicked man. Baxter. Hopefully, he was alone.

Wyatt outdistanced Mason. If anyone had to kill or be killed, it was going to be him, not a man with a wife and son back home.

Fear sucked Charlotte into its ugly grasp. Wyatt could die never knowing she loved him. Why hadn't she realized it sooner, so she could have told him over and over until he believed her? Why had she held back, in her head and in her heart? All the things that she'd thought obstacles became trivial.

He might die.

Holly drew her back to the table. "They're smart, strong men."

Which didn't matter in a gunfight. Charlotte felt helpless. "What can we do? I can't just sit here knowing Wyatt's in trouble and do nothing. I don't know how you can be so calm."

"Oh, I'm not calm inside. Not entirely. I know Mason is in the Lord's hands, but I do pray he returns safely."

Charlotte struggled to accept Holly's words. "How can you let him walk into danger?"

Holly laughed. "I don't *let* him do anything. Mason is his own man. He has a job to do, and yes, it could be dangerous. I have to rely a lot on the Lord."

"And that works?"

"You'd be surprised." She extended her hands. "Shall we pray for their safety?"

Charlotte could do nothing else. Every other option had been removed. So she grasped Holly's hands and bowed her head.

"Father in heaven," Holly prayed, "You hold each of us in Your hand. We, Your children, lift our voices in prayer, trusting that, as Your Word states, where two or more are gathered in Your name, You will be also. So we ask in faith that You be with Mason and Wyatt. Guide and protect them from evil, and bring them home to their families." She squeezed Charlotte's hands. "And help my friend to know that You are at her side, helping to bear the burden."

God at her side? Impossible. Why would the all-powerful Creator be with her, a terribly flawed person? Charlotte prayed, attended worship and listened carefully to the sermons. She tried to live as the Bible instructed. She'd been baptized and accepted Christ into her heart, but never had she considered that God would be right next to her. Yet after Holly said the final amen, Charlotte felt a surprising sense of security, like when she'd curled into her papa's arms as a child and all her worries vanished. In his arms, she'd felt secure and safe. She'd known everything would turn out all right. Could her Heavenly Father be like that?

For the first time in her life, Charlotte suspected He could.

Baxter threw his hands in the air when Wyatt leveled his pistol at him.

Mason followed, his gun also at the ready.

"You're under arrest," Mason growled, and Wyatt sensed the sheriff had kept his anger under control until that moment.

"For what?" Baxter whined.

Mason didn't hesitate. "Arson, destruction of property and attempted murder."

Baxter's eyes rounded. "I didn't try to kill anyone. That's a false charge. I want my lawyer."

Wyatt held his gun on Baxter while Mason circled the massive oak desk. Papers spilled off the top, and an open satchel held more documents. Probably money too. Baxter wasn't the type to leave without grabbing his cash.

"We'll send for your lawyer from the jailhouse," Mason informed him as he placed the handcuffs on Baxter.

Baxter managed to work up his indignation. "My friends will hear of this, and you'll pay. The mayor won't stand for it. Neither will the city council. They're not going to let you arrest a law-abiding, taxpaying citizen."

"I don't care who you know," Mason growled. "You're

coming to the jail for questioning and will be held there until your hearing before the judge."

As Wyatt looked at the papers scattered on the desk and the files spilling out of the cabinet drawers, he got an idea.

"You could answer a few questions right now, Mr. Baxter." To emphasize the point, Wyatt pointed his pistol between Baxter's eyes.

The man began to sweat and tremble. "Lower that thing. It's not like I can go anywhere since your sheriff has me trussed up like a common criminal."

"Oh, you're not common, are you, Mr. Baxter?" Wyatt lowered the gun, but kept it at the ready. "I'm sure these papers will tell us a lot about your operation here."

Baxter paled.

Mason picked up on Wyatt's train of thought. "Suppose we go through these papers right now, before heading to the jailhouse?"

Baxter licked his lips. "Now, that's not necessary."

"It wouldn't be," said Wyatt, "if you'd tell us a few things. For instance, how many orphans do you have here right now?"

Baxter looked relieved at the question. "Just one, an older boy. He showed up today and is more trouble than he's worth. Please, take him off my hands."

"We will," Wyatt assured him.

Mason cocked his head toward Wyatt. "While Mr. Reed fetches the boy, you can answer a few questions about where you were this morning around eight-thirty."

Wyatt hated to miss this, but Mason seemed in full control of Baxter. He scoured the ground floor, opening every door to find only empty offices, the kitchen and a dining area. No sign of a boy. The bedrooms must be on the two upper floors.

He headed for the stairway at the end of the hallway.

The door at the base was locked, but the key hung on a nail pounded into the frame. Wyatt fit the key in the lock and turned it, but before he could touch the doorknob, a tall and lanky boy of around fourteen burst out of the stairwell. While Wyatt recovered his balance, the boy dashed down the hall and out the back door.

Stunned, Wyatt stared at the departing boy. His hair was the same color as Heidi's, but it was curly. Could this be Jakob?

"Hey, come back," Wyatt yelled. He raced after the lad and pushed out the same door. It opened onto an alley bordered by privies and outbuildings.

Wyatt looked left and then right, but the lad had vanished. A toppled pile of garbage indicated the boy had headed to the right. Wyatt bounded down the stairs two at a time and raced down the alley. His longer strides should close the distance between them quickly, but when he reached the busy street, he realized he'd lost the boy. Between the pedestrians, wagons, carriages, buggies and countless buildings and alleys, he stood no chance of finding the boy without a full-scale search.

Wyatt growled with frustration. Why had the kid run? He'd wanted to help, not hurt him. Then he looked down. He was still holding his gun.

An oath bubbled up, but he stifled it. He was a new man now, one who didn't let foul language cross his lips no matter how angry he got.

He'd let the boy get away, but at least they had Baxter. He hurried back to the interrogation room to find the man looking cowed.

"Did you find the boy?" Mason asked.

"Slipped out the back and vanished into the crowds. By now, he could be anywhere. If we want to find him, we'll have to search the whole city."

Mason frowned. "Don't suppose you got a look at him."

"Not much of one, but it could be Jakob."

Mason turned back to Baxter. "What's the boy's name?"

"I don't know. He just showed up asking if the train with the orphans had arrived yet, and I sent him upstairs to wait."

It had to be Jakob.

"Did you tell him the orphans were in Evans Grove?" Mason demanded.

"Not exactly," Baxter sniveled. "I still expected them to come here."

Mason's gaze narrowed. "Because of the fire?" When the sheriff got angry, he could be terrifying.

Baxter blanched and then rallied. "You can't prove I was anywhere near that fire. I left last night on the stage, like I told Reed."

"Too bad you didn't tell the hotel clerk. He said you stayed over."

"I saw you in the dining room," Wyatt prodded, hoping to get Baxter to admit what they'd already learned from the hotel's dining staff. "You were talking to someone. Who?"

"Who I dine with is none of your business."

"It is when you're involved with a crime." Mason's jaw tensed. "What did you and Miss Ward discuss?"

Baxter visibly shrank. "Nothing important. She just didn't want the orphans to stay in Evans Grove."

"And you figured you could help her." Mason glared. "Did she suggest you burn down the school?"

"I told you. It must have been an accident. I wasn't anywhere near that building."

That's when Mason pulled the ace from his pocket. He turned over the watchcase so Baxter could see the initials. "We found your watch next to the schoolhouse steps."

Baxter sputtered. "I—I must have set it down and some-one stole it. That's who dropped it there."

Wyatt knew a flimsy excuse when he heard one. "Like someone from the saloon?"

Baxter brightened. "That's it. I met a man there. What was his name? Can't recall, but he looked like one of those professional gamblers."

Wyatt smelled the stench of lies, but it was Mason who took control.

"You can tell that to the judge," Mason said. "You can also tell him why you didn't fetch your horse until just after the fire was started this morning."

With every word, Baxter cowered lower and lower. All his alibis had been dashed. The evidence nailed him to the crime, but Baxter was a slippery crook. The moment Wyatt thought they had him, the man came up with a new angle.

"Maybe we can work out a little deal." Baxter's grin made Wyatt sick.

"No deals," Wyatt growled, "not for child killers."

"I never killed anyone," Baxter shot back. "Unlike some people here."

The accusation stung, and before today it would have started the nightmares, but Wyatt had made Jesus his commanding officer. Mason said the slate was now wiped clean. Maybe Baxter deserved the same opportunity.

"Speak your piece," Wyatt said.

Baxter stood a little taller, confident now that he could weasel out of trouble. "There are others."

"Others?" Mason yanked Baxter so he looked into his eyes. "Accomplices?"

"Not accomplices. Other orphans."

Wyatt had been right. His blood heated, and he grabbed Baxter by the collar. "How many and where are they?"

Baxter coughed and gasped until Mason made Wyatt let go. He wanted to throttle the rat, but Mason had made it clear that the rule of law must prevail.

"Well?" Mason prodded. "Out with it. How many?"

Baxter acted like he was counting. "Maybe twenty or so."

Twenty orphans?

"Where are they?" Wyatt demanded. "I know they weren't placed around here because I checked."

Baxter's lips curled into a cruel grin. "That's where the deal comes in. You let me go, and I'll tell you where to find them."

Wyatt looked at Mason. The sheriff was not the type of man to make deals with criminals. But if he didn't, twenty children would suffer. He surveyed the scattered papers.

"It must all be written down."

Baxter's grin never faded. "The only place it's written is in my head."

The weasel had them in a bind.

Chapter Twenty-Three

Since Charlotte didn't know when Wyatt was returning, she filled the time with cleaning and cooking and playing with Sasha. But when the sun dipped below the horizon and Sasha drifted off to sleep, the night became too quiet to bear.

That's when she took her cue from Holly. Not from what her friend said but from what she did. Holly acted on faith. So, too, would Charlotte, and there was one thing that needed to be done before she and Wyatt could become a real family.

So she balanced a lamp in one hand and climbed the ladder to the loft. She passed the bed with its memories of Wyatt and went directly to Charles's trunk. In the past, she couldn't face giving away his clothes, but there were still townspeople in need after the flood. These clothes could be put to good use elsewhere. She'd ask Pauline after Sunday worship.

To her surprise, Charles's clothes no longer generated the ache they had before. She could look on them knowing that Charles would approve. He'd been generous with his time and skills, always helping out in the community. He would be pleased his clothes went to the needy.

Charlotte packed the candles, too. Though she could have used them, they still carried too much meaning. That left

Gloria's photograph and the baby spoon. It was too late to bury them with Charles, but he was with Gloria and his son now. Knowing that, she could look at Gloria's image without the sense of inadequacy and resentment that she'd carried for too long.

"He loved you so much," she whispered before putting the daguerreotype and spoon into her apron pocket.

After descending the ladder, she walked to the table and opened Charles's family Bible. Pulling the ink pot and a pen from the desk, she noted the date of Charles's death and the death of his son. Lastly, she tucked Gloria's photograph in the back.

This belonged in Charles's family. He'd spoken of a brother in Missouri. She'd search correspondence for an address and send the Bible to him. Perhaps Mel Hutchinson could meld the spoon into a memorial marker for the baby, which she'd put on Charles and Gloria's graves.

Then, if Wyatt returned, they could start anew.

Mason gave no ground to Baxter. "If you tell us where to find the orphans, I'll put in a good word with the judge."

"Not good enough," Baxter insisted.

Wyatt would have twisted the man's arm until he screamed in pain, but Mason used more civilized tactics.

He yanked Baxter toward the office door. "Might as well get you in jail then. I'm getting hungry." In an aside to Wyatt that Baxter could easily hear, he added, "Sure hope they've solved their rat problem. Those train robbers I brought here last month got so sick from the bites we weren't sure they'd make it to trial."

Wyatt cocked his gun. "Maybe we'd better put him out of his misery now."

"Now, hold on," Baxter squealed, digging in his heels. "I can be reasonable."

Mason paused. "I'm listening."

Baxter licked his lips. "You promise to talk to the judge?"

Mason nodded.

Baxter wasn't finished. "And you'll make sure Reed doesn't shoot me in the back?"

Wyatt released the hammer.

Even with that threat removed, Baxter's hands trembled. "You gotta understand that they're not gonna want to let 'em go." His polished speech vanished. Apparently, Baxter didn't come from any highborn background. "And they're gonna deny they got anything to do with me or orphans."

Wyatt had no doubt of that. Baxter was dealing with the type of men who enslaved children. That type of no-good scoundrel had no conscience.

"Let us worry about that," Mason snapped. "You tell us what you know."

Baxter drew a deep breath. For a second, Wyatt thought the man would renege, but he finally named several mining operations in Colorado as well as three of the larger farms in the area, including Star Plains.

Wyatt thought back to the plow boy's fearful glances toward the grove of trees. He'd rescue that boy first.

Baxter then admitted that he kept a ledger detailing where every child had been sold. The buyers were listed as acronyms, which Baxter deciphered. Only nine places, but they ranged across a hundred miles. It would take time and effort to find those orphans.

Hours later, as he and Mason pieced it together over supper in the hotel dining room, Wyatt finally came up with a gut-wrenching total.

"There's eighteen of them still underage." Wyatt rubbed his head in frustration. He might be a new man, but the plight of those poor kids weighed on him. "Eighteen. How am I going to get them all back?"

"You?" Mason eyed him gravely. "This matter crosses state and territory lines. Only a federal marshal can handle it."

"But it could take days to get a marshal on the job. Meanwhile, those children are in danger, and once the men who bought them find out Baxter is in jail, they'll get rid of those kids as fast as they can. If we wait for the marshal, we'll never find them."

Mason strummed his fingers on the tabletop. "The only solution then is to get you named deputy marshal. For that, we'll need to see a judge."

Wyatt stood. "Let's go."

Mason didn't budge. "Even if you are authorized to go after the orphans, what do you intend to do when you find them?"

"Free them."

"And then?"

"Bring them home."

Mason tapped sugar into his coffee, a luxury Wyatt never indulged in. "They're orphans. They don't have a home."

In Wyatt's rush to solve the problem, he hadn't fully considered the outcome. "Baxter's orphanage is empty."

"And who will run it?"

The only staff the man had hired was a housekeeper, who cooked and cleaned when children were in residence. According to the ledger, no orphan stayed there more than a few days.

"Until we find another solution, the housekeeper could stay on." Wyatt knew that wasn't a perfect solution. Aside from the problem of money, the woman would be spooked when she learned her employer had been arrested. "Maybe Miss Sterling could talk to the man who runs that orphan society of hers. Maybe they'd take them in."

"Maybe. If the judge can get you named deputy marshal, then I'll have a talk with her when I get back to Evans Grove." Mason leaned back with an exhausted sigh. "The deputy sheriff said Judge Broadside is in town, but we'll probably have to wait until Monday morning to talk to him."

"Monday? We can't wait that long. We need to find him now. Tonight." Wyatt rose again. "Where's he staying?"

Mason pointed behind Wyatt to a nearby table. Sure enough, there sat the judge, eating dinner with an impeccably dressed businessman, whose back was to them. "I suggest we wait until he's done eating, though."

Wyatt didn't wait well. He strummed his fingers. He tapped his toe. He drank far too much coffee.

Mason seemed to be enjoying Wyatt's impatience. "We'll have to spend the night in any case." He leveled his piercing gaze right at Wyatt. "I suggest we attend worship tomorrow. You and those kids could use the extra blessing."

"Well, for the orphans, maybe." The old worry tumbled in Wyatt's gut. Would any preacher even let him in the door? God himself might strike the church with a lightning bolt.

Mason laughed. "Don't look like you've been sentenced to hang. A little preaching and praying will do you a heap of good. It's best to have God on your side." He grew serious again. "Baxter was right about one thing. The people who took the orphans won't give them up without a fight. I doubt they'll even admit they have any orphans, because it'd mean admitting they did wrong. Men like that will shoot before asking questions."

Mason was warning him he could die, but Wyatt knew that.

"I have to do this. I've never been more sure of anything in my life. Don't you see? It's my penance."

Mason's left eyebrow lifted. "God forgave you when you repented and confessed."

"I know, but that doesn't mean I don't have to pay a penalty. Every sin has its price. This is mine."

"What about Charlotte and Sasha?"

He hadn't had a lot of time to think about it, but deep down he knew the answer. "I'm leaving, just like we planned." There was just one problem. That letter of his would have cut the ties, but he'd gone and asked Amelia Hicks to tell Charlotte that he'd be back. Now she'd be expecting him. He'd have to break it off all over again. Still, it had to be done. "It's better that way," he stated flatly.

"Better for who?"

"For them." In Wyatt's line of work, emotions could get a man killed. He couldn't afford emotion, and neither could Charlotte and Sasha. "They've just lost a husband and father. Better they don't get too attached, in case I don't make it back."

Instead of criticizing Wyatt's choice, Mason nodded. "You'll still need to talk to Charlotte."

Wyatt knew that. He also knew it wouldn't be easy.

Judge Broadside set down his napkin. Supper was over.

Wyatt stood. "Let's go see the judge."

The businessman across from Judge Broadside pushed back his chair, rose and shook the judge's hand. When he turned to leave, both Wyatt and Mason froze.

What on earth was Curtis Brooks doing here?

Reverend Turner's words during his Sunday sermon touched Charlotte deeper than they ever had before. When he said that God made straight the path for those who put their trust in Him, she was sure He'd bring Wyatt back to her.

"It's all going to work out for the best," she told Holly.

As usual, the orphans congregated to catch up on all that had happened. Today they had a lot to talk about after the fire. So did the adults. Everyone was still buzzing. Well, everyone except Miss Ward, who looked strangely subdued. She'd hurried past Holly and Charlotte without a word. Small blessing! The rest of the congregation more than made up for Beatrice. Several stopped Charlotte to tell her how brave Wyatt had been when he thought the children were trapped inside. Apparently, he'd tried to storm into the schoolhouse, and it took several men to hold him back.

Charlotte had nearly burst with pride for him. The town had adopted him as one of their own. Now, if he could only see that. She'd have to tell him when he came back. If he came back.

She had to stop herself. The future was in God's hands. She'd placed it there, and, as Reverend Turner had said, there was no sense taking it back.

As they watched Rebecca talk with the pastor, Holly nudged her. "I got to thinking last night. You know how Rebecca lost everything in the fire?"

Charlotte nodded, not sure what Holly was getting at.

"All her lovely dresses." Holly sighed. "Gone. She only has the dress she's wearing."

Charlotte saw where this was headed. "You'd like to give her the dress I'm making for you."

Holly grinned. "If you can make it fit. She is a lot taller."

Charlotte had to smile at her friend's generous spirit. "There should be just enough fabric."

"Good." Holly squeezed her hand. "Thank you. It means a lot to me. Let's tell her now. Why don't you and Sasha come for Sunday dinner this afternoon? Perhaps you can fit her then."

Rebecca teared up when Charlotte and Holly gave her the news. "That's so generous of you." She mustered a weak smile. "Maybe it's the start of good things. Maybe your husbands will find Jakob in Greenville."

"We can certainly pray about it," Holly urged.

Rebecca smiled demurely, but she looked as skeptical as Charlotte had been yesterday. "At least I've talked Mr. Armstrong into letting me stay a little longer, until we have some idea what happened to Jakob." She glanced at Heidi and nibbled her lip. "If only…"

She didn't have to finish for Charlotte and Holly to understand. If only someone would agree to take in Heidi. And Jakob, for if and when the boy appeared, they'd have to stay together or the same trouble would arise.

"Evans Grove is such a wonderful place to raise a family." Rebecca sighed. "I was saying that to Mr. Brooks the other day. It's just perfect."

"Sounds to me like you'd like to stay, too." Holly shot Charlotte a knowing smile.

"Oh, no." But Rebecca's light blush and averted eyes belied her words. "My family is in New York. That's my home. I only meant that I wish Heidi and Jakob and any other child who needs a home could stay here. Mr. Brooks understood what I meant. He said the Greenville orphanage looks cold and forbidding. I don't want any orphan to end up there. Here everyone would take them in with open arms and hearts." She glanced at Beatrice Ward. "Well, at least most of them would. If only the orphanage was here."

Charlotte felt the depth of her plea and wished with all her heart that Rebecca's dream could come true. Beatrice would fight it, but the greatest obstacle was even harder to overcome than a meddling spinster. Money. The town simply didn't have the funds to build an orphanage. They couldn't even hire Wyatt to search for Jakob.

Holly, however, was undeterred. "Another thing to pray about. And it wouldn't hurt to ask Mayor Evans. Maybe when all the rebuilding has been completed, there'll be enough of the loan left to build a small orphanage."

When Amelia Hicks approached, Rebecca and Holly

drifted off to gather Liam and Heidi before heading to Holly's house.

"Mrs. Reed?" Amelia's voice broke, and she averted her gaze.

Charlotte felt for the skittish woman. She looked so pale and defeated. Charlotte shuddered to imagine how her drunken husband treated her last night.

Her drawn face and downcast eyes inspired Charlotte to give her a hug. "It's not your fault."

"But it is," the woman cried. "I forgot to tell you yesterday. I'm so sorry."

Charlotte had no idea what she was talking about. "Forgot what?"

"Y-y-your husband." Amelia's gaze darted up to check if Charlotte was angry. "He wanted me to give you a message, but I forgot, what with bringing Vern home and all."

"I understand." Charlotte automatically said the words, but she wished Amelia would get to the point.

"H-he said he'd be here."

"Here?" Wyatt clearly hadn't attended worship.

"No." Amelia shook her head. "He said to tell you that he was coming back."

Coming back? It could only mean one thing. Praise God! Wyatt was coming home.

Chapter Twenty-Four

Charlotte's fingers flew over the fabric for Rebecca's dress. By Monday afternoon, she was ready to do the final fitting. Holly wanted to see the finished gown, so after makeshift school let out, Charlotte and Holly headed to the hotel with Heidi and Sasha.

Rebecca met them on the porch, a peculiar flush in her cheeks. "I can't believe you finished it already. How can I ever thank you? Many ladies offered to give me their old gowns, and I don't mean to be unkind, but they're rather in need of repair."

Charlotte understood. No one in Evans Grove had the sort of wardrobe Miss Sterling was used to. "Show them to me after the fitting, and I'll see which ones I can fix." It was the least Charlotte could do after all of Rebecca's help securing the necessary documents to adopt Sasha.

"Charlotte is the finest dressmaker in Evans Grove," Holly insisted.

It was Charlotte's turn to blush.

"I can see that," Rebecca said. "You should open a shop."

A shop? Charlotte looked around at the stores in Evans Grove. "I never considered making dresses for others."

Holly added her voice to Rebecca's. "You were looking for work, weren't you? This would be perfect."

Charlotte had intended to look for work, but those days seemed so long ago. And now that Wyatt was coming home, she'd stopped fretting over money and started dreaming of a family again. She blushed at the thought of holding a baby of her own.

"Charlotte? What is it?" Holly had that knowing smile on her face.

Charlotte shook her head. "Nothing. Just a dream."

Holly squeezed her arm. "Dreams can come true. Mine did."

"Mine might too." Rebecca showed again the spark that Charlotte had noticed when they first walked up. Her gaze drifted back to Heidi, who was keeping a good watch on Sasha at the end of the porch. "I received a surprise in to-day's post."

"Holly! Can I have a word?" Pauline Evans bustled toward them, a frown on her face and papers in hand.

Holly started down the steps, but Pauline waved her back. "Good morning, ladies," she said when she got to the top. "Have any of you seen Curtis Brooks?"

Charlotte tried to think back. "He was at the hearing on Friday. Did he help at the fire?"

Pauline confirmed that he'd worked beside her in the bucket brigade.

"He wasn't in church Sunday," Rebecca noted.

"Nor could I find him Saturday," Pauline said. "What is that man up to? And now this." She shook the papers. "I don't know what to make of it. Money. From nowhere."

"Nowhere? For what?"

"See for yourself." Pauline handed the papers to Holly, who quickly read the contents.

"It's a banknote for—" Holly gasped at the sum.

"That's right," Pauline said. "This has to be Curtis's doing."

Holly frowned. "But the note is from the Greenville office of the Prairie Trust Bank. Mr. Brooks works out of Newfield."

"It's still his bank," Pauline fumed. "Who else knew about the fire? Who else could send a note so quickly?" She waved the remaining papers. "This is outrageous. Am I supposed to accept such a sum? I don't see how I can refuse, but what strings are attached? What is he going to want from us in return?"

Charlotte looked at Holly to see if she understood what the mayor was saying. Clearly she did not, for Holly posed the question that was in all their minds.

"I can see this is a banknote, but for what?"

"To build a new school."

At first they all stared, then Rebecca squealed. "Me too! I received a banknote to build an orphanage right here in Evans Grove. Isn't it wonderful?"

Pauline frowned. "Perhaps too wonderful. There must be a catch."

But when Holly and Rebecca cried out in protest, Pauline conceded defeat.

"Who am I to turn down money to better our town?"

"Then you'll take it?" Holly asked breathlessly. "That much will build an even larger school."

"Well, I intend to take the money for the orphanage," Rebecca said.

"All right. All right," Pauline said. "You win."

"When can we begin? Who will draw the plans?" The questions flew from both of them so fast that the mayor put up her hands.

"One step at a time, ladies."

"Of course," Holly and Rebecca said in unison. Then,

looking at each other, they burst into giggles and hopped around like schoolgirls.

Rebecca clapped a hand to her mouth, but it couldn't smother her joy. "An orphanage would solve everything. If I could get Mr. Armstrong to agree, Heidi—and Jakob if we find him—could stay right here until we find a family for them. Maybe other children not chosen off the trains could stay here, too. It would be wonderful. Mr. Armstrong has to see it's the perfect solution. I'm going to wire him right away."

Holly followed with her own plans for a new and improved classroom.

Charlotte watched, excited for her friends. Everything *was* working out for the best for those who loved the Lord.

Maybe it would work out for her, too.

Wyatt didn't look forward to facing Charlotte, but he had to come clean with her. She deserved to know everything he'd done in the past and everything he intended to do now that he'd been sworn in as deputy marshal. Once she heard that he probably wouldn't make it home alive, she'd accept going their separate ways.

After his first Sunday service since the war, he and Mason had met with Judge Broadside, who readily agreed to wire the federal marshal for the Nebraska District. They then spoke with Curtis Brooks, who confirmed that none of Evans Grove's supplies had been purchased from Baxter. Monday morning, Mason straightened out Greenville's deputy sheriff.

"I should have given the man more oversight," Mason said to Wyatt, once they'd left. "If it doesn't work out with the marshal, I'd love to have you take over here."

"Tempting offer, but I've got to get those orphans." *Marshal or no marshal.*

Thankfully, Wyatt didn't have to go outside the law.

Approval came that afternoon. By two o'clock, they were headed back to Evans Grove.

"Should arrive in time for supper," Mason mused aloud. "Too bad we missed Sunday dinner. Holly planned fried chicken, my favorite. Maybe she's holding off until my return."

Wyatt remembered the roasted chicken that Charlotte had made last Sunday. He'd tasted better-seasoned birds over the years, but none had warmed him the way hers did. The way she set the fowl before him and asked him to carve. The eager look of anticipation as he took his first bite. The pure joy when he said it was delicious. Each memory bored deep into his soul.

Sweet stars, he loved her.

More than anything he wanted to stay with her, to live in peace and take his place in a loving community. But he had to pay for his sins. It wasn't for God's sake—Wyatt knew with a bone-deep certainty that the Lord already forgave him for his sins, with no payment required other than his faith. No, Wyatt needed this quest to remind him that he could use his abilities to do something good, to help those who needed his protection. Only then could he truly let go of the past, and take a chance on a new beginning. But until then, what did he have to offer to Charlotte? He couldn't promise her a life together today when tomorrow he might die.

Meanwhile, Mason had been extolling Holly's cooking. "She'll fatten up this old bird," he chuckled, rubbing his lean gut, "and she'll get some meat on Liam. That boy is thin as a desert coyote."

They splashed through the creek where Wyatt had committed his life to the Lord. The nightmares had stopped, and he finally knew peace. He shook his head over his fool stubbornness. He should have gone on his knees years ago, but he hadn't been able to see the path from the thicket. Now it was plain as a stagecoach road.

"Why don't you and Charlotte and Sasha come over for supper?" Mason asked. "Holly won't mind."

Wyatt shook his head. Mason had been trying to talk him out of his plan to leave Charlotte and Sasha, and Wyatt figured supper at the Wrights' would only bring one more voice nagging at him. "I need to talk to Charlotte."

"You have a responsibility to her and Sasha."

"That's right, I do. But I also have a responsibility to save those kids. Maybe if I survive, she'll let me come back, but she's suffered so much loss. It wouldn't be fair to leave her mourning again."

"I can see where you're comin' from," Mason said, "but we can't protect our loved ones from everything."

Wyatt set his jaw. "I can protect her from grief."

"Don't you think she oughta have a say?"

Wyatt had heard the argument so many times that he had to rein in the urge to lash out at Mason. The man didn't understand. "It's for her own good."

"Charlotte might seem delicate, but she's a strong woman. Let her decide."

Wyatt couldn't. He'd felt her tears and despair. He'd held her trembling body, and he couldn't bear to think of putting her through more pain.

After Pauline left and Rebecca quieted enough to stand still for the fitting, Holly and Charlotte and her daughter headed home. They walked together up Third Street. At Liberty, Holly would head for the teacherage.

"Papa?" Sasha asked, a worried look on her face.

Charlotte hadn't found a way to tell her Wyatt might not return. She prayed she would never have to. "Soon." She took her daughter's hand. "I'm sure he'll be back soon."

"Since we haven't gotten any word from Greenville, everything must be all right," Holly reasoned.

Charlotte hoped her friend was right.

"Papa!" Sasha tugged on her hand.

"No, Papa's not here," Charlotte patiently told her.

But then Holly shrieked, "Mason!"

Her cry of joy tugged Charlotte out of her worry. Holly was already running toward the corner of Liberty. No buggies or wagons lumbered toward them, just two horsemen. Mason and…

"Wyatt!" Charlotte cried. She picked up Sasha and started running toward him.

At first Wyatt halted, still on horseback, while Mason dropped to the ground and rushed to Holly. The sheriff swung his bride around in a circle and kissed her madly. Only then did Wyatt slip off Dusty, but he didn't run toward her. He walked slowly, grimly, with excruciating heaviness.

He wasn't going to stay.

Charlotte's heart sank, and she stumbled. After catching her balance, she let Sasha down and struggled to breathe life into her weakened limbs.

All things work for good for those who love the Lord.

Holly's favorite verse popped into Charlotte's mind.

Please, Lord. I do love You. I do trust You. Please help this work for good.

"Papa!" Sasha ran toward Wyatt, arms outstretched. "Papa. Papa."

Her cries tore a hole in Charlotte's heart. How could he leave his little girl? He must know how much she would miss him.

Of course. From the mouths of babes. Charlotte took a breath, and strength returned to her legs. She rose as Wyatt scooped Sasha into his arms. The little girl wrapped her arms around his neck and hugged him tight, showering him with unconditional love. Holly's advice coursed through her mind. *Love him as he is now.* That's what Wyatt needed from her right now, to know that she loved him. No questions. No demands. Just love.

Joy bubbled up. She could love him. She did love him. Without heed to what anyone might think, she ran to Wyatt and wrapped her arms around him. Though she felt him stiffen at her touch, she couldn't let doubt distract her from what needed to be said.

"Wyatt. You're safe. I'm so thankful to God for answering my prayers."

He cleared his throat and broke away. "We need to talk."

She wouldn't let him stop her. Before anything else he needed to know how she felt, so she blurted it out. "I love you."

He looked stunned and then distressed as he disentangled himself from Sasha and set her down.

Charlotte's confidence tumbled.

"There's a lot you need to know," he said stiffly.

"Such as how he captured Baxter without a fight." Mason walked near. "And got him to confess."

"That was your doing." Wyatt didn't much care for accolades, even in front of the woman who'd just declared her love for him. He hated breaking her heart. He hated it even more now that he knew she loved him. Adding in Sasha's devotion made it worse still.

Mason clapped him on the back. "Nonsense. Best deputy I ever had. Too bad I'll be losing him."

Charlotte paled, but Mason grinned.

"Don't you worry, Mrs. Reed, it's an honor. Your husband is now a Deputy U.S. Marshal."

Charlotte's stunning hazel eyes rounded. "Deputy Marshal?"

Wyatt scowled. He'd wanted to explain this all to Charlotte in the privacy of her house, not in the middle of the street.

"That's right." Mason wrapped an arm around his new bride. They looked so happy that it pained Wyatt.

"I have a job to do," he tried to explain to Charlotte. "Baxter was running the orphanage as a front for child labor. He shipped the kids out to mines and farms. I intend to find them all and bring them someplace safe. Haven't figured that part out yet. I was hoping to talk to Miss Sterling."

"The new orphanage," Charlotte breathed, looking to Holly.

"It's perfect," Holly agreed.

"What new orphanage?" Mason asked before Wyatt could spit out the question.

"Rebecca got a banknote to build a new orphanage right here in Evans Grove," Holly said. "And the town got money for a new school, too. Can you believe it? Right when the need is greatest. If you ask me, God had His hand in this."

Mason stared straight at Wyatt as if to confirm his wife's assertion. "That's what happens when you put Jesus in command."

The women looked to each other and Mason in confusion, but the sheriff left this revelation to Wyatt.

The words felt awkward after so many years of denial, but Wyatt knew he needed to say them. "I finally came to my senses and turned my life over to the Lord."

The joy on Charlotte's face could outshine the sun. "Oh, Wyatt." Her arms stretched out to embrace him, but he couldn't let her get too close.

He held up his hands and backed away. "You need to know some things about me first."

Holly tugged Mason off to retrieve his horse. That left

Wyatt and Charlotte alone with Sasha, who was eying Dusty from a safe distance.

Charlotte squared her shoulders. "I know all I need to."

He shook his head. She stood too close. The touch of her, the smell of her, the sight of her filled his senses with longing. He wanted a life with her. The peace he'd sought since the war was right here, but first he had penance to pay.

"I killed people in the war," he blurted out.

She didn't flinch. "I expect most soldiers do."

"Not just Rebel soldiers. Civilians. Innocents. Women and children."

Distress flickered in her eyes.

"We were ordered to burn everything in Atlanta. The people were supposed to evacuate the city, but not everyone left. I saw them. I saw their shadows in the flames. You see, I set the fires. I burned down their houses. I heard those people cry out, and I didn't save them." He couldn't bear to look at her. "I told myself they supported Rebel soldiers. They'd turned their men against their own country. If they hadn't sent their husbands and sons into battle, my friends wouldn't have died." A jagged cry tried to rise but he stuffed it down. "Johnny died in my arms. I'd talked him into enlisting." He had to choke off the emotion again. "It's no excuse. I should have checked the houses. I should have tried to save them. I was a coward." Truth hurt. It cut clean through, worse than the bayonet wound in his shoulder, worse than the bullet in his knee.

He heard her draw a breath and had to look. Surely she hated him now.

Instead, her eyes glittered liquid in the sun. Her words fell soft as spring rain. "You're the bravest man I know."

She forgave him. Like God forgave him. But as unwarranted as that gift was, he still couldn't open his heart to her. "Those people in Atlanta…there's nothing I can do for them now. But the children from Baxter's orphanage are still out there. I can still help them. I can't bring back the dead, but I can save the living."

Her eyes glowed as she grasped his hands. "Of course you can."

"You don't understand. It's dangerous. I could get shot." He paused to let the impact sink in, but the woman stood strong.

"I don't care."

He tried again. "I don't want you to suffer through another death, so I'm giving you the chance to hold to our agreement. I'll leave. The money is yours, like I said in the letter, but at least—"

"Stop this instant," she barked in a tone he'd seldom heard from soft-spoken Charlotte. Her index finger poked into his chest. "Do not think you can shirk your responsibilities, Mr. Reed. You have a wife and daughter who love and adore you. I don't care what foolish argument you come up with. We are never leaving you. Understand?"

He blinked, stunned by her reaction. "But I could die."

She was sick of his feeble excuses. In the past few days, she'd learned a lot. All things *did* work for good for those who loved the Lord. She would put her faith and her future in God's hands.

"Yes, you could die." She folded her arms across her chest. "So could I. None of us knows what tomorrow brings, but I know right here and now that I love you, Wyatt Reed, and I will never stop loving you. If you leave us, do it for yourself and not because you think you're protecting me from anything."

Sasha's brow crumpled. "Papa leave?"

For the first time since Charlotte had known Wyatt, he looked like he couldn't piece together his thoughts. He gulped. He looked to Sasha and then to Charlotte as if he didn't know what to say.

When at last he spoke, it was with disbelief. "Do you mean it?"

She nodded, hoping her smile convinced him. "I do."

Wyatt had never thought it possible that she could not only forgive his terrible past but also accept an uncertain future.

He touched a finger to her soft cheek, and she curled toward his hand, kissing his rough fingers. The simple gesture shattered his plans and his doubts.

He made a last feeble attempt. "Are you sure? I might not make it back."

She lifted her eyes. "Each of us has only this moment. Charles died suddenly. The flood came upon us without warning and left families without children or parents. There will always be heartache, but we must also hold on to joy. I know what gives me joy. You. Sasha. Us."

His heart swelled until he thought it would burst. She loved him. This beautiful, God-fearing woman loved him with all her heart. He almost couldn't take it in. Everything he'd ever wanted was right here.

He lifted his gaze to the now-familiar buildings of Evans Grove. Charlotte's house—their house—was just up the street. The sheriff's office. The town hall. The church. Praise God for that church where he'd married this wonderful woman.

"For better and for worse, in sickness and in health," she said, her eyes glistening again. "As long as we both shall live." The words she'd been unable to say that day now spilled out with confidence.

Wyatt had always been decisive. This decision took no thought. He dropped to one knee, right there in the middle of the street, and took Charlotte's hand.

"Charlotte Reed, will you stay married to this ornery, stubborn fool of a man?"

She dropped right down beside him. It must be the angle of the sun, because he could swear her face glowed.

"I will, Wyatt Reed."

"I don't have a ring, but I promise I'll get one."

Her pretty little chin jutted out. "Who needs a ring when she has a man's word?"

No pronouncing was necessary. Wyatt pulled her into his arms and kissed her like a man ought to kiss his wife.

"Oh, my," Charlotte gasped as she came up for air. If she'd had any doubts before, they were gone now. He loved her. He'd committed to a lifetime together. She could have jumped and skipped like a little girl.

"Papa stay?" Sasha tugged on Wyatt's sleeve.

He grinned and swept her into his arms. "Yes, Papa will stay. I love you, Sasha. I will always love you."

Charlotte could hardly keep back the tears. They were a real family now, Sasha's forever mama and papa.

* * * * *

Dear Reader,

The 19th-century concept of sending orphans from city slums to Midwestern farm families has fascinated me for some time. Those of you who've read my other books know that I touched on what came to be called Orphan Trains in *The Matrimony Plan*. That story took place toward the end of the orphan train experience while this one is much closer to the beginning, when the idea was fresh and the outcome hopeful. Some children (not all were orphans) did end up in wonderful families while others became little more than unpaid laborers.

I am greatly blessed with two loving parents and thank God for that every day. Like many children, I went through a rebellious phase and threatened to run away. I packed a few belongings into a blanket, like a hobo, and set off. Before I reached the end of the street I realized how much I'd miss my family and came crawling back full of regret. My mother welcomed me without a single word of reproach. Her grace imprinted in my mind forever the way Our Heavenly Father accepts us time and again when we turn away from Him and try to set out on our own. Charlotte and Wyatt both try to take matters into their own hands, yet God welcomes them back, as He welcomes all His children. I hope you enjoyed their story. I'd love to hear from you, either by mail sent to Love Inspired or through my website at www.christineelizabethjohnson.com.

Blessings,
Christine Johnson

Questions for Discussion

1. Wyatt states he won't get emotionally involved, yet Sasha's tears draw out a tender side. How does he attempt to hold on to his emotional distance while helping the little girl?

2. Why do you think Charlotte struggles to grieve the sudden loss of her husband? Have you ever experienced sudden loss? What was your initial reaction? How did you cope over time?

3. Why does Charlotte put her entire focus on Sasha? Is that healthy? Why or why not?

4. Wyatt insists on taking the orphans to Greenville even after he learns Sasha is one of them. Why does he stick to this plan? What repercussions do you think he'll endure based on his subsequent decision to let some stay?

5. Why are the citizens of Evans Grove so desperate to keep the orphans there, even though all of them haven't been placed in homes yet?

6. When Charlotte learns she must remarry at once in order to keep Sasha, she hasn't yet mourned her husband's loss. How does this complicate matters? If you faced such a decision, could you marry someone you didn't know?

7. Why would Wyatt agree to marry a woman he just met?

8. Do you think it's wrong to marry outside of love? Why or why not?

9. Sasha takes to Wyatt immediately in a way she never did with Charlotte's late husband. Why do you think Wyatt feels "safer" to her?

10. Though Charlotte married only to keep Sasha, she soon expects Wyatt to behave like a "real husband" and resents his riding off without telling her where he's going and when he'll be back. Do you think Wyatt should keep her informed or is she asking too much of him? Why does he not tell her what he's doing?

11. War has a terrible effect on those who fight and must take the life of another human being. Wyatt struggles with his role in the Civil War. How can he put those memories behind him? Do you know a returning soldier who struggles with memories of war? In what ways could those of us back home reach out to them?

12. Why does Wyatt think he needs to leave Charlotte and Sasha?

13. What could Charlotte have done to change his mind?

14. The schoolhouse fire triggers Wyatt's deepest fears, but it also spurs him to act rather than run. Have you ever faced a life-changing moment? How did it alter your course?

15. Forgiving yourself can be terribly difficult. Before

Wyatt can become a husband to Charlotte and a father to Sasha, he must forgive himself for what he did during the war. How can faith help overcome this hurdle?

REQUEST YOUR FREE BOOKS!

2 FREE INSPIRATIONAL NOVELS
PLUS 2
FREE
MYSTERY GIFTS

Love Inspired
HISTORICAL
INSPIRATIONAL HISTORICAL ROMANCE

YES! Please send me 2 FREE Love Inspired® Historical novels and my 2 FREE mystery gifts (gifts are worth about $10). After receiving them, if I don't wish to receive any more books, I can return the shipping statement marked "cancel." If I don't cancel, I will receive 4 brand-new novels every month and be billed just $4.74 per book in the U.S. or $5.24 per book in Canada. That's a saving of at least 21% off the cover price. It's quite a bargain! Shipping and handling is just 50¢ per book in the U.S. and 75¢ per book in Canada.* I understand that accepting the 2 free books and gifts places me under no obligation to buy anything. I can always return a shipment and cancel at any time. Even if I never buy another book, the two free books and gifts are mine to keep forever.

102/302 IDN F5CN

Name   (PLEASE PRINT)

Address   Apt. #

City   State/Prov.   Zip/Postal Code

Signature (if under 18, a parent or guardian must sign)

Mail to the **Harlequin® Reader Service:**
IN U.S.A.: P.O. Box 1867, Buffalo, NY 14240-1867
IN CANADA: P.O. Box 609, Fort Erie, Ontario L2A 5X3

Want to try two free books from another series?
Call 1-800-873-8635 or visit www.ReaderService.com.

---

* Terms and prices subject to change without notice. Prices do not include applicable taxes. Sales tax applicable in N.Y. Canadian residents will be charged applicable taxes. Offer not valid in Quebec. This offer is limited to one order per household. Not valid for current subscribers to Love Inspired Historical books. All orders subject to credit approval. Credit or debit balances in a customer's account(s) may be offset by any other outstanding balance owed by or to the customer. Please allow 4 to 6 weeks for delivery. Offer available while quantities last.

Your Privacy—The Harlequin® Reader Service is committed to protecting your privacy. Our Privacy Policy is available online at www.ReaderService.com or upon request from the Harlequin Reader Service.

We make a portion of our mailing list available to reputable third parties that offer products we believe may interest you. If you prefer that we not exchange your name with third parties, or if you wish to clarify or modify your communication preferences, please visit us at www.ReaderService.com/consumerchoice or write to us at Harlequin Reader Service Preference Service, P.O. Box 9062, Buffalo, NY 14269. Include your complete name and address.

LIH13R

Love Thy Neighbor?

After years of wandering, Daisy Johnson hopes to settle in
Turnabout, Texas, open a restaurant, perhaps find a husband.
Of course, she'd envisioned a man who actually likes her. Not
someone who offers a marriage of convenience to avoid scandal.

Turnabout is just a temporary stop for newspaper reporter
Everett Fulton. Thanks to one pesky connecting door and a
local gossip, he's suddenly married, but his dreams of leaving
haven't changed. What Daisy wants—home, family, tenderness—
he can't provide. Yet big-city plans are starting to pale beside
small-town warmth....

Texas Grooms

The Bride Next Door

by

WINNIE GRIGGS

Available June 2013

www.LoveInspiredBooks.com

LIH82967